MW00779688

RED DOG FARM

ALSO BY NATHANIEL IAN MILLER

The Memoirs of Stockholm Sven

RED DOG FARM

A Novel

NATHANIEL IAN MILLER

LITTLE, BROWN AND COMPANY

New York Boston London

Little, Brown and Company
Hachette Book Group
1290 Avenue of the Americas, New York, NY 10104
littlebrown.com

First Edition: March 2025

Little, Brown and Company is a division of Hachette Book Group, Inc. The Little, Brown name and logo are trademarks of Hachette Book Group, Inc.

The publisher is not responsible for websites (or their content) that are not owned by the publisher.

The Hachette Speakers Bureau provides a wide range of authors for speaking events. To find out more, go to hachettespeakersbureau.com or email hachettespeakers@hbgusa.com.

Little, Brown and Company books may be purchased in bulk for business, educational, or promotional use. For information, please contact your local bookseller or the Hachette Book Group Special Markets Department at special.markets@hbgusa.com.

Book interior design by Marie Mundaca

ISBN 9780316575140
Library of Congress Control Number: 2024949388

Printing 1, 2025

LSC-C

Printed in the United States of America

For my own pabbi and mamma,
charter members of a mutual admiration society

PROLOGUE

Every few years—we get itchy if it's been too long—Iceland remakes itself. The land may look stony and immutable, but without fail a fissure opens and the earth's hot blood comes bubbling out, sometimes in a jet and sometimes an ooze. Smoke fills the air, tourists fill the airport. When it's all over, we lean forward to behold the new landscape. Maybe a mountain where a town once stood, or an island where before there was only ocean.

It's an Icelandic paradox: The very stubborn nature of the place is change itself. Not always adaptation but alteration. It's written into our rocks and our bones.

I believe the same could be said of my father and, perhaps, of me.

We don't all become our parents, but their lives and wounds built the houses we live in. Theirs are the hammers and rough chapped hands that hung every window and lopsided door. Whether the rain rots our clapboards eventually, whether the flying red sand pries loose our metal roofing and sends it off to Greenland or leaves it dull, dented, and intact, that's a reflection on their work. I mean a metaphorical house, of course—my pabbi and mamma's construction skills were limited to rudimentary things: a coffee table, a fence, a paper airplane.

I've been a farmer for over twelve years now. It no longer feels presumptuous to say, even though the old-timers around here will persist in treating me like a novice and giving unsolicited advice until they're finally croaking out, "Orri, the thing to do is—" in a death rattle and I have to lean in close and ask them to repeat it but they can't because they're dead.

They counsel me about child-rearing too. My own kid—a daughter, I'm told—is soon to be born. I intend to ignore all the advice until it suits me not to. I intend to abjure bows and skirts and frills in favor of rubber boots and leather gloves, to have her changing oil filters and filling bovine syringes by the time she's three, so she recognizes all those ubiquitous farm-themed children's books as absurd and asks, "Why aren't they filthy like our place?" and if she ever says she wants to work the farm herself, to "be a farmer," she'll know precisely what she means.

I'm not going to say the farm has been a success. I don't know yet, I can't make so weighty a determination and that would be unlucky. Besides, in farming, you hemorrhage cash even when you're making it, so these things can be very hard to tell.

My father, my pabbi, taught me to farm. His father was a farmer too, and yet Pabbi managed to slither out from under his father's heavy shadow. I'm not like that. I don't define myself in opposition the way Pabbi did. Every day I become more like him, and like Mamma too. I might have, say, a cursory exchange with a slaughterhouse employee, and I feel that same implacable silence coming out of me, a void in the air as I refuse to chat or remark on the weather, and I don't hate it, this emptiness between us, though the slaughterhouse employee surely does.

And I am changeable, like Pabbi. I make adjustments, adhering to as few principles and dogmas as I can, including his. He would approve, I think. To change is to embody one of his finer parts, though decades of friction against the mean left him raw and abraded. Maybe it was harder for his generation. Or maybe the cold truths of farming are, at their core, undeniable.

So there's this difference between us: Despite Pabbi's great love for my mother and me, and his genuine fondness for animals, he experienced life as a slow leak, a gradual drying out of hope. I think I'm otherwise. Or trying to be. I see the same furrow lines converging across my brow like spring-flush rivers when I look up from spitting toothpaste. I see, just like his, the corners of my mouth dipping toward the earth when I'm engaged in something menial, something decidedly non-cerebral, like chipping ice from beneath a frozen gate or ladling turds from a water trough. But resembling a bitter old farmer—we age prematurely, it's established—is not the same as feeling like one.

And Pabbi's well of hope was never so deep to begin with. If it was already filled in halfway with mud and sharp igneous rock by the time he left the Westman Islands, that wasn't his fault. If my own well has the greater reserves, or is always so stocked with clear glacial melt that I don't notice it's leaking, that's only because my parents dowsed and dug it with their bare hands so it would endure like Írskrabrunnur, the Well of the Irish.

A farmer needs to endure a great many things.

1.

I witnessed the birth of Dagmar, gentle lady. She became our herd boss.

It's not my first memory. My first would've been around 1997, when I was five years old, though maybe it's just the memory of someone else's memory. I know that I drank an ounce or two of *brennivín* after mistaking it for water. I can still bring to mind the pervading sense of shock, like my palate and esophagus were on fire, and then onward throughout my digestive tract. I coughed extensively, but I kept it down.

"You survived the Black Death!" Mamma liked to say. Some parents enjoy recollecting the near misses, provided they were not too near.

It was an unlikely occurrence, brennivín being rare in our house. If Mamma felt like spirits, she generally stuck with her potato vodka—only potato, mind you, cold and torpid in the glass or the bottle, whatever receptacle was nearest at hand, she would countenance nothing else.

"If I wanted to smear rye bread with moss and then liquefy it," she'd say, "well, I wouldn't."

Pabbi was the brennivín drinker, for old times' sake, although not by nature picky with his alcohol, and he'd mostly abandoned the strong stuff by March 1, 1989, Beer Day, when Iceland finally legalized beer after its ridiculously long prohibition, and he never looked back.

So Dagmar is my second memory. Later that same year, or thereabouts. The sweet, slightly fetid smell of fermenting hay in the barnyard. The cow prone, breathing heavily. And then the tiny yellow hooves, so incongruous, and all at once the calf squelching out onto the ground.

Pabbi, next to me, exhausted from his endless watch but happy, I think. Mamma laughing, a little grossed out. And me, in my shrill delight, "She pooped it!"

They say it's usually the heifer calves who rouse first, and Dagmar was on her feet almost immediately, tottering around, getting licked and unslimed by her mother, who was also on her feet, finding the best teat within five minutes in this world, sucking contentedly, tail wagging like a dog's.

And we made this a tradition. Two years later I saw Dagmar's first calf born, a massive sweet-natured bull with one lopsided scur on his head, and because Dagmar was so calm and easy and would often allow herself to be led into a clean stall before calving, sometimes even in the final hours of her labor, I saw almost all the rest of her children born too, always hale, always thriving, never the hint of a problem.

That was our very first calving season, Pabbi and Mamma having moved to the farm only a year or two before, and of course it posed its challenges. The next calf after Dagmar was a bull who ran straight through a three-strand barbwire fence in abject terror when he saw Pabbi for the first time, had to be tackled and dragged up the hill — he was fine — and another calf never came to be; it was aborted spontaneously about a month before, deposited in the corral looking for all the world like a wet cat. The mother had somehow contracted a parasite that we later learned would be passed from cow to heifer calf ad infinitum, causing lesions on the placenta, and the whole line had to be culled.

And a decade later, despite her many good years as imperturbable boss, Dagmar left us. She bloated out when she lay down in a small ditch and couldn't get back up for several hours, smashing her head on the ground so many times in an effort to stand that her wits were never quite the same, and neither was her reproductive system. She couldn't get pregnant again under any circumstance, and who could blame her, but she had to be culled too, and that was a hard blow for everyone, Pabbi most of all.

And maybe I wasn't always the best farmhand. I liked fetching tools for Pabbi, learning a socket wrench from a pair of locking pliers, but he said I moved too slowly at times of need and complained whenever I had to use a leg muscle in any way whatsoever.

Adults ask kids what they want to be when they grow up, and for a long time I said "farmer." But Pabbi took pains to disabuse me of romantic notions, and if I thought a task was at all difficult, and I expressed this dissatisfaction, he was bound to remind me that farming was made up of unpleasant tasks, one after another, and eventually I stopped saying it.

I didn't really know the place, the work. That wouldn't come until much later: 2013, the year I turned twenty-one. Maybe I arrived late. Maybe I took too long to understand, to mature—it's a maxim about bull calves, why shouldn't it be true for bull children? But a kid takes his surroundings for granted. He's not aware of the labor, the sacrifices, or even that a farm is something singular, a world unto itself. How can he embrace the thing when he can't see well enough to wrap his arms around it? And there was no guarantee that I ever would. Farm-raised children don't grow up to farm much more often than farm-raised eggs grow up to be chickens. Anyone who spends more than a moment looking backward knows that inevitability is a fiction. No Norns, just opportunity, blood, and choices.

But still, in those bright, snow-blind early days of Dagmar and her ilk, there was a great deal of life, and an abundance of care, and the two seemed to intermingle successfully more often than not. We took a lot of photographs. Mamma took the best ones, she didn't even need a filter, and the cows always came right up to her because cows prefer women to men, it's a universal truth. People liked our beef, they liked knowing where it came from, they said, and we liked it too — I was raised on it, after all — but we liked the animals even more.

I was young. It seemed that farming could be simple. It certainly seemed that it could be beautiful.

2.

$\int$ pring 2012. I was home on furlough. Mamma is the one who called it "furlough," self-imposed. She said it with empathy, knowing too well the ways academia could grind a person down, or preserve them in a state of suspended discontent. Pabbi called it "fucking off."

I'd made it much of the way through my first year at the University of Iceland in Reykjavík, studying who knows what. A bit of psychology, a touch of law. Certainly not a career path of any kind. Other kids from our part of the country often took a year or two off to figure their lives out between high school and the loftier halls, if they ascended at all. Many didn't. I jumped straight for it with unclear but trite motivations: feeling stifled by the rural life, by the weekend farm labor, by the fact that we never went anywhere. Or maybe just because it was expected that I would.

Mamma understood. She never pushed, or even subtly intimated that I should study at Bifröst University, where she taught. It was fifteen minutes away, after all, and I could live at home and help Pabbi out in the mornings and evenings. But she knew the city was pulling me. She said it would be worth the price of tuition—admittedly very modest for locals and EU members—just to live in a place where one could eat sushi or pho every week. And I could stay with my grandmother, Amma, rent-free in her elegant, austere apartment. She didn't approve of every youthful indiscretion, and that meant some lecturing and judgmental looks, but she doted on me, forgiving most minor trespasses, and besides, she hadn't retired yet so was often away at work.

But to my shock, I missed home terribly. I quit sleeping that first semester. Or rather, I lost the ability to conjure sleep, which I'd always taken for granted. On the farm, there was perfect silence at night if you didn't count the wind, the intermittent banging of a gate or a chain, the ragged bellowing of a weaned calf. And even in the dead of winter, we didn't keep a single outside floodlight switched on, as most farmers did. Pabbi found them annoying—said the cows don't give a damn, they can smell their way from feed to water to bed and back again. I had to agree. And so, with blackout curtains for the summer sun, I grew up sinking into an inky pool every time I closed my eyes to sleep. Now faced with streetlights shining in every window, and drunk people laughing, and neighbors shouting, and all sorts of unwelcome nighttime stimuli, I was forced to conceptualize sleep for the first time, to analyze its necessary conditions and components, which is the very worst way to succeed at conjuring. For what is sleep but magic?

Amma tried to help. She saw me decompensating when I'd been in the city for only a month or two. The lights and sounds never bothered her—she grew up in Vilna, after all—but she tried to adapt the apartment to my needs, buying heavier shades, turning certain obnoxious household items off and others on. Nothing worked, and I proceeded to lose my mind. I stumbled around in a miserable daze and fell asleep in class. As evening approached, I became seized with anxiety, dreading the very sight of my restless bed. I was Tantalus and night the false promise, extended again and again. In the end, nothing worked but downers. Amma, a physician at Landspítali, pulled a few strings and got me a benzodiazepine scrip from her friend, the chief of Psychiatry.

Possessing the unique faith in medicine — and her own ability to dispense it — that most doctors seem to have, she didn't think it necessary to consult a sleep specialist or a psychiatrist, and neither did the psychiatrist himself. She was right, of course. Sedatives were the knock upon the head that I apparently required for city living.

By the start of the second semester, having recovered my senses somewhat over the winter break, I was sleeping better, mostly coping without chemical assistance, but still fundamentally lost. Neither Amma nor Mamma proposed that I follow them into their respective fields. It's not that I didn't have the head for it, more that I lacked the ambition. The sum total of the knowledge I acquired in Reykjavík, the self-growth of a baffled young adult, was that I missed the company of animals — their pace and uncomplicated needs. Many farm kids know from early on that they want out, and when they finally achieve it, the liberation is gratifying, even if their illusions of a bigger, faster life turn out to be just that. Others fall into the cliché of only realizing what they love once it's in the rearview mirror. I was one of those.

So I was primed for exodus when Mamma called the apartment that night in late February 2012. Amma answered, speaking Yiddish for a minute, and then handed it to me.

"I'm worried about Pabbi," Mamma said, after receiving her usual reassurances about my health. "He seems depressed."

"Did he say he was depressed?"

"No, but I can tell when he is. His voice turns into a mutter, and he won't look me in the eyes."

"Doesn't he often mutter?"

"I guess. Not like usual, though. I can't understand him."

"It's that Vestmannaeyjar accent," I said. "He sounds like a pirate."

"He does!"

We laughed a bit, as mothers and sons can do together even when things seem dire, and Mamma made a remark in Yiddish, but whispered it, as though the secret language — secret from Pabbi and me — were insufficient, its meaning divined if overheard.

Then Mamma asked if I was still planning to come home for my weeklong holiday in March. Of course, I told her, I wanted to help with the calving.

"Good," she said, and she sounded genuinely relieved. "Two weeks? That's not so far off. He'll be happy to see you."

I tapped my toes on the floor and glanced across the room at Amma, who was looking at something on her laptop, pretending not to listen.

"I could just leave tomorrow," I said, sort of to both of them. "Then I'd be home for three weeks instead of one."

Call it a family emergency—my professors wouldn't really care, so long as I kept up with the reading and turned everything in on time. That part was simple. And by then I had my own car, an old salt-fuckered Renault Twingo with two brash holes in its muffler and a rear hatch that wouldn't open under any circumstances.

Mamma didn't think there was any harm in it, and Amma conceded that maybe her lunatic uncultured son-in-law, whom she adored, could use a boost.

So I drove home the next morning, and for the first two days I was back, Pabbi seemed tolerably well. He showed me some small machines he'd brought into the shop—one had its carburetor excised, cracked open like a complicated fruit and spread across the floor. He was pleased about a brand-new heifer calf, Vinur, who had arrived earlier than expected on a brutal night but stood and nursed within minutes, before she was even licked dry. In winter, most newborns are sluggish, especially the boys. Vinur had a ferocious will and was untroubled by matted, shit-covered fur and engorged teats.

We chored together, Pabbi and I, taking our time as one should in winter, leaning against the wind, me entertaining him with a few lengthy monologues about the idiosyncrasies of town folk and him occasionally holding forth in his laconic way. I searched his eyes when they were focused on other things. I may as well have searched the sky.

Mamma was an immigrant—a first-generation Icelander and a Jew—genetically disposed to be in touch with her emotions. Pabbi, on the other hand, came from a long line of Icelandic farmers, dating as far back as you'd care to look, and Icelanders like to look, though they make it hard for themselves by insisting on patronymics instead of family surnames. Most farmers, despots and subjects of their little realms, have a degree of stoicism, but Icelandic farmers take this predisposition even further, battered as they are by meteorological cruelty from one day to the next. They prefer never to acknowledge their vulnerabilities, even if they are bleeding out on a hillside somewhere.

But Pabbi was different, somehow. He appeared more threadbare, as though wind were getting through the cracks. It could've been simply that I'd gone away and come back and was seeing him with new eyes, as when you don't notice a dog growing, or a child, until you stop watching it for a day or two, and then you look again and say, *My, how big you are,* or in this case, *My, Pabbi, how tired you are.* In my lifetime he'd seldom seemed happy—that was not a word one would use to describe him—but maybe Mamma was right, maybe he was unhappier.

Finally I asked him outright whether he was depressed, and of course he said no. I thought, *He is lying,* but couldn't be sure, as parents are very good at lying, they have to cultivate the skill from the moment you're born or they risk killing you with exposure. They must be pillars, and so they are, right up until the moment you realize that they're not.

3.

Always a bitter morning when the calves drop. The mercury stoops overnight to its late-season nadir, and the rising sun has no discernible effect. The ground, the air, the machines — all intransigent. And somewhere in there, about two or three hours before the farmer gets up to check on everyone, the cow finishes her long labor. The typical response to this obnoxious timing is to blame the cow. Clearly she has done it out of spite, going into labor just as soon as the farmer has turned his back for the night, reluctantly, of course, because if he could make do without sleep he'd keep watch forever. So he retires, leaving his pregnant patient either out on the hard frozen ground, where the calf will begin dying as soon as it emerges, or, if the farmer is endowed with luck and foresight, in a marginally warmer, hay-bedded barn stall, where the calf will land nose-first in a steaming pile of shit and then get stomped by its oblivious mother.

You can avoid the March–April calving nightmare if you are talented at coordinating bovine intercourse, but there are downsides to every time of year, and centuries of farmers, who can never agree on anything, mostly seem to have agreed that frozen ground, on the heels of winter's worst abuses, is preferable to the poisonous muck of a thawed barnyard, or to flies.

This is how it goes. Or so Pabbi has said, anyway, on many occasions, I am basically quoting him. My own experience was too intermittent, and too colored by childhood curiosity, to produce such a jaded outlook. But Pabbi kept a great deal from me. He wavered perpetually between a desire to keep farming joyful—to protect me from its wounds—and a compulsion to rob me of my illusions.

He waffled as usual, on that morning in March, when Fús got dystocia. Fús was a first-calf heifer, and you always have to keep a closer eye on those. But her labor ended before dawn, and by the time Pabbi got outside, the calf was stuck, only halfway out and all the way dead. Pabbi was out there for a while, and then came back inside with his head down. I had slept a little late, as kids do when they're home from university, and was just slouching down to some breakfast when he came into the kitchen with hay chaff on his socks.

"Everything okay?" Mamma said. She tried to hand him a cup of coffee but he wouldn't take it. His eyes wandered around the room and wouldn't meet hers.

"No, everything is bad," he said, and then muttered the particulars. "Can you help?"

She couldn't, though she wanted to. She was already late for a morning meeting with the rest of the faculty in her department.

"I'm coming, Pabbi," I said.

He looked at me bleakly. "You haven't eaten."

"Neither have you. I'll meet you out there in a minute."

We stared at the situation. Fús was down, and starting to look fairly bloated. Her eyes rolled back in her head, and all four legs stuck out straight, as though she'd paused in the middle of a big stretch. The dead calf, with a lolling tongue as long as its head and two thick-jointed forelegs preceding it as they should, lay partway flopped on the floor, covered in hay and shit and amniotic slime. Its eyes were still shut tight—lucky, maybe, that it never got a glimpse of any future indignities the world had in store.

"I don't get it," Pabbi said, as though we'd been in conversation.

"Her frame is so big." He meant Fús. Fús was the daughter of our herd boss, Skynsemi, a fairly enormous cow for a Galloway. Skynsemi made us all proud—she had a sleepy-eyed complacence, and took her job seriously—but she threw big calves, and her teats were large and pyramidal, making it hard for newborns to nurse. At any rate, Fús should've been fine with a calf of this size. But for whatever reason, it got stuck.

"What do you want to do?" I said. The reek of blood and indoor manure passed easily through the neck warmer I'd pulled over my face.

Pabbi glanced at me. He was chewing his lip. I don't know if he was thinking, then, about whether I was ready to engage in such a horrific task. Ready in the sense that my soul was fully formed and therefore able to withstand the abrading it was about to endure. I certainly didn't hesitate. Of course everyone thinks they're ready for everything, until they face it for the first time.

"Grab some ratchet straps," Pabbi said. "The big ones. We've got to get the calf out."

We never had a real calf-puller, the kind with hooks and chains that veterinarians bring. Maybe we should have—our veterinarian lived about ninety minutes away, so an emergency visit was neither financially nor temporally feasible. But Pabbi didn't want one around. He said that sometimes owning a tool manifested the need for the tool. He could be superstitious that way.

While I secured one end of the strap to a metal eyebolt, Pabbi wrestled the other end around the calf's slippery legs, trying in vain to avoid the frenetic whip of Fús's dripping tail. Then he stood up and started ratcheting. At last the calf slopped out in a wet tangle. Fús moaned, writhing, twisting. Pabbi grabbed hold of the calf and dragged it from the stall, leaving a viscous record. I heard him shouting at Rykug, our dog, to keep the fuck away.

"A nice bull calf," he said, shaking his head ruefully, when he came back.

"What now?"

"We have to get her up."

I'd seen him pull bloated cows off the ground a few times before, with the tractor and chains, but that was outside, with plenty of room. In the barn, there was little we could do. We tried tying the halter to the ratchet strap, and Fús's heavy head came up, kinked against her body. She was thrashing so hard now that I could feel it through the concrete. The air was full of her steam. But thrash as she might, she couldn't rise.

After several minutes of this, Pabbi let go of the rope and hung his head, breathing hard. The strap kept Fús's head in the air. Her eyes were bone white.

"Paralyzed," he said.

If calves got stuck, or spent too long in the birth canal, the fetus pressed on its mother's spine, or pinched a nerve, Pabbi wasn't sure which. In any case, the pregnant cow's lower half would go completely numb. Every so often they could come back from this, given time, but they had to get on their feet first, and that was nearly impossible. Especially inside a stall.

"Watch her," Pabbi said. "I'll get the zapper." I winced. I'd been trained to hate the electric prod, having heard enough stories about hasty, irresponsible farmers and slaughterhouse workers who couldn't be bothered to wait more than three minutes for beeves to make up their minds before reaching for the goddamn prod. But we had one, as every farmer must, a little blue thing about the size of a cordless telephone, and Pabbi kept it locked up, in case any little kids should come over and mistake it for a toy.

He shuffled back into the stall—I could tell he was moving slower now, despite the urgency. This meant that things weren't looking good.

"You pull," he said, and started zapping. The prod sent out a high-pitched whine as he pressed the button, and then, when he pushed it through the heavy winter fur on Fús's bloated flank, a muffled crack. Her skin twitched and her legs waved and her eyes retreated even farther into her head, but she was still emphatically down. Pabbi tried only two or three more times. I knew each attempt was another wound in him.

"All right, I'm firing up the tractor," he said. I stood watch and heard Kolkrabbi turn over without too much protest. Good thing it was March, not January. The old coughing dinosaur, an 85-horsepower Valmet, had been starting hard lately—Pabbi thought the in-line fuel filter was clogged with congealed diesel snot.

When Kolkrabbi was warmed up enough, Pabbi inched it forward. A rope was tied to Fús's stiff legs by a complicated labyrinth of cables and snatch blocks, and she started to slide, barely protesting. A bloody smear collected in her wake. I barked at Rykug to stay out— she had crept forward, like one of those horror-film mannequins that move closer every time you turn away.

Things took a swift turn for the ominous when we got our first unhindered, daylight look at Fús's hind end.

"Goddammit," Pabbi said. It was all too clear that what we'd both assumed was her placenta, in the obscure light of the barn, was nothing of the kind. Her uterus had prolapsed. The set of options afforded to Fús were now considerably narrower. Even if we managed to get her up, we'd then have to shove the uterus back in, but also somehow keep it clean during the process—impossible with her lying down; almost impossible with her standing up.

But Fús wouldn't rise in either case. She seemed to have given up. She no longer moaned or kicked. Who knew if bloat was reaching its lethal apotheosis, or the pain and paralysis had proved too much, or what. I looked at the ground. I felt raw, scraped out.

"Jæja," Pabbi said. *Well.* He had a particular style of saying it that was crushing in its finality.

Without looking at me, he trudged back toward the house, muttering that I should come inside and eat some breakfast, as though that were foremost on my mind. Maybe it was, god forgive me.

"No, Pabbi, I'll stay and help."

"There's no need for you to see this."

"If I'm going to farm this place someday, there is."

He stopped in his trudging, as though I'd said something too thorny to untangle while in motion. I thought maybe he'd say some word of approval, or mild encouragement, or blatant dismissal, but instead he just scrutinized my face for a quick moment, then shrugged and kept walking.

The gun, a heavy Sako 85 rifle that seemed far too dramatic for the job, nonetheless did its job well. I stayed close for the final act. It was the first time, in all my years, that I'd done so. I'd always been ushered back to the house, or at least behind the barn. Pabbi placed the muzzle just a few inches from Fús's great head. She didn't look at him. The report was a thick *woof,* like the sound of an ice shelf sliding off the roof, the kind Mamma always said would decapitate me.

Smoke wisped out of a black smudge in Fús's curly forelock. She shuddered, and her head sank down. Blood frothed discreetly from her lips. I thought in that moment how strange it was that bovine heads seemed tailor-made to absorb bullets.

I consented to going inside. Pabbi followed me in about ten minutes later, looking utterly destroyed. He'd used Kolkrabbi to drag the enormous corpse a good ways off, rolling her into a ditch full of old bones. There, the ravens could do their work.

"Sorry, Pabbi," I said.

"She was a good one," he replied, and then somehow we threw together a full breakfast of fried eggs and toast and juice and coffee, our hands engaged in their usual motions, and somehow we ate it.

Outside the day was warming by incremental degrees. By noon the snow would be slushy underfoot, the driveway perilous, the great ice sheets launching themselves from our metal roof. The sky was low and gray. Faintly visible from the kitchen window, Baula and her sister, Litla-Baula, blond volcanic cones and sentries of our world, loomed through the fog like chipped canine teeth.

4.

The dog heralded Ketill's arrival before any of us knew he was coming. She whined and clattered her toenails and huffed at the window. It was Saturday, late morning, which found the three of us hiding from the feeble, low-slung sun, each in our respective chairs, each with our respective books. Pabbi had already accomplished his chores and checkups on the bovine maternity ward and seemed relatively content to do nothing for a little while, since Mamma was home. We were one of those rare families that liked being together.

Pabbi groaned when he saw the ratty old flatbed rolling in. He disliked Ketill, but had to stifle it because diplomacy was perhaps his core value, and because Ketill was a neighbor whose years of hard-won dubious experience in homesteading and machine maintenance were occasionally called upon in times of emergency at our place, and because Ketill was unfailingly, maddeningly generous.

"I'm not at home," Pabbi said. I could never tell when he said this whether he was quoting Bilbo Baggins or had simply become Bilbo Baggins.

Mamma gathered up her book and made for the back room. "I'm

not either," she said. She didn't need a reason to dislike Ketill, and though she taught politics, diplomacy was not her thing.

"I guess that leaves us," I said to the dog, cramming my bare feet into a pair of insulated rubber boots and taking a heavy down jacket from the overburdened rack.

Rykug preceded me, barking with menace and joy, and she scrabbled her claws all over Ketill's paint job. Fortunately Ketill did not give a damn about his paint job. The old farmer unfolded himself like an arthritic insect, lanky and unbending, his false teeth clacking in his mouth. He grinned at me.

"The prodigious son returns!"

"Hey, Ketill."

"Home from the big city, I see. Slumming it with the peasants."

This was one of Ketill's favorite tactics: calling attention to his erudition with facetious mockery of his ignorance. It was a sword with an impossible number of edges.

"You on break?" he said.

"Not for another couple of weeks. Just thought I'd bring some classwork home, start vacation early." I was careful, always careful, to avoid any suggestion that Pabbi needed help. Not only would it inspire scorn from Ketill—worse, it might inspire his help.

Ketill nodded knowingly. He produced his plastic flask of *neftóbak*, Icelandic nose tobacco, tipped a line of the coarse snuff onto his hand, and disappeared it in a couple of hearty contemplative snorts.

"How is the beautiful lady of the house?" he said, with a leer in his voice. Mamma may not have needed a reason to dislike him, but if she had, his insistence on calling attention to her appearance would have been sufficient. Sometimes he worked in bizarre references to her background when delivering his lascivious compliments. He once called her a *"framandi hornkýr,"* or *exotic horned cow.* We'd spent weeks afterward trying to decide whether he understood the anti-Semitic implications, or if he referred only to the rareness of horns among

Icelandic cows. That was a regular game in our house: Did Ketill know what he was saying?

"Fine. She's in the shower," I said, and then instantly regretted it, assuming Ketill's mind would jump at the opportunity to picture her there. "What are you up to, old man?"

"Ah, just picking up some hay for the critters." Ketill, who had no outbuildings that weren't stuffed with machine parts, stored his square bales at our farm. In return, we used a few as bedding in the maternity ward. "Any babies on the ground?"

I looked over his shoulder, as though I might see a calf lying in the barnyard instead of the gory smear from Fús being dragged off. I'd always been mystified by how blood could leave a tenacious stain in concrete, snow, gravel, dirt.

"Nope."

We stood in companionable silence for a minute, Ketill watching with a look of beleaguered amusement as Rykug chased his little Icelandic sheepdog, Gúrka, around the buildings, humping him relentlessly. It didn't matter, of course, that Rykug was female. This was her place, and she would express her dominance however she saw fit. She hadn't been socialized particularly well, way out in the sticks, and she also seemed to resent the fact that Gúrka was uncut, oozing useless hormones. They still liked each other, but in a toxic way.

"Your dog is a rapist," Ketill said. "Where did Viðir ever get such a horrible thing?"

I let the insult wash over me. Rykug was Pabbi's dog, but whenever I was back home, she was mine. Pabbi sometimes made a show of objecting to this, calling her "traitor" when, in the morning, he discovered that she'd slunk from my parents' bedroom and relocated to mine, the better to nose me at the first sign of waking.

"You abandoned me," he would say to her. "Fickle beast."

But we both knew, and we knew Ketill knew, that Rykug could run literal circles around the rest of the country's native canine stock. In theory, she could outperform the border collies that now outnumbered Icelandic sheepdogs, at least among pragmatic farmers. Border collies only worked the head, and were of course deeply neurotic, seldom able to acknowledge when the workday was over.

Rykug was an Australian kelpie, rust-red and long-legged, and though her coat was wholly unsuited to the climate, her intelligence and drive made her an indispensable farmhand, or would someday. Pabbi had worked long and hard to find a pup of her breeding, rare outside of Australia, and to wade through the rigid bureaucracy that tried to prevent her immigration. Then he'd waited impatiently during her long quarantine on Hrísey. Maybe it was on the cusp of paying off. She was three years old now. They say kelpies never tire, not ever. They can work the heel just as well as the head, depending on what's required. Pabbi showed me a video once where a kelpie disappeared into the scrum of a chute packed with nervous sheep only to reappear moments later on top of the herd, using their wooly ovine backs as a promenade. Rykug was untested in that regard, but she certainly knew how to conserve energy: Once indoors, warming on the floor, she turned it off like a switch. The only things that made her somewhat disagreeable were horses. She didn't do so well with them: They hated her, and she hated them. Fortunately we didn't have any. Also, she was an incorrigible yapper. Pabbi trained her not to do it in the house, but she just replaced the barking with whines and whistles and other alien sounds of the same volume and pitch, and in such speech-like intonations that she seemed part raven.

Ketill could cast his aspersions if he liked. I'd known the old man since I was an infant, when he held me in one arm and bellowed Icelandic folk songs, which I apparently found reassuring. His retrograde fumblings about ethnicity and religion could be chalked up to a lifetime spent among Icelanders, along with a perverse, ill-conceived desire to prove to everyone just how enlightened and unintimidated he was. As far as he was concerned, his admiration for my mother's appearance was just more evidence of his progressive attitude, and therefore allowed him liberties in his speech. He allowed himself many liberties. And case in point: Weren't he and I great friends? Wasn't he, for all intents and purposes, my godfather? He certainly thought so.

After a little while, Rykug came back in a lather and collapsed at my feet, conserving her spirit until the next big thing. Gúrka, looking spent, retreated to the cab of Ketill's truck. Neither of us was in a hurry, though I'd begun to feel the cold through my thin cotton pants.

"Ah, the farming life," Ketill declaimed.

We stared toward the Þverá, where a feeble cloud of steam was rising from the ice. The wind got hold of a cracked plastic bucket and bounced it into a ditch.

5.

"What did he want?"

Pabbi was suited up for work, overheating in his winter gear while he waited for Ketill to leave. His face was flushed and dour.

"Picking up hay," I said.

"You didn't let him near the tractor, did you?" My father lived in fear that if his vigilance lapsed, Ketill would take it upon himself to "help" with the animals or the machines. His help had to be tightly regulated or it would turn to destruction. It had happened before. Once, learning that Kolkrabbi had a coolant leak that my father couldn't find the source of, he'd come over, found us not at home, unscrewed a bunch of things from the old tractor, but then got stumped or was missing a necessary tool and departed, leaving behind a pile of important-looking bolts, two flattened washers, and a radiator that still leaked just as much as ever.

I knew he reminded Pabbi of his own pabbi. Both Steingrímur and Ketill were old-school farmers, and Pabbi hated the old school.

Pabbi stepped outside, his head still hanging, and he didn't ask for help or company.

"Mamma," I said. She murmured but didn't look up from her book. "Do you think Pabbi is peculiar?"

Now she looked up.

"Is that what Ketill says? Well, he's right. Your pabbi is peculiar. He's always been peculiar."

I considered this.

"He doesn't seem that peculiar to me."

"That's because you're used to him."

"Aren't you used to him?"

Mamma put down her book with a sigh. She guarded her reading time jealously, even when I was home. It meant the day hadn't really started yet.

"Let us review," she said in her most professorial tone. And then she began to enumerate all the ways in which my father's choices diverged from those of most other Icelandic farmers. He kept no sheep, for example, and no horses. That meant no wool to sell, and no majestic rides in the sunset, no tourists. Pabbi rode the boundary on an old coughing Yamaha dirt bike.

As for cattle, he insisted that his herd be composed of slow-growing Galloways, one of only a few breeds you could get in Iceland that were tailored exclusively for beef. He didn't believe in cross-purpose or dairy cows, which meant no Icelandic cattle, so we never had any milk to sell, and the beef market had to be cultivated with care. The only time he milked cattle was in dire nursing emergencies, which meant getting kicked by animals unused to having their mammaries manhandled. And there was Rykug, of course, the canine anomaly. All these choices I'd taken for granted until somewhat recently, feeling pride, if I noted them at all, in my father's independent streak.

"You mean he is mulish, like Bjartur," I said, thinking of the miserable antihero of *Independent People,* a book as detested by Pabbi as it was loved by Mamma and everyone else. He found it too depressing to stomach; she found it hilarious. But maybe that was the heart of the matter: Pabbi had lived inside one or two facets of Laxness's bleak gem. You could almost say that he defined himself in opposition to it.

"No," Mamma said. "He just wants to do things a better way, even if it means financial ruin."

I considered this. Lately Pabbi had begun to veer even further from the farmer's mean. This year, for example, he had sold our bull and failed to procure a new one. After the spring crop of calves, unless he found a new bull by summer or tried artificial insemination again, which was almost always a colossal waste of time and money, we'd have a year with no offspring. Was it a plan or was it lassitude, or something else?

"So he's a contrarian, then." I didn't like the way it sounded after I said it. "Obstinate?"

"Maybe," Mamma said. "But if he were simply contrarian, he would revel in other people's reactions. Instead, he hides from people, as you can see. He genuinely finds their old ways embarrassing. Not that he himself is embarrassed—he's embarrassed for them."

I was starting to feel a bit ashamed that we'd been talking so long about Pabbi behind his back, but if we'd tried it in front of him he would've left the room anyway.

"You think it's innate, his weirdness?"

"Some of it, certainly. But his childhood was odd. Certainly it always sounded odd to a city person like me. But maybe it was odd even for Icelanders, who are an odd people."

"You are an Icelander, Mamma."

"Thank you, I know, but don't be obtuse. I grew up in Moscow and Reykjavík. Your father grew up on Heimaey, a far tinier island than Iceland, and yet still lived apart from most of the people there. And he spent a summer alone on Elliðaey, a puny little rock that makes Heimaey seem almost big."

"I didn't know that."

"Then there was the eruption, of course. The evacuation. I think it damaged him. It certainly made an impression, or maybe it makes more sense to say that it left an imprint. A brand? Is it the same thing? Is that what the expression means? I am lost. In any case, I don't think your father has ever gone back there."

"What about the rest of his family? His brothers and sisters?"

"As far as I know he hasn't seen or spoken to any of them since he was young. They went their separate ways after Steingrímur died."

"Pabbi doesn't talk much about that stuff."

"No, he doesn't."

Mamma picked up her book. The conversation was over.

6.

All thawing had ceased by the following week. Nighttime temperatures were steady at about −24°C, and everything froze over hard again. No more "mixed precipitation," no more steam from the river ice or from the paddocks crusted over with old snow; no more standing around the barnyard without your insulated overalls. Winter was jealous and had come back to reclaim southwestern Iceland. It seemed to enjoy delivering this cruel reminder.

Pabbi and I hunched against the wind, dancing from foot to foot, our shoulders raised in a perpetual expression of ambivalence. But he wasn't ambivalent today, he was very pissed off. The block heater in Kolkrabbi had died that winter, and rather than endure the monumental hassle of swapping it out right away, Pabbi decided to limp through the last few months of bitter cold, moving Kolkrabbi into the garage so he could heat it ambiently a few hours each morning, which left our forlorn truck out in the elements.

He'd been through three heaters in the last ten years, an endless source of irritation. Other farmers seemed mystified: Maybe something was wrong with the electricity current? Maybe he left it plugged in too long? Ketill liked to crow that he'd never replaced his, and his tractor was approximately four hundred years old. Another farmer down the road said that he never used his heater anyway—he just started it cold. Kolkrabbi wouldn't start cold in 0°C, let alone −18°.

Now it groaned and groaned and refused to turn over. I knew that the prospect of replacing the heater was playing before Pabbi's inner eyes like a scene from a horror film. To do it, you had to drain all the coolant from the engine block before you could attack the heater itself, which sounds easy enough, maybe, but which on Kolkrabbi entailed a whole slew of hand-breaking mechanical and physical difficulties, not to mention that the heater was buried under a snarl of metal hydraulic lines, and coolant is unpleasant, it reeks like old tires and rotting fish and can't be spilled in any volume lest dogs and barn cats discover it, because they find it delicious, and if they drink it they will swiftly die. Of the tractor-related tasks Pabbi resented, this was high among them. It may even have surpassed the abject misery and expenditure of life force required to wrestle on the ice-pick tire chains every November.

I came outside because I heard Kolkrabbi trying, cranking, failing. If it went on long enough, Pabbi might start kicking things, which was invariably how he hurt his feet. And if it went on past that, he might consider calling Ketill for help. Then the situation would be very dire indeed.

"What do you think?" I shouted. The wind vibrated the barn's loose battens and metal roofing in a discordant symphony.

"What?" Pabbi shouted back without turning around. We were both deaf beneath our thick wool hats, and he was occupied, glaring at Kolkrabbi in impotent wrath.

After a few minutes he conceded defeat, and we did a few small chores, checking that the heater still functioned in the cows' water tank and that they hadn't taken a five-kilo dump in it—this was something they did on a somewhat regular basis, for reasons that were baffling at best. When we came back, Pabbi got into the cab and turned the key. Kolkrabbi moaned for a long while in that sleepy, anesthetized tempo, but at last the engine began to huff and cough as the frigid, semi-congealed fuel tried to compress, and then with a final effort it turned over.

I felt triumphant. But triumph was clearly not on Pabbi's mind. Maybe a touch of relief? His jaw had unclenched just a little. He lurched down from the cab and we stood back, listening to the idle as it evened out. Black smoke slithered in the eaves.

"Fuck," he said.

The subtext being, *I have postponed this god-awful problem for one day. Tomorrow I will face it again.*

He fed out three round bales while I tried to make his life easier, leading the cows and yearlings into their neighboring paddocks, opening and closing gates, dragging off and trashing the big wads of plastic wrap. The whole thing took about an hour. Afterward we checked on the two cows who were indoors, ensconced in their steaming stalls because calving seemed imminent. No action.

"What's next?" I said.

"Well. I'm hungry, but it's not lunchtime yet."

"You're always hungry at ten thirty."

"You're right. The cold makes me hungry."

"Why don't you just eat?"

"Because then I'll be starving again in four or five hours. I think I'll have a smoke."

7.

Pabbi switched on the heat in the shop, which sent wood dust flying, so he switched on the exhaust fan too. Then the buzzing fluorescent tubes. It was loud but livable, and a perfect little refuge for Pabbi, who was not allowed to smoke in the house.

Our rubber boots left puddles of shitty melt on the concrete floor. Wood shavings rose to the top and eddied around. From where we sat on stools, looking out the window, I could see Baula, pallid and portentous, but no cows. The sun was carving out a meager corner of the sky to the northwest.

Pabbi extracted a pressed tobacco flake from a fastidiously labeled mason jar and started breaking it up, making a tidy pile on the cleanest corner of the workbench. The leaves were dry as bone and more or less crumbled into chips and dust. He glanced up at me briefly in the midst of his preparations, peering through his eyebrows.

"I hear you're smoking cigarettes now." There wasn't much disapproval in his voice. It was as though he were reporting on moderately bad weather.

"No," I said, trying to sound convincing and nonchalant. "Not really. I mean, I've tried them a few times. How did you hear that? Did Amma say something?"

"If your Amma knew, you'd be in deep shit."

"Then how?"

"Mamma spies on you on the internet. Some idiot friend of yours posted a photo from outside a bar. You looked drunk."

"Well, I wasn't," I said. "Not very."

In an elaborate process, Pabbi extracted the metal lighter from deep within his layers of clothes, where he kept it close to his body so the butane would work. He spun the spark wheel a few times ineffectually before his stiff fingers remembered their old routine. Wind pushed through the poorly insulated, single-pane shop windows, causing Pabbi's flame to dance around the bowl of the pipe for a while before getting caught in his draught. He leaned back, puffing.

"I used to smoke cigarettes," he said. His voice always took on a lower, pinched timbre as the smoke whirled around his mouth. "As a kid, back in Vestmannaeyjar, and later when I was driving trucks in Reykjavík."

"I didn't know that. I figured you always smoked that thing."

"No. My father smoked a pipe, but nobody my age did in the '60s, and I never wanted him to think for one second he was my hero. He wasn't. Plus it's damn hard to light a pipe while you're driving. Or in the wind. It's always windy in Vestmannaeyjar."

I looked out the window, where the landscape was now wholly obscured by a squall of hard drift snow blowing sideways: no Baula, no mountains, nothing to guide home the lost landlubber. Pabbi caught my meaning.

"It's worse there."

"How come we don't visit? You almost never talk about the place."

Pabbi furrowed his brow, maybe at the question, maybe at his pipe, which had gone out. He tamped it lightly and relit.

"Cigarettes are worse for you," he said. "Because you inhale, and they're full of nasty chemicals."

"I know, Pabbi. I only had a few. Actually I was thinking I'd like to try a pipe myself."

He regarded me with sardonic amusement.

"Because I'm your hero?"

8.

With only two days left in my school break, Pabbi wrenched the hell out of his shoulder. The joint was already bad—an old injury, scanned and probed and steroided but nebulous and idiopathic, as with so many things in the body, and intermittently re-aggravated. Pabbi always said it was the kind of pain you had to forget about, because if you remembered it when it wasn't hurting, it would start hurting again.

I wouldn't have known anything was wrong, except that Pabbi came back into the house and shut the door gently, not looking irritated, as he often did, so much as defeated. He stood in the mudroom with his boots on.

"Everything okay out there?" Mamma said, for it was Saturday again and she was home.

"No," he replied. "Didn't you hear me hollering?"

"I didn't. Are you hurt? Did you need help?"

"Yes!"

I knew that Pabbi would occasionally give vent to his rage at farming's cruel vicissitudes, in a way that might suggest he required assistance, but without ever framing the word "help." This frustrated him, as it did us, because he clearly desired help—or moral support at least, since there was generally little we could do by that time—and would've liked us to anticipate this desire without him needing to come back to the house and ask for it or bellow impotently from one hundred meters away. It was a paradox.

Pabbi consented to having his coat hung up for him and his sodden gloves draped on the towel dryer, and now, appeased with kind words and a cup of decaf coffee, since more than his single morning allotment of caffeine would cause him to vibrate, he related the morning's events. He'd heard Pylsa lowing insistently when he first checked on everyone. Noting the goopy dangler of placenta that hung from her rear end, he realized he was too late as usual, and he should've found her a place inside the barn. But it was always like this: not enough stalls for everyone, and some pregnant cows gave you no warning when they were imminent. Experienced farmers knew to watch for the "freshening," but sometimes teats stayed shriveled until the calf was halfway out, or all the way out.

"Just like a person," as Mamma was fond of saying, even though she wasn't keen on the language of bovine anatomy and obstetrics being applied to human females.

The other thing you looked for was an engorged vulva, which... of all the subjective, hard-to-quantify things. And as Pabbi was just as fond of saying, "If you spend all your time staring at cow vulvas you start to see them when you close your eyes."

So Pylsa calved out on a shit-strewn hillside. It would've been okay except the weather had warmed up marginally the day before, and it had been pissing cold rain since about 5 a.m. If the calf were still out there when the rain turned to ice, as it inevitably would, she'd be dead. Also, the hill had turned to glass. When Pabbi spotted the heifer calf out there and stepped tentatively over, she seemed to have given up on her brief life already. She lay like a pile of wet laundry, shivering and breathing only a little. Pabbi gauged that she must have been there on the ground for hours, because Pylsa had given up trying to rouse or dry her, and instead wandered back to the hayrack to eat, where she stood gargling out the occasional disconsolate moan with her mouth full.

So Pabbi sprang into action, but he sprang too fast. It was predictable, in a way. Many farming mistakes and injuries are predictable, because you're doing things that you've done a thousand times, so you get complacent or lazy. Picking a calf up off the ground and carrying it any distance is always a recipe for disaster. They're heavy, sometimes as much as forty-five kilograms, and there's no intuitive way to hold them. It's easier when they're mostly dead, as they don't kick or put up a violent protest, writhing and twisting, but when they're sodden and limp and still coated in slippery afterbirth, you can't win. So if you rush, and you're also navigating treacherous ground, as Pabbi was that morning, something is bound to stretch, snap, or tear. That day it was Pabbi's bad shoulder—the worse bad shoulder. He conceded that the agony was immense. But he got the calf into a stall somehow and gave her a quick rubdown with a nasty old dog towel, and Pylsa followed him inside, lowing in his ear. This is when cows can be the most dangerous, so rather than risk trying to tube the calf with some colostrum replacer, Pabbi deemed it preferable to get out of there fast. They'd have more luck, this new pair, if they were left alone together for a while.

Now, somewhat warmed up and composed, Pabbi said it felt like someone was jamming an ice pick into his shoulder joint if he so much as cut a pat of butter.

"You need to take it easy for a few days," Mamma said.

"Can't," Pabbi said. "I've got calves dropping left and right, and stalls to clean, and stalls to bed, and hay to feed out, and one calf that's still on replacer, and the barn is flooding every time it thaws..." He trailed off. There was no need for more entries in the litany, we all knew the list was never-ending.

"'I can't go on, I'll go on,'" I said.

Pabbi gave me a look of irritable incomprehension.

"Beckett," Mamma explained, flashing a smile, but Pabbi shrugged with disinterest so we went no further. This wasn't the time for literary exegesis.

"Pabbi, what if I stayed home and helped out for a while?"

Mamma's smile evaporated.

"What about school?" she said.

"I bet my professors would let me finish out the semester from home. I could tell them it's a family emergency. Or if not, I can just take an incomplete. Either way, it's no big deal. I'll just start back in the fall."

It wasn't that I'd planned these words, but they'd clearly been brewing. They felt natural—at home in my mouth.

Mamma and Pabbi looked at each other. I couldn't read their faces. I think maybe they were trying to reconcile the temporal disconnect of having a child, subordinate to your will for a period of years, and then suddenly finding that your child is a real person with real agency. Or I don't know, maybe they were thinking about what to have for lunch.

9.

Seven p.m., Pabbi's head was on the table and his back rose and fell in complacent rhythm. He did this often. Maybe because he rarely allowed himself to sit down during the day, so when he finally arrested his forward momentum, warmed by the heat and the food and the beer, his body gave in. His eyelids would start to droop just as soon as his plate was clean, his speech became a barely intelligible murmur and his responses sporadic, and then he'd lower himself down to the table, or occasionally all the way to the floor itself, with a smooth motion and a *huff* like a balloon landing.

We usually gave him about ten minutes. Any more and it would compromise his night's sleep—a phenomenon I now understood well—but he tended to rouse on his own at the right time, creaky and slow, fighting gravity, and ease back into consciousness by switching on a record and washing the dishes. He claimed he could hear everything that was said in his absence, but it came to him as a dream.

"Did he talk to you?" Mamma said. Pabbi was in his third minute of slumber. We'd moved over to the kitchen and I was transferring leftovers to the fridge. It didn't matter if I banged the pans around, he'd sleep through anything, unlike Mamma, who'd wake to the sound of the rain getting harder, or less hard, or a mouse in the wall, shifting around in its fiberglass nest.

"About what?"

"About being depressed."

"Not really. I did ask him, though."

"Ask him what?"

"If he was depressed. He said no."

"Well, of course he said that."

"I told him you thought he was depressed."

"You told him?"

"He said you're always projecting that stuff onto him, but he's fine. The farm has been hard lately, that's all."

"I'm not projecting," Mamma said, clearly irritated by the jibe, or perhaps just its inaccuracy. "I'd have to feel depressed in order to project it, and I don't."

Mamma had no real interest in farming—in fact, no real fondness for the country life. She considered it a sacrifice to have relocated from the city, being a city person herself, and to be reduced to neighbors who did not wash themselves as thoroughly or as often as she would prefer, and a perpetually filthy mudroom, and an even filthier car, and a dog that left ovoid impressions of caked grime wherever it happened to lie down. She also lamented the provincial culinary offerings—only a handful of restaurants in Borgarnes, serving only the usual, and a supermarket there that boasted every conceivable kind of biscuit but no fresh vegetables and a dismal array of fruit. But she would be damned if she'd blame any of it on Pabbi. She'd chosen him, she said, and whatever came with him in the bargain, even if it meant she had to wear muck boots 350 days a year, even at work.

Maybe there was a time when she thought Pabbi would settle in the city, but I doubted it. He was not city material any more than she was country. One of them was bound to compromise.

She told the story this way: They met in 1988, when she was checking out a book at Borgarbókasafnið, the Reykjavík City Library.

Pabbi, thirty-two, was briefly, fortuitously employed there, not as a librarian, though he liked to refer to himself that way, but as a kind of book-adjacent customer service technician. He said it had been his dream job until he actually landed it, because he thought it would afford him a great deal of time to read books, but instead he was expected to fill his day shelving and stamping books, as well as taking them from or handing them over to people with a moderate degree of civility. He said it was like being an impoverished bank teller.

In any case, he wasn't very good at it. He occasionally re-homed books according to his own peculiar philosophy about where they belonged, and disappeared others that he deemed overrated or otherwise unacceptable, like *Hinn mikli Gatsby*. And when it came to the library's patrons, he found it difficult to assume the correct expression of bland friendliness, or to utter the required words. The forced goodwill chafed him. So patrons often found him surly or glum, and everyone bore witness. Alternately, if he'd read someone's book selection, he might extend the verbal exchange far beyond the expected length, and a line would develop behind the patron while Pabbi engaged or imprisoned them in a debate about the finer points. He hadn't been a reader for very long, and his well was shallow in comparison to the hordes of students and aesthetes who came through every day, but his mind was thirsty and far ranging.

So when Mamma, age twenty-five, stood at the desk and passed the Icelandic translation of Walter Benjamin's *Reflections* across it, Pabbi regarded the book, and then lifted his head and regarded her for longer than was strictly necessary. He stamped it, but hesitated before giving it back to her.

"You've read this?" he said. His voice sounded judgmental.

Mamma glared at him. Her walls were always in place, in ways that remained mysterious even to her own mother, who had so much more reason and who yet hoped for her child to live a life free of constraint. But the walls were there, nonetheless, and though they were old, draped with moss and ivy, encrusted with ancient bird shit, they

could still be fortified and bristled with weaponry at the slightest hint
of siege. There were very few Jews in Iceland at the time. Very, very
few. Judaism wasn't even acknowledged as an official religion by the
Icelandic government. This meant a fairly regular exposure to uncon-
scious anti-Semitism — confusion and blithe ignorance — if and when
Mamma chose to reveal herself. She did not often reveal herself.

And there was something presumptuous about the way Pabbi
had addressed his question that put her on edge. Maybe he was one of
those who thought that Jews read only Jewish writers, or that all Jews
were Marxists. Maybe, since he was clearly Icelandic in every conceivable way, she should ask him if he'd been reading Laxness.

"Why?" she said. "Because I'm a Jew?"

Pabbi flushed. He looked like a man who had stepped out of a
sauna. It was suddenly very quiet in the library, which is not as quiet
as people think. The patrons behind Mamma stopped shuffling. The
book-adjacent technicians beside Pabbi quit stamping.

"I didn't know that," he said. "How would I know that?"

"Because of my name?" From the embrasures, arrows were
notched; from the turrets, hot oil sloshed and bubbled.

Pabbi looked down at Mamma's library card, clearly scrutinizing
it for the first time. Then he seemed to become irritated by the whole
situation.

"It's not an Icelandic name, but it means nothing to me. You're
Finnish? Russian?"

Mamma grimaced. The strange man was digging himself a hole.

"Lithuanian, thank you very much."

Pabbi suddenly brightened. "Ah! Like Teodoras Bieliackinas."

"Yes, like him," Mamma conceded, trying not to show that she
was a little impressed. "But wasn't he a bit of a fascist?"

"Oh no, no. Not at all! The Icelandic Communist Party painted
him that way because he was anti-Soviet. You would have to be, coming from Lithuania, right?"

"That's true, you would."

"They wanted to get rid of him. And anyway, he can't have been a fascist: he was friends with Laxness."

"Oh, I love Laxness," she said.

"Of course you do."

"What's that supposed to mean?"

"Just that all the students are reading Laxness again. Everywhere I look, it's Laxness, Laxness, Laxness. You can't get a drink in peace without some pretentious twerp plopping down at the bar to read Laxness ostentatiously. They might as well be holding the book upside down."

"I'm not a student," Mamma said. "Anymore."

"Well, I never was," Pabbi retorted with absurd pride. "So have you read the Benjamin?"

"If I'd read it, why would I be checking it out?"

"Maybe you liked it enough to read twice."

"Is it that good?"

"I don't know. Maybe. To be honest, I'm not sure I get it. It just seems like the only people checking it out are stoned kids who heard of 'Hashish in Marseilles,' and they think it's going to be some far-out trip, and then they come back looking disappointed. But you didn't seem like that type. And there's so much more to it."

He flipped some pages. "Like this one, 'The Destructive Character.' Every time I read it, I think I'm finally understanding. Then I get to the last line and realize I don't have a clue."

In a loud voice he read a sentence about the "destructive character" being someone who hates life but finds suicide to be too much bother.

"This from a man who killed himself!" he said, looking up expectantly, as though Mamma might very well possess the analysis he lacked. It was at this point that she began to see him less as an obnoxious know-it-all and more as an irrepressibly curious eccentric.

She held out her hand for the book. When he passed it over, she said, "I'll let you know what I think. I'm teaching it in a month."

"You're teaching it and you haven't read it yet?"

But she'd already turned and vanished behind the now-very-long line of irked patrons.

She did come back. She waited two weeks even though she'd read the Benjamin in two days, because she had things to say and the peculiar feeling that she wanted to be ready for this non-librarian. She thought the conversation might be lively, even heated, and when she ran through the turns and ripostes of their imaginary debate, sometimes she found herself very annoyed, as if she were arguing with a real person, and sometimes she smiled.

But when she showed up again at Borgarbókasafnið, he'd been fired, and no one behind the counter had any wish to discuss how or why or where he was working now.

"I've heard this story so many times," I said to Mamma. Pabbi was awake now, listening and nodding at the various things he'd said that he still agreed with. "But I somehow forgot that you two didn't actually get together when you first met."

"That's right," Mamma said. "I didn't know where he was, and I wasn't going to look for him and ask him out on a date."

"So what happened?"

"I found her," Pabbi said. "I remembered her name and I looked her up. I was making deliveries again, so I just detoured a bit from my route that day and stopped by Amma's apartment. Your mother answered the door. I was dressed in my ridiculous uniform and I don't think she remembered who I was."

"I remembered," Mamma said.

"Then what?"

"Then your father stood at the door talking about Walter Benjamin until I finally interrupted him and told him to take me out on a date."

10.

*M*ud season. We call it spring. In April, there are unmistakable signs that spring is coming. I suppose, if you were a resigned person, you would ignore what the rest of the world thinks spring is and just redefine it, thereby orienting your mind toward the real.

Pabbi was not a resigned person. He grumbled and resented and stomped. And if I scrutinized our world from a certain angle, I empathized.

When the big thaw finally showed up—showed up to stay, that is, rather than here and gone again like a sailor—water suffused us. If we had snow remaining, which we did that year, it melted into coursing rivers from any elevation. And I don't mean the Þverá alone, gray and bloated, angry with runoff. That was its own problem, for it was prone to surging over its banks if rain persisted for longer than an hour, and we had to keep a close eye on stray calves who ducked under fences and wandered in search of their swift ruin. And smaller streams rushed from all sides to feed the Þverá, which in turn paid tribute to the mighty Hvítá, and so on to the sea. Some of these brooks came from high up in the mountains and others bubbled from capricious holes in the ground that had been quiet and dry since the previous summer, hidden beneath their moss comb-overs but now spewing and sulfurous.

We were also swamped by the monoliths of filthy snow we'd plowed and piled up throughout the winter, for they now shrank by centimeters each day and their meltwater pooled on top of the still-frozen earth or ran wherever it could. If there was a hill, or even a barely perceptible decline, the water ran until it carved a rift and then it ran through that. Our road grew treacherous and striated in its curvier places, and axle-deep with sludge in the flats, pooling gray-black as the melt mixed with volcanic gravel and filled every rut. Folk in Borgarfjörður had to replace their suspensions about twice as often as people in Reykjavík, and two years prior, one of the wheels on Mamma's car had been yanked off entirely. It took half a day to extract her dismembered vehicle from the jealous mud.

It didn't matter that Pabbi paced the road, pickaxe on his shoulder like an itinerant hand, hacking channels into the mud, splattering his pants, trying to coax the water into a ditch. This was generally in vain. The road surface was like fresh *skyr,* but the dirt and ice scraped up along either side were still frozen, and they acted as bulwarks, keeping the water from the ditch and turning the road into a canal. Also the culverts were half choked with mud and ice, so any water that did find the ditch generally accumulated there instead of making its way down to the overburdened Þverá.

The barnyard, however, was the worst. A person can grow accustomed to the perpetual odor of manure and ammoniac piss. Some farmers even grow to like it, god help them, and marketers of wine or tobacco will occasionally liken the aroma of their product to "barnyard." But the barnyard in spring is something to avoid.

Our situation was rare among Borgfirðingar (the people of Borgarfjörður), in that we overwintered our cattle outside, according to Pabbi's dictum. Most cattle or sheep farmers kept their stock indoors for the long winter—with access to the barnyard and open air, of course, but in a limited way. Their springtime problems were legion but different: manure pits full to overflowing because the fields were too wet to drive upon; deep bedding in desperate need of excavation; animals driven mad with boredom, scratching their mange-ridden hides on anything with an edge or hard corner until they were stippled with open sores.

Pabbi believed in doing the opposite: essentially, in treating our herd like reindeer or musk oxen. They had access to shelter when they really needed it, of course, but they seldom made that choice, stoically bearing almost every kind of weather except for freezing rain, which they disliked, knowing perhaps that it was uniquely qualified to kill them. The thick wooly coats on our Galloways grew even thicker in November. Occasionally the animals would get itchy and drive Pabbi mad, pushing fence posts over in their single-minded determination to scratch, but their curly fur seemed to protect them from the worst abrasions and lacerations. We had some indoor cleanup to do come springtime, but it was mainly in the maternity ward, where piss, shit, and other stray bits of anatomy would get buried in the bedding and carry on a potent fermentation.

Our cattle overwintered in what we called the "sacrifice yard" — not because they were being sacrificed to Odin, or that their lives were a sacrifice, both of which may have been true, but because that paddock was a wreck. Year after year the cows dwelt there in the inclement months. The frozen season was not so bad, they simply stood around warming their engines with hay and leaving stiff, frozen turd formations in a close radius from the feeder, esoteric architecture like doll-sized modern art exhibits. But in the fall and spring, the wettest seasons, their hooves punched the ground into a cratered morass. Water ran, or bubbled up, and pooled everywhere. The melt could seldom find an outlet, blocked as it was by frozen manure and hay, and brown waste pits sprung into existence like vernal pools. If we moved with any speed greater than that of a tick, we were sure to experience the particularly unpleasant sensation of frigid slurry coursing over the top and down into the boots, soaking our socks. As it was, the integrity of the boots was often compromised by exposure to cow shit, which will eat through anything.

Splash, squelch, slop. That was the way of it. If you somehow managed to keep your pants dry during the briefest of chores, you were likely to catch it when you unwrapped a bale, for the big sheets of moldy plastic came away and flapped on the ground, acquiring a liberal veneer of liquid manure, and the wrap would always conspire to get you somehow, some way, whether in your legs or face as it kited, swinging in the stiff wind, or along your cuffs and sleeves as you crammed it into the dumpster. Pabbi often ran through his inventory of work pants in under a week, this time of year. Soiled clothing piled up in the bathtub closest to the mudroom until it began to ferment in its own juices and require immediate intervention.

So this was not an ideal time for a calf to be born, or to take its first shaky steps. Farmers in Borgarfjörður have a rule, almost an adage, that "a calf should find the teat before it finds a mouthful of shit." Pabbi was always scrambling, sliding, sloshing around in the mire, trying to rescue newborn calves and move them inside, while the mothers bellowed and charged and splashed him and whipped their tails across his collar. Sometimes a calf couldn't or wouldn't nurse. This was, perhaps, Pabbi's greatest source of frustration. He'd try it all, dragging the calf to the udder and forcing the teat into its mouth over and over again, while the mother tried her best to kill Pabbi or the calf or both, or resorting to foul vanilla-reeking fake colostrum in a bottle or, worse yet, an esophageal tube. It was seldom worth the effort.

I think, for all these reasons, that Pabbi resented springtime even more than winter. Its false promise was a personal insult. He looked about him and saw only mud and shit and death and anxiety.

I saw it otherwise. I saw everything otherwise. Pabbi had insulated me from much of this wet work over the years, whether because I was often at school or he didn't wish for me to loathe the farm or he was a man who never believed a job would be done well if someone else did it, I don't know. All those reasons, probably. But I was home now. His shoulder was injured, and the ankle he'd sprained badly in a dirt-bike fall the previous summer was plaguing him again, aggravated by the disordered terrain, so I helped with or in some cases took over these same foul tasks, slogging through the same conditions, and I found something like joy in all of it.

In Reykjavík, I had been a sleepwalker—not literally, of course, for a sleepwalker must sleep. The city stultified. All things seemed draped in gauze, and every meal took on the consistency and flavor of boiled rice. Music, previously a reliable refuge, became dangerous— it lost the power to elicit anything but pain. Now that I was rested and back in the fetid embrace of farmland in springtime, my senses were awake.

The more putrid, the better, it seemed. The squelch and suck as my boot was claimed by deeper layers of submerged muck, and my socked foot hovered perilously in the air, was a source of great amusement. The oily slick of standing wastewater shimmered with rainbows. Rykug's pleasure at the filth was irrepressible and contagious: She ran in tight circles, kicking up a spray of mud that dripped from her belly and haunches, and tried again and again to sneak around the other side of the barn and consume a rotting placenta. Even the pervasive stench that rose from the mud—very unlike fresh manure in that it was brinier, funkier, and fermented—could seize and shake me with its appalling novelty. And the sound of Pabbi's dirt bike starting up after a long winter of disuse, coughing and sputtering in objection to the clogged carburetor, the old gas, the carbonized spark plug, was like the throat clearing of an old friend.

Other pleasures were undeniable. Warmth crept into the day for longer and longer. I could feel it under my skin, down deep in the muscle and bone, the moment I stepped out the door, for the house was now colder than the world. The cows grew lazy as soon as the sun hit their flanks; they ate less and lounged more, groaning under their weight. Steam lifted continuously from the river, and from the earth itself. Fence posts relaxed. The weather was probably just as uncertain, but I could almost swear that the sun appeared for longer intervals, as though at any minute it might decide to stick around.

And then, of course, there was the *lóa,* or golden plover. The herald of spring. I think this was the first time I'd ever paid much attention to it, at least since I was a kid. The plover generally arrives first in the southeast, coming from its winter grounds in Europe, and then makes its way across Iceland to its various nesting spots. One song about its arrival, almost a nursery rhyme, begins: *"Lóan er komin að kveða burt snjóinn." The plover has arrived to banish the snow.*

So on that mild afternoon in early April when I finally heard the trilling *tuu-tuuuu* and caught sight of a mating pair, looking for all the world like honey badgers in bird form and standing in contemplation over our cleanest stock pond, I felt something crack open. It was genuine and unaffected, and I thought that I understood, at last, why we'd made up so many ridiculous songs about this very ridiculous little bird. This glorious bird.

"Sólskin í dali og blómstur í tún," I thought — *Sunshine in the valley and blooms in the meadow* — and absurdly, like a character in a musical, I sang the line out loud.

Pabbi came around the side of the barn.

"Ah yes, farming is very romantic," he said. "Maybe we should open a bed-and-breakfast."

"Maybe we should."

He gave me a scrutinizing look.

"I hope you're joking. You must *never* open a bed-and-breakfast."

"Why?" I said with a laugh. I knew Pabbi was not the type of man who wishes for the company of more than, say, three people he knows very well. But this sounded more like a conviction.

"Because a real working farm isn't a tourist attraction," he said. "It's not cuddly lambs and horses shaking their manes in the afternoon light. It's grit and misery. Look around. Does this seem like something city folk would pay to see up close?"

Pabbi shuffled away, eyes on the ground.

I gazed about me. The plover was peeping in agitation.

"Hún hefir sagt mér að vakna og vinna," I sang to myself. *She has told me to wake up and work.*

11.

"Your phone is ringing."

"I hear it, Mamma."

"So do I. Why don't you turn the sound off if you're not going to answer?"

Why indeed? The truth was, I'd shunted most of my cursory Reykjavík existence to some isolated mental outpost. Here it was late April, with only a few weeks left in the academic year, and I'd barely had any contact with my life back there. Professors had accepted my unelaborate excuse of a "family emergency back home" and—one of them grudgingly—allowed me to call the coursework complete so long as I turned in my final essay on time, along with a few extra "response" papers in lieu of class participation. These I had done with minimal effort and even less reading.

The rest of it felt just as distant. My friends (few, and were they friends? maybe they were "associates") vanished like cotton candy in the mouth. It wasn't their fault. And the person calling was a whole other story.

In the months before I'd left for university, I was deep in the throes of a dramatic teenage relationship. It was exceedingly serious, the way only nineteen-year-olds can be. We'd cried in each other's arms and vowed to be true. Sóldís wasn't going to university, not yet. She didn't feel ready, and wished to accumulate some life experience first so she didn't waste her time and money. She was practical that way. Maybe in all ways. And I knew she was right: I would've done the same if I hadn't been so curious, or so aimless, or both.

But as it happened, the mundane requirements of life had stepped in the way of her journey of self-discovery, or else routed it in a bleak direction. Sóldís had no money for travel. So now she worked the checkout aisle at Bónus, the largest supermarket in Borgarnes. This meant that I never went to the largest supermarket in Borgarnes, and my reluctance was a source of perpetual irritation to Pabbi and Mamma, who could've used more help with the grocery shopping. But there was no way around it. I lived in terror of running into her.

With every good intention, I'd gone off to Reykjavík and called her at least once a day. But sustaining long-distance love is not easy for adults, let alone teenagers. I quickly became absorbed with myself and my miseries, and found the phone calls tedious. I didn't wish to describe my classes or my meager social life. Sóldís updated me on the various doings of everyone I knew back home, which scarcely warranted the effort, since nothing ever changed. So we were left with proclamations of increasing emptiness. How many times can you tell someone you love and miss them until the words lose their meaning, and the meaning loses its meaning?

When I broke it off with Sóldís, she howled into the phone. She demanded a reason, and I offered none. She told me she would never trust another man, and would never love again, not ever. I was nineteen years old, and I felt like the worst person in the world. I surely was the worst person in the world.

I'd moved on, more or less, but Sóldís had not. She still called sometimes, looking for clarity or I don't know, I didn't answer. Mamma found the whole thing annoying. She wasn't your stereotypical mother, always feeling that her son's paramours are unworthy. She adored Sóldís, and she couldn't understand why I wouldn't answer the phone, or shop at the one store in Borgarfjörður that carried organic tomatoes.

"The grocery list is getting longer and longer," she said. "Your father is up to his ass in calving, and I'm up to my ass in grading. How do you even know Sóldís will be there?"

"Exactly," I said.

12.

Typically Mamma raced home for lunch, Bifröst University being only about a fifteen-minute drive from our place. She preferred eating in the relative peace of her kitchen to the company of her fellow educators, who were, like her, overworked, underpaid, and prone to the gossip and drama that plague academia worldwide. One or two of them were her friends, but with them Mamma always had to juggle conversation, and the creeping suspicion of seeds or dried basil in her teeth, with her enjoyment of and investment in the lunch itself. Not a great atmosphere for digestion.

Today, however, we made a plan to meet at her office and hike Stóra-Grábrók, eating a picnic at the rim regardless of the wind's unfriendliness. She had an oddly lengthy gap between classes, with no office hours scheduled and nothing pressing. Plus, the road home was so muddy now that every pass felt like it could be her little car's last. I certainly wasn't going to risk it in the Twingo—Pabbi had no need of the truck that day, and no interest in joining us. It seemed, sometimes, that the more time elapsed between his excursions off farm, the more he needed to get away, and the less able he was to do it.

Mamma and I trudged up the steps in companionable, miserable silence. The weather in Iceland knows when you are planning something. We'd barely begun the ascent when a vicious squall blew in, obliterating all memory of the sky that I could've sworn had been almost blue just minutes before, and pelted us with sleet and hail. All visibility gone. We might have been scaling some medieval tower, or a lighthouse in the midst of a gale. The saving grace was the precipitation's frozenness—I think if we'd been soaked early on, we would've turned back. Instead the sideways torrent mostly just bruised our joy, our will, our enthusiasm. You learn to forgo such things.

But we kept our heads down, grim pilgrims, and grasped at times for the intermittent railing to avoid being blown off the side, or into the crater. We made it to the midway point, where there's a rest landing, and we kept on. The hike is not long, after all, maybe one and a half kilometers there and back, and we were determined to eat at the top. Besides, we weren't going to concede defeat when we were being passed by cheerful students who practically danced their way up the stairs.

Mamma had the ornery motivations of the perpetual outsider, the immigrant, and she had passed them on to me. She may have resented the famous stamina and imperturbability of native Icelanders, coming as she did, instead, from a rich heritage of complaint elevated to a kind of art form, but she was just as hardy as they were, and if she wasn't moaning about the hellish conditions, then neither would I.

We scarcely knew when we'd reached the loop that encircles the rim of the old crater. Stumbling against each other and clutching at the rails, we were at risk of pitching headfirst into it. Surely the scabbed hole has claimed its share of picnickers that way. So we planted ourselves in a random spot and huddled together, clinging to the tinfoil that wished to take flight, our faces pointed toward what we hoped was east, and home.

At first, we could see only our immediate surroundings: the little red and black lava rocks like those clumps of crystallized sugar that line a coffee cake, only less delicious. Much of the surface was covered with pale gray-green lichens. The bottom of Stóra-Grábrók's crater was so close as to seem positively shallow. We peered into the impenetrable air.

And then, in a moment of fickle benevolence, the storm departed. It was a strange sensation to gaze about and instantly forget the prominence of Stóra-Grábrók from the ground, the portent of the humped black monolith, standing vigil over Bifröst and Route 1 like a giant's weathered tombstone. From up here, we had the dead giant's vantage. And yet we too were dwarfed by Baula behind us. She loomed, blond in the sudden sunlight, an upended canine tooth, a little broken at the top from nighttime grinding or a particularly tough piece of bone. Down below, the rectangular hayfields made a pleasing dissonance with those that were shaped into the natural oxbows of the Norðurá. Agricultural altars, old and new.

Off to the side lay Grábrókarfell, or Rauðabrók, the sister volcano to Stóra-Grábrók. She had a more derelict appearance. Her crater was obscured and partly filled in, looking as though she'd closed up and swallowed her victims forever, a surly old god. To the right of this sunken cake were the leftover signs — rock-wall paddocks, stone foundations — of a farmstead intelligently abandoned. The slightly more modern settlement of Bifröst, with its university, sat right below us: a hodgepodge, if not quite a blight, and in the grand old Danish colonial tradition of finding a sublime backdrop and then lobbing some ugly, almost brutalist, utilitarian structures into a north-facing, shade-stricken pile at the bottom. Mamma had shaken her head when the university built itself up in the 2000s, rapidly expanding its student housing, only to face the crash in 2008 and the hard truth that most students could only afford to be virtual. So most of the dormitories stood empty, but unlike the old farmstead and its ghosts, these rooms were inhabited only by the ghost of a fool's hope.

West of town, the clear waters of Lake Hreðavatn, formed when the molten Grábrókarhraun flowed into the valley and dammed the Norðurá, reflected the sky in moving tandem. These days the lava field was sedate — mossy and ancient, like the craters that had spewed it.

In this abrupt clarity, we could watch the Norðurá snaking away and away southwest, growing thinner and then fatter again as it rushed toward the meeting of rivers and the mouth of Borgar-fjörður, and the sea. And standing sentinel above that far-off patch of salt water, which was distinguishable from the sky only by the way it glittered, was Hafnarfjall, blunt-faced, holding back the entire weight of Skarðsheiði like the steadfast captain of some unruly Asgardian platoon.

"So you and Sóldís are done for real?" Mamma broached from behind a mouthful of bread and peanut butter.

I groaned, nodded.

Mamma chewed pensively. "Another broken heart convulsing in your wake."

It was harsh poetry but true, like many of the things she said. But there was no condemnation in her tone, or in her eyes. She felt for everyone, that's all.

We ate in silence for a minute or two. I thought I might be in for a treatise on why I should grow up and make peace with Sóldís, or at least get over myself and do the grocery shopping. But that wasn't on Mamma's mind.

"Do you remember Rúna, Stefán's daughter?"

"Drunk Stefán the sheep farmer? From over by Grimsá, on the shitty side of the road?"

"Yes, that one."

"Of course. She was a grade or two behind me in school. As far as I know, she never spoke."

I tried to piece together what little I knew of her. I had never seen their place but remembered that Rúna was an easy target for taunt-ing. Her farm was notoriously poor. In an area like ours, where des-titution is no particular novelty, her circumstances stood out. It was rumored that they still had no toilet indoors, and that the outhouse had to be moved every year because the farm had never been ditched properly, so the pit was always filling with water, and Stefán would rather scrape by in prehistoric style than spend a penny improving his infrastructure. Who knew how much of this was true? Children are cruel. They will seize upon anything if they think they can belittle you for it, or if they think you're a soft target. Rúna was often absent from school, and the kids liked to crow that she was digging for buried treasure on her farm—the buried treasure, in this case, being shit.

"I saw her the other day. She came with Stefán to buy some hay. I guess they didn't have enough to get through this winter."

"Damn," I said. "That's rough."

"Yes," Mamma said.

"And...?"

"And what?"

"And why are you asking me about her?"

"She asked about *you*."

Now I had some idea where this conversation was headed, and I wasn't pleased. I kept chewing.

"She wanted to know how things were going at university. I didn't say you were miserable down there. I told her you were home for a while. I suggested that you two go out sometime."

"You did what?"

"Not like a date—don't worry. You know, a walk in the mountains, or whatever you country people get up to in your spare time. Lunch on the tailgate of a truck, a few hours of fishing..."

"Fishing, really?"

"Don't give me that look, please. I swear I'm not trying to set you up. She's just—I remember that you were nice to her back when no one else was."

"And this is what I get for being nice."

Mamma ignored me. "And she seems lonely, that's all. Like she could really use a friend."

"So this is a guilt trip. I came in to meet you for lunch and we hiked up Stóra-Grábrók for a guilt trip."

"A little guilt never did any harm," she said. "Sometimes a person's empathy needs a jump start. Particularly a young person. And besides, she's grown quite beautiful."

"You mean beneath all the dirt?"

Mamma chuckled. "No, she is very clean now. Cleaner than Stefán, anyway. But she still smells like a bag of greasy wool."

13.

We sat in tolerable awkwardness on the tailgate of Pabbi's truck. The takeout from Hverinn was already cold and globulous, but we ate efficiently and without too much judgment, as Icelanders do.

Rúna and I had decided, in the world's shortest phone call, that I'd pick her up at the end of her road, since the vehicle she shared with her father was in surgery. The hardpack was still far from hard, a grayish stew. Too mucky for the Twingo. Pabbi seemed low that morning, indifferent to comings and goings, and said he didn't give a damn if I used the truck today or any day, so long as I didn't get it mired.

On the way to Rúna's, I'd rehearsed a few iterations of what I might say.

"How have you been?"

The answer could not be good.

"How's your old man?"

Also not good.

"You look the same."

Easily interpreted as an insult.

"I barely recognized you."

Same.

Fuck it, I thought. *Maybe she'll do all the talking. But what if she asks me about university?*

In the end, neither one of us said more than a few words the whole ride, and most of those revolved around whether we should get food from Hverinn or try farther afield. Rúna, who did look entirely different now, as it happened, and who I was relieved to find had made no more effort than I had to clean up — we'd both left our foul coveralls at home but remained in our shitty rubber boots, tracking clods everywhere — did not seem to care where we ate. Her introversion was unchanged, and it amplified mine.

But now we were eating, feeling the benevolent effects of the fuel and gratefully sucking down the bottles of beer she had suggested we buy, to my surprise and delight. It was 11 a.m., when farmers eat lunch. We were parked on the northwest side of the Hvítá bridge — not the old, long one down on Hvítárvallavegur, where the tourists like to block traffic while they look for the aurora, but the short, economical one-laner up by us, on Borgarfjarðarbraut — watching the spring flood as it did its best to murder an island just downstream. The water almost drowned out Rúna's voice.

"Your mom said I should give you a call."

"What?"

"Your mom said I should give you a call."

"No, I mean, I heard you. Did she say why?"

"Just that you were back home, maybe at loose ends. And something about you having a nervous breakdown in Rcykjavík."

I coughed. I was inclined, for a few moments, to feel intensely pissed off, but the beer was in its pleasantest stage, and besides, this was only Rúna, she didn't talk to anyone. I might need to have a chat with Mamma later, though. She wasn't usually a gossip.

"Well, I don't know about that. But it's funny: She said the same thing about you."

"That I had a nervous breakdown in Reykjavík?"

Rúna looked up briefly, chuckling into her sandwich. Her eyes were dark gray and speckled like a skua's head, and she already had little wrinkles around them. No money for sunglasses, I thought. Or no use for them. I realized then that I'd been underestimating her. She had a far clearer idea about this rendezvous than I did.

Now we exchanged a knowing glance. Knowing but shy.

"I have a proposal," Rúna said.

"I'm listening."

"This lunch is turning out less painful than I expected, so can we, maybe, just skip all the bullshit?"

"Yes, please," I said. "There is already far too much in the world."

She tipped back her beer and glugged a few times. Her brows were furrowed, as though the bullshit were hard to dispense with and the true genuine thoughts were tricky to parse. The sun had graced us for a few minutes and deemed that more than enough. Now it was gray and spitting a little—I shivered, thinking I should've grabbed my coat from the cab before this conversation had started. I had more than mild trepidation about what might come. I thought it might be the confession of a long-harbored crush, or else the request for a long-overdue apology for some forgotten schoolyard slight. It was neither.

"You were always nice to me," she said. "When it really felt like nobody else was."

"Should've been nicer. I think I stood by for a lot of bullying. Maybe could've stopped it."

"I doubt it. Anyway, you'd be surprised how far a little kindness goes when it seems like the whole world is shitting on you."

I nodded gravely.

"So here's how it is. I'd thought I might ask you for another favor."

The alcohol was doing that awful trick where it leaves your body faster than you can replenish it. I felt tired and cold. But whatever Rúna was grappling with, it was clearly taking courage to untangle in my presence, and I thought I owed it to her to maintain a look of serious consideration.

"You know how small it is around here. How everyone knows everyone else's business. Look, I don't want to be your girlfriend."

"Okay." I wasn't sure, in the moment, whether I felt relieved or a little crushed. I tried to look disinterested—not at all thrown by the abrupt lurch this sort-of-date had taken. Rúna picked at the sodden label of her beer, peeling it back and then pasting it on again. She stared into the dregs.

"I see Sóldís every time I shop at the Bónus, and when I mentioned your name once last winter her face turned kind of pale and sweaty and her smile went all rigid, and even though she sounded friendly and said she hoped you were having a good time in Reykjavík, I got the impression that she was angry. I just wanted to get my groceries and get out of there. Honestly she terrifies me a little."

"Yeah," I said, shaking my head. "Me too."

"I think I'm still bullshitting."

"Then don't."

"Okay, so it's like this. You're just, not my type? No offense."

Why am I here? I thought, hoping Mamma could feel my righteous irritation in some telepathic maternal mind wave. *I only agreed to this lunch to be nice.*

Rúna shook her head, as though she'd heard me. "I'm screwing this all up. Look, to hell with it. I know you weren't in the city long, but I was hoping you might've met some queer people there, or maybe you're connected on social media? And could maybe, um, connect me to them? Gay women, I mean."

My brain felt sluggish. "Lesbians?" I said.

She winced, as though the word were one with which she'd fought more than a few losing battles. Her whole body was now slumped against the wheel well. Slumped and hunched at the same time. Like an animal in pain.

"Right, whatever. That's me. I'm that. And, well, this will come as no surprise to you, but the dating pool is fairly limited in Borgarfjörður, especially if you don't want everyone in your shit."

I tried not to examine her face. That's the thing about Iceland, or most of it. You are often very alone with the person you're talking to. You can't step out of the conversation when it gets tricky. You can't disappear into the woods—there are no woods. I wondered when Rúna had figured this out about herself. I wondered who else knew, and whether she'd ever dated anyone at all. Should I feel privileged to be trusted with the information, or was I just the potential key to Reykjavík's healthy queer scene? If the latter, she was in for a disappointment.

"I might know two or three folks I could connect you with," I said, "and they might know a few more. The truth is, I didn't meet many people in the city. I'll let you in on a little secret: It's hard to make friends when you're having a *nervous breakdown*."

She looked up at me and smirked briefly.

"Anything you can do," she said. "I'm a bit desperate, as you can see."

"How about Sóldís? She said she was never going to love a man again."

"Very funny."

We sat in silence for a minute or two. The wind was whipping away every sound and smell of spring—the banter of two or three bored gulls, the frothy turgid Hvítá, the saturated riverbank with its incipient midge clouds—and flinging it out toward Borgarnes and the sea. Everything in a mad hurry to be gone.

"There's something else," Rúna said. "Another favor I wanted to ask. Really, the main reason I wanted to see you again."

"Ask away."

"Did you ever hear of a 'beard'?"

I rubbed my hand along my sparse chin bristles. "Yeah, I've heard of a beard. I hope you're not casting any aspersion on my meager attempts. It'll grow in eventually. These things take time."

She threw her balled-up tinfoil at me.

"You know what I mean or not?"

"I really don't."

"A 'beard' is like a fake hetero partner for a queer person, so people think they're straight."

"Oh," I said. "But why 'beard'? What's the significance?"

"I think it's meant for gay men. Never mind. You get the idea."

I thought I mostly did. "So you want a 'beard.' And, if I'm understanding correctly, you want me to be the hairy accessory in question. But why? Who cares what people think? Aren't you 'out'? We Borgfirðingar may be fairly backward still, but we're coming around."

Rúna groaned and inspected her bottle again. I couldn't tell if it was my naïveté irritating her or something rockier.

"I'm kind of out," she said after a long pause. "Well, I'm out online. My dad doesn't know. My aunts and uncles and cousins don't know. I'll tell them eventually, I guess, or they'll find out. Right now I just don't want to deal with it. My family is old-school. Religious too."

That was the thing about Drunk Stefán. He may have been a fool, showing up at meetings or in town with piss-stained trousers, but he was not a comic fool. Everyone knew he was a tyrant. It's a paradox, Mamma told me once—a shaky hand can still make a hard fist.

I didn't ask my next question: *Why me?* It could've been any number of reasons. Maybe because I was nice to her a few times in the past; maybe because I was living back home and single, but marginally more enlightened than the average young farmer; maybe because she didn't know or speak to anyone else. The answer might matter to me, to my ego, but it didn't matter here.

"What are we talking about exactly?" I said. "Limousines and red carpets? Fine dining in Borgarnes? Or more like cuddling and groping at the sheep roundup? I'll have you know I charge by the hour."

Rúna leaned across the truck bed and punched me hard in the biceps. It hurt like hell. She was smiling now.

"Jerk. Just call me now and then when I'm at home, or answer when I call. Maybe we can run an errand or two together, or work on a machine? I'm not asking you to pretend anything. If someone asks you directly, I wouldn't want you to lie. Just maybe, you know, don't deny it?"

"So I think what you're asking is that I be your friend," I said. "A luxuriantly bearded friend."

On the way back to her place, Rúna rolled her window down, so I had to roll mine down to balance the discordant air currents. Then she said Pabbi's CD was terrible, and she put on the radio, hitting the tuner until a pop station out of Reykjavík came on. The songs were appalling—chirpy and lugubrious—and she sang along in a fine alto. She knew all the words.

When we bumped up to the old homestead, I saw Drunk Stefán on the porch in his long johns, watching us, or watching the world, with bleary hostility. He raised his hand in a nominal greeting. In the passenger seat, Rúna took a deep breath, as though for a plunge into very cold water, but her expression seemed milder than earlier that day, less burdened. She gave me a tiny half smile.

"Talk to you later? Thanks for lunch."

Then she stepped out and walked around to the barnyard without uttering one word to her father.

"Goodbye, my love!" I called out the window.

She barked a quick laugh, shaking her head, and disappeared behind the round bales.

I drove home, took a thirty-minute nap, and went back to work.

14.

Middle of May, the air full of birdsong, insects hatching in clouds of precocious horniness from river, pond, and puddle, Borgarfjörður positively brimming with life after so many long months of dormant stillness, and yet six lively, cheerful steers were due to meet their cruel maker the following day. It was time to slaughter.

Time for us wayward would-be cattle barons, anyway. Most of Iceland slaughtered in September and October, when it was appropriate for sheep to die. (The horse ranchers seemed to slaughter whenever it was convenient for a roundup, or high time to cull.) But Pabbi did not want to contend with the hordes of sheep farmers all scrabbling for slaughter dates in autumn, or jockey with their lines of bleating trailers as they snaked through the back roads and queued up to unload. Also, we kept the slow-growing Galloway longer than most people keep steers—two years at the very least, or they'd be so lean, so low in intramuscular fat, that every customer would need to tenderize their steaks with a mallet as if it were octopus. One more winter usually did the trick.

And the Icelandic abattoir system was a bottleneck. Not enough facilities — not enough clean, reliable ones anyway. Pabbi had tried out a couple of local options and was not pleased. He was picky, of course, and held them to a high standard. He felt that the amount of care and effort he put into raising these difficult animals and giving them lives of decency should be reflected not only in the manner of their deaths but in the meat created from their muscle and bone. There were so many ways a slaughterhouse could fuck it up, and they invariably did fuck it up. So Pabbi drove our animals the two hours to Selfoss, where there was a large, relatively clean, well-inspected operation. They still fucked things up sometimes, but they fucked them up less, and they knew Pabbi well. This meant it was easy to schedule his off-peak dates whenever he wanted them, and in May they had the cooler space to let our beef hang for a solid three weeks, which it needed.

But regardless of the season, the abattoir decreed that animals be unloaded by 7 a.m. — a requirement that Pabbi found arbitrary and irritating — so he had to perform the delicate maneuvers of loading large animals the day before.

This was the first time I participated in earnest. I'd watched from the sidelines, of course, held the two-way radio while Mamma conveyed trailer directions to Pabbi in the truck, heard the cursing and entreating from Pabbi, the lowing and snorting and nervous shitting from the beeves.

Sometimes the process took six hours. Today it took two, which Pabbi and I considered pretty good. I did my best to keep my breath calm, my emotions collected, as cows — maybe all prey animals — have a keen sense for these things, and so nothing went too awry, even when a big steer tried twice to kick me in the knees as it walked past, and another made a few half-hearted attempts to jump through a plate-glass window.

We made the steers as comfortable as we could — hay, alfalfa pellets, water — and then we went over the directions together. They were easy. Pabbi reminded me to set an alarm for 4:30 a.m. — preferably two alarms. He reminded me to adjust the strength of the trailer brakes before I got to the main road, and to adjust them again when the trailer was empty. He reminded me to hand my cut sheet to the one employee he knew to be semi-competent. He reminded me to take the truck out of four-wheel drive when I left dirt, and to use the engine brake as much as possible, especially since the rotors were perpetually fucked from rust and damp, as warped and jagged as a cheese grater, and there was a real chance the brake pads were already scraped right down to the metal.

"You're not getting up with me?" I said, a little apprehensive.

"What would be the point of you doing the slaughter run if I still had to get up at the crack?"

Ten minutes before the alarm, I jerked out of bed, heart racing. My stomach was closed, but I forced down some toast and made coffee to go. I thought maybe Pabbi would crawl out of bed to proffer a few more sage words, but if he was awake and concerned, then he was doing it silently.

The steers stood up and stamped around a bit when they heard me coming. I switched on the inside trailer light and peered in at them. Wide-eyed as always, but calm, adjusted to their new quarters. Their last quarters.

I did the first part of the haul in silence, attentive to the harsh music of the trailer: the creak as it shifted and swung; the emergency chains banging against the hitch; the whine of the electric brakes; the metal clangs as the steers jockeyed for position and lurched into the walls; the occasional bellow. They say, for the purposes of animal well-being and subsequent meat quality, that a drive to the slaughter-house should be as short as possible. They are undoubtedly right.

I mused and tried not to drink my coffee all at once. I thought of Pabbi relinquishing this task. Was it hard for him? Or was it a relief? I knew he hated everything about it, particularly the emotional rents and the deeply unpleasant labor of cleaning the trailer afterward, which he'd made it clear I would do alone. And thus the new, recurring question: Was he welcoming me aboard, or passing the torch, or trying to scare me straight? Straight, in this case, being a life of gainful employment in almost any field but farming. Impossible to know. Or too tricky to untangle.

A little way past Thingvellir, with about forty-five minutes to go, the sun came up. I put the stereo on, my old iPod plugged in by an aux cable. I was cresting a hill, the truck chugging doggedly, and just as a blast of dawn light pierced my left eyeball, I heard the opening bars of "For Those About to Rock (We Salute You)." The song always seemed like it was building toward something and never quite got there, even when the cheesy fake cannons started firing, but maintained this kind of satisfying, head-nodding, low-tempo bombast. I turned it up.

By the time I pulled into Sláturfélag Suðurlands, I was wide-awake. The coffee was running through my veins, and so was the music, and so was this heady draught of independence and capability. I backed the trailer up to the loading dock with abnormal precision. The employee who came outside, smoking, grunted his approval and said, "Nice." When I opened the rear door the steers backed away, looking alarmed, but I walked in calmly, keeping close to the wall, and they filed out. No one threw a kick—not even Safi, who'd tried to jump out of a window sixteen hours earlier.

"That a bull?" the man asked, eyeing Safi with approval.

"No, just a steer."

"Well, he looks like a bull," he said. "He looks *good*."

I nodded my thanks, the joy of the compliment suffused with a condescending glow at the man's profound ignorance, since bulls look nothing like steers and he clearly couldn't tell a cow from a goat.

The steers walked placidly inside, and I handed off my cut sheet. It was 7:01 a.m. A horse farmer—Pabbi called them "horse people"—had pulled in behind me and was privileged enough to witness the whole thing.

This is what satisfaction feels like, I thought, and then got back in the truck. Within ten minutes I was back on the main road and deadly tired. A raw chasm had opened up in my torso. Was it hunger? (I was exceedingly hungry, I realized.) Or pain at playing such an intimate hand in this latest betrayal? I knew Pabbi took these slaughter trips hard. He always came home looking destroyed, and required a large hot breakfast and at least three hours of rest, with maybe a nap, before donning his rubber boots and wheeling out the pressure washer.

But I didn't feel destroyed. Not yet. The steers had enjoyed a good, albeit truncated, life, and now they would have a quick death without terror, and their flesh would enliven the repasts of many grateful eaters. Wasn't every line of work full of trade-offs? It all depended on what you were trading.

15.

Early summer evening. Only faint smells on the wind—that's Iceland for you. Fermenting barnyard if you're lucky enough to live near one. Fish and seaweed along the coast. The rest is blown off with little to obstruct it.

Windows wide-open to let in the fine breeze. No screens, of course—we don't do screens. It isn't backwardness, we just don't stoop to their level. So, black flies congregating around my desk lamp, or scuttling across my computer screen, along with a few of the innocuous long-legged things we call horseflies and the rest of the world apparently calls mosquito hawks or mosquito eaters. I didn't mind the intrusion. I was on the internet.

I swear my intentions were good. I'm fairly certain my intentions were good. Pabbi and Mamma in bed, asleep or reading, me down the hall in my old room, I thought I'd do a little scrolling on Rúna's behalf. Not a dating site—I didn't think either one of us was quite there yet—just plain old social media. But I'd skittered from profile to profile, following some senseless, grubbing muse, and so far failed to find anyone I might be even remotely connected to, and this was employing at least four or five liberal degrees of separation. No one who might be even remotely promising for Rúna. Of course I didn't know her very well yet. What sort of woman was she looking for? Most of the people our age with any sort of active web presence were either urban or rural masquerading as urban. Would Rúna be comfortable with people like that, who didn't understand or embrace farm life? Maybe she wanted to leave it all behind. Bury it, like so many former countryfolk did when they moved to the city. But even if she wanted to, it wouldn't be easy. The farm was written all over her. She tracked it across the floor of every room she entered.

"Didn't give me much to work with," I said to Rykug, who was snoring at my feet in a box that used to hold the tractor's ice-pick chains and was now filled with ratty old towels and a warm dog.

So I let the blind muse wander. Soon, inevitably, I was scrutinizing the faces and profiles of people I'd never heard of, but with a more selfish eye. Maybe I was still doing what I set out to do—maybe my preferences could be helpful in determining Rúna's. Probably not.

And then, following the thread of a brilliant, semi-obscure Kiwi musician I particularly liked, and pulling it, and pulling it, I found her: Amihan Cruz, Proud Pinay, student at the University of Akureyri, "If you tell me to smile I will stab you in the face." If she was in her photos, and she wasn't in very many—not a fan of selfies, apparently—she was always at least partly obscured, or distant, or half out of the frame. The best I could see of her was this: scowling a little, brows furrowed, looking annoyed at the photographer, or the lens, or the world, but her eyes alive with amusement. She was about half a meter shorter than everyone else. About two years older than me. Good taste in music, clearly. Snooping didn't get me much more. I couldn't tell what the story was with her schooling—was she still enrolled?—or her job, which was maybe at a hotel. A few photos showed her with a young boy of about six or seven, the two of them glowering at the camera in affectionate tandem. Could it be her kid?

Most of the other photos were of animals, classic Icelandic animals in classic Icelandic tableaux. They looked like they were taken by the side of the road, sometimes from a moving vehicle. Horses in a scattered line, the foals showing their asses as they ran from the stranger. Sheep huddled morosely in a ditch. An Icelandic cow with its head sticking out of a barn door, face rendered ridiculous as it chewed cud, jaw off-kilter and huge, questing tongue. A fox looking back over its shoulder, as if to say, *What?* A raven on a gut pile. No captions to any of these.

And she seemed to really enjoy camping. Or was, at the very least, intrepid. Several shots of a tent — was it a one- or a two-person tent? — being pelted and smothered by various weathers, the rain fly in the process of living up to its accursed name. Sometimes it was set up in a boggy-looking moor, the stakes set deep against the wind. Elsewhere she'd pitched it like an ill-equipped astronaut amongst the unforgiving black moonscape, likely up in the high country, and the guylines were tied to rocks.

Without quite knowing what I was up to, I penned a private message. "Hey, cool photos. No love for the lowly Galloway?" I stood up and paced around the room. My heart was hammering absurdly. Should I add an emoji to indicate facetiousness? I didn't believe in them, as a rule, but it was hard to deny their practicality when addressing someone whose sense of humor I'd yet to plumb. What did it matter? It was out of character, that's all. People sent messages to each other all the time. That was the modern world. It's how we became a less isolated society. Or maybe it was how people crossed ancient boundaries, invading a space that should've been private, and somehow wasn't anymore.

I stooped and grabbed hold of the loose skin around Rykug's neck, giving it a gentle shake. She snorted out of sleep, unkinked her neck, and lifted her head over the rim of the tire-chain box. She blinked once or twice before shining the high beams of her deranged yellow eyes at me, her ears reaching up and up until they were at full attention. This was a dog who listened.

"What am I looking for?" I asked her. She gave two half thumps of her tail and let her spade-shaped satellite dishes pivot 10 degrees to the side and rear. This meant, I think, something like *Give me a few scratches while I take a moment to consider your question.* I'd found recently that speaking to Rykug in my head was insufficient—she wasn't telepathic, despite her strong powers of empathy, and she didn't know she was being addressed. Sometimes it felt a bit silly, talking aloud to her about things she didn't have the language for, but then you saw old farmers doing it all the time. They were probably onto something. Also, there was that story in the news about the border collie—Chaser? terrible name—who had learned over one thousand words, and according to Pabbi, anything a border collie could do, a kelpie could do better. She just might be a little less showy about it.

Back at the scene of the dubious epistle, two horseflies were having sex on my laptop, or just touching butts, I wasn't sure.

"I'm not an entomologist," I said.

Rykug groaned and settled back into her box. I knew her feelings on the matter. Bugs were fine for eating, and good fun to catch out of the air, like the occasional songbird.

I shooed off the lovers and deleted the note. The cursor blinked at me—how could a pulsing line appear so exasperated?

"Delaney Davidson is the best," I wrote. "Do you like the new album? That's Fanfara Kalashnikov backing him up on 'I Slept Late.' I found a bunch of their songs online. Could send if you're interested."

Pedantic, I thought. *Intrusive, presumptuous.* Again, I deleted most of it in disgust. Now what remained were the only bits I could stand: "Hey, cool photos. Delaney Davidson is the best."

I rapped my fingers on the desk, ran them through my hair until it had sprung out in all directions like that of a cartoon man being electrocuted.

"Fuck it," I said to Rykug, then added "Right?" to the end of my missive so that it might encourage a reply, and hit SEND.

The next morning, after a restive night, I opened the computer first thing. Nothing. Mildly disappointing but expected. Three days later, still nothing, and I cursed myself for stepping past the invisible boundary, vowed never to do it again. On day four, a message came back: "Yeah he is. 'I Slept Late' is my favorite. Trying to learn it on guitar. Sounds fucking terrible." To this I replied with a very, very long letter about music obsessions and what I was doing back at the farm, along with a few cow stories I thought she might find amusing or horrifying, and I sent it before I could make it go away, and then felt so fluttered and nauseated that I couldn't eat breakfast and Mamma asked if I was sick. Two excruciating days followed in which I didn't think highly of myself.

Then the dam broke. A letter from Amihan came back. If it wasn't quite as lengthy, quite as revealing—well, it was considerably more guarded—I was sanguine about that. In fact I couldn't have been happier. And the messages started to flow between us, faster and faster, longer and longer, sometimes two or three a day, and now I knew all about her musical tastes and her family and her life without really knowing anything. She said to call her Mihan; only teachers and doctors called her Amihan. The kid was her sister's, it turned out—and what confusing relief for me to hear—who she spent a great deal of time with, helped raise in a way, as the dad wasn't in the picture, wasn't in fact a dad of any kind. Mihan was still in school, Media Studies, but part-time. She was working a lot at the front desk of the hotel where her mom also worked, only taking a class or two at the moment—I felt a twinge of recognition at her evasiveness on this subject—and this left her not much time to do what she loved most, which was camping in the wilderness, as far as she could get without drowning her mom's car in the river, and did I like camping? I did not but hedged my answer to that one.

One week and about four hundred letters later, we switched to the telephone. The telephone seemed more practical; there was so much to say, after all. It started because the internet was shitting the bed at our farm, maybe the router or something, except I failed to mention that it was perpetually shitting the bed, our internet slept in a shitty bed, but still it was true enough. I gave Mihan my cell phone number, just in case she wanted to tell me something, that unlikely scenario, and couldn't reach me online, because, you know, data is expensive, etc. And this felt like another step too far, a nauseous step, but within fifteen minutes I received a text from an unknown number that said, "Hey it's Mihan!" followed by two emojis: a cow and a hot dog. And if I leapt at the opportunity to talk to her, if I found her voice—strangely low and gravelly—entrancing, well that was just how friendship went sometimes.

We talked for hours at a stretch. There is much for good friends to catch up on when they've only just met. And we spoke with animation on every subject we could think of, usually late into the night. This was a source of consternation to Mamma, who was no more a deep sleeper than I was, so I began to call Mihan from the barn if it was raining or the field if it wasn't, from which she could hear the occasional irritated call of a cow or melancholy moan of a calf as they sought each other in the blueish half dark, and this delighted her. And anything that delighted Mihan delighted me, and her laughter, brash and rowdy, was, I thought, the finest sound in the world.

16.

It's bloody hard to make hay in Iceland. So hard that it's almost comical. And you don't have to be from Iceland to know it, anyone who's read Laxness can testify.

Two innovations made it marginally more feasible for us. The first was mechanized ditching, pure and simple. Back before the Americans showed up here in 1941 and, in a patronizing move that still irritates us, took over our "defense," our agriculture was basically medieval. Slow, poor, grueling, laced with futility. Because who in their right mind—I'm looking at you, Vikings—would take their first steps onto our steaming black rock and think *farmland*? I guess they had to be coming from some tough places.

So for about a thousand years we farmed the same way, horses and hand tools, we stuck with what worked. The problem was that it didn't work very well. Being that our fertile season is shorter and wetter than most, and being that most of our ground is like the gods' own mining operation with, if you're very, very lucky, a paper-thin layer of tussocky grass thrown over it, we have certain hurdles to overcome. It's handsome and all, but *farmland*? Maybe a person will take on any agricultural indignity if there are no big animals to

eat and he's tired of fishing some of the most lethal waters known
to man.

It's a leap from tailings to timothy. Our bottomland, our flattish
and relatively fertile valley floors, were all floodplain, marsh, and bog.
Wet ground becoming ever wetter as it's pounded by rain throughout
the short growing season will not produce an Icelandic winter's worth
of livestock feed. So we ditched. We ditched and ditched and ditched,
but there's only so much ditching a human and horse can do, particularly when the ground is *grýtt,* with precious little dirt between the
razor-sharp rocks, and there aren't many humans to begin with, and
only the most wealthy among them might own a horse, and how are
they feeding the horse anyway? Horses can't survive the long dark
months on salt cod.

But then the Americans showed up in the '40s and they were
like, "Jesus Christ, haven't you ever heard of a tractor?" And in their
supreme benevolence they gave or sold us a few Masseys, Farmalls,
John Deeres, and Internationals, and all of a sudden we were ditching the hell out of the place. We drained so many swamps and moved
so many rocks in our madness to create hay ground that most of the
birds departed—the expression is "for greener pastures," but in this
case they'd preferred the soggy bogs. That left us with a great many
fertile fields in perfect rectangles, because they were shaped by man,
not god.

Pabbi said that in parts of the world, such as the western United
States, people dig ditches so that they can run water through them
and *intentionally* overflow the banks, thereby flooding the flat land.
They call this irrigation. Irrigation is a foreign concept in Iceland, like
"suntan" and "fruit."

The other major invention didn't occur until about fifty years
later. It's called plastic wrap—you know, the marshmallows. Until
sometime in the 1990s, we did it like everyone else, trying our best
to dry the cut grass so it would hold stable for the long winter and not
turn into a science experiment. In the old days this meant piling the

hay into esoteric little sculptures before moving it under cover. Usually we failed in this. Icelandic skies don't like to give a person more than a day of meteorological respite, we might get complacent otherwise. Once again, see Laxness.

In more recent years we figured out how to blow loose green hay into the barn and then vent hot air through the floor, so the drying process could cheat time. But we still had a devilish time of it making bales, large or small, which everyone will agree are the most efficient method for moving feed from the barn to the mouths of hungry beasts.

Then came plastic wrap, the farmer's friend (also the friend of the petrochemical executive, the enemy of the farmer's bank account, and the flapping, disintegrating, wind-driven scourge of ocean and glacier). With rolls and rolls of the fabled wrap on hand, we could finally use the European fixed-chamber round balers, which can handle wet grass or dry grass or any kind of grass without plugging up, and we could take those big beloved bales and place them gingerly on mechanical spinning tables. These, in turn, would rotate each bale with a horrific squeal as the wrap unrolled, music to our bleeding ears, leaving the bales coddled and concealed like Christmas presents for sheep, cow, and horse.

At this point they could be stored outside, freeing up untold square meters of barn space—precious, particularly, in a climate where any tool or machine left outside is beset by water, salt, and flying volcanic sand, resigning it to a half-life of far shorter duration. Unplanned early obsolescence.

But most importantly, once "ensiled" in their individual gnocchi, the bales could skip the drying process altogether. There, catching meager rays but no life-nurturing oxygen, they ferment. Green hay wrapped at the right time—and it's a generous window—will preserve its finer qualities, namely protein, better than dry hay ever could. End of science lesson.

So Iceland became viable farm country at last. This presented us with a decade or more of wild abundance: bales piled as high as Heiðarhorn, increased herds, government grants flowing like spring runoff, upgraded and modernized dairy infrastructure — things were looking good. But it wasn't good at all. We'd already cratered our market in the late 1980s by aping the Danes and their top-down style. That colonized mentality sticks around like an oil stain. We stood by while the suits in Reykjavík took control of everything — the stores, the abattoirs — and the Kaupfélag Borgfirðinga, the buying union that had once brought farmers together and made them powerful, or relatively so, went bankrupt. Pabbi used to tell stories about the "meat mountain," a nightmarish monument of backlogged flesh that accumulated at the Kaupfélag when distribution and sales screeched to a halt.

And that was only the preamble, of course. The gentle first notes. Farmers treaded water for a while, as farmers do, some invariably sinking, some scrambling out so that they might kick others in the face, stomp on their bloated, white-knuckled fingers, and send them down, leaving very few on the dock, no one wants to share the dock. We are full of grim oceanic metaphors and can take them far. But we farmers, we liked this new capacity for production, and we bought many machines, and we poured many concrete floors, and we built many new buildings, and to do this we took out many loans.

Then, in 2008, the crash. Farmers didn't stand a chance. The banks failed, and in their death throes they dismembered small-scale agriculture. Debt has always been the way of the farmer. It's a tenuous way to live, but people get used to it. And when it ruins them, for one reason or another, it does so with quiet indifference. Each time Iceland made the news during those two cruel years — and not for a volcano, finally — it was all about the greater economy and the upheavals in government, or people on the streets in Reykjavík. You didn't see international journalists moaning about the old-timer on the dry side of the Grimsá with five hundred sheep and twenty milk cows and thirty horses who went tits up and drank himself to death.

Some oldsters hung on to the land even though they weren't farming it for profit anymore, just raising some horses, because their mortgage was paid off and their machines, lovingly tended, still ran. Many more sold out to bigger operators. Pabbi said that in Borgarfjörður, at least, there are so few active small farmers left that the wind doesn't even whistle between them.

17.

We made our first cut in late June. It wasn't a task that Pabbi could turn over to me entirely—there were just too many complicated things I needed to learn first—but I took on a more active role than I ever had before. Usually he did everything himself, from start to finish, with the exception of the wrapping, and stumbled back into the house each night in a state of unparalleled filth, half dead.

It had been fairly dry the day before, so the grass would be manageable and the hayground solid enough for us to drive over it approximately one thousand times without rooting it up like a pigpen. Pabbi had been checking the weather app compulsively, cursing its notorious worthlessness, and now we had two days ahead of us that looked moderately clear, two days to complete about a quarter of our first cutting.

Each task began with both of us cramped inside Kolkrabbi, switching back and forth in the driver's seat, Pabbi demonstrating the perils and pitfalls. In a hoarse shout over the diesel roar, he talked me through the mowing, raking, baling, wrapping. The things to listen for. The frequency with which an operator should turn around and assess the implement behind them—so frequent, it turned out, that a person existed for two days at a time with their back and neck in a twist, their eyes looking in both directions like a cow. Pabbi's spine resented this. Mine was more forgiving.

After an hour or so with each new step, Pabbi would jump out and watch from the sidelines. His look of appraisal was stern. At times he'd wave frantically for me to stop and then he'd climb in, correcting whatever grave error I'd committed, but without too much harsh judgment unless I really seemed obtuse. There were a few "What the hell were you thinking?" and "Haven't you been listening?" but not many. Every time we went through this, Rykug, who had also been observing, but with a look of bemusement, ran over and jumped through the open cab door. Then she'd squeeze beneath the clutch pedal and, with her toenails digging into the rubber mat, affix herself to the spot like a tai chi master. It took some coaxing to get her out again. Harsh words were of no use—had to be entreaties.

"Why is she being so neurotic?" Pabbi said. "I never let her in there."

"It's my benevolent energy," I said. "Irresistible."

After a while, I'd look up from deep concentration on the rows before me and find that I was alone in the field. Pabbi had taken the four-wheeler back to the house, or was observing from a secret vantage somewhere. And then I began to experience surges of self-worth that I'd seldom known. I'd note the neat swaths, the rigid rows, the sweet din of well-oiled machines behaving tolerably, belts and chains spinning the way god intended, and all of it making such harmony with the wider world—the river still running high, insects rising from the swampier parts, once in a while a wayward seabird, Baula mild in her supervisory role—and I'd think, *Goddamn, I can do this. I am competent at something.* And another voice in my head would nag that many, many people were competent at this, many who were not in fact very smart or capable in other ways, but that voice wasn't strong at the moment, it lacked volume.

Once or twice I even stopped and took a photo of myself in the tractor, or hopped out and framed Kolkrabbi against the sky, too picturesque not to, I guess, machine and nature, work and worth, and posted it online, where it generated a few hearts and a few unanswered comments like "Amazing! What are you doing? Let's catch up!"

I mowed and raked on day one, accomplishing the latter in one of our smaller, more agile, and fuel-efficient old Deutz tractors. These, which lived outside in the ignominy of the outdated, were open-station German relics that made the haying a louder, grittier, more tangible, and allergenic experience. They couldn't handle a baler or a round bale, but they could rake with the best of them.

On day two, we baled and wrapped. By splitting these up into two discrete processes, we were purgatorial. Not quite old-school — we wrapped in plastic, after all, and our baler was under ten years old, therefore newish — but already antiquated. Borgarfjörður had begun to see a number of, if not yet a preponderance of, the expensive machines that baled and wrapped in one long mysterious two-part chrysalis. The crop was consumed as a windrow and excreted as a perfectly wrapped bale. These made Pabbi nervous. He said it was because their workings were obscured; you couldn't open them up and manually intervene.

My first experience with baling proceeded without incident, which is never to be taken for granted, as balers have a fondness for breaking down, plugging up, catching fire, or tearing your arms off. When things went well, you knew simultaneously that the stars were aligned and that you were going to catch it in some other way.

So with the field full of bales — a fine sight indeed, when everything was still grass-colored, and before the pleasing barrels had a chance to slump — we commenced the job of wrapping. In the past, Mamma had worked the wrapper, a somewhat derelict specimen that showed every inch of abuse it had taken, while Pabbi drove Kolkrabbi back and forth over the field a hundred times, moving the bales. Mamma used the truck to haul the wrapper around; having its own little engine and hydraulic pump, it required no tractor. But this arrangement could be problematic if haying occurred on a day when Mamma was at work. Mamma was the best at wrapping—she always found the right speed for spinning the bale, always paid close attention to the number of rotations, always dumped the bale with great care so the wrap wouldn't puncture. She was a conscientious machine operator, a conscientious person in general, and Pabbi knew it better than anyone. So if someone else did it, there was bound to be some frustration. Harsh words, harsh reflections. Everyone unfamiliar with the device tended to make the exact same mistakes, and the maddening consistency of this could be read across Pabbi's face as clear as if it were in words. Ketill had wrapped for us a few times, as had a few other local farmers. Even Amma had wrapped—she wasn't bad but objected to the noise.

Now we'd entered a new epoch, however. Here I was, driving Kolkrabbi around and loading the bales onto the wrapping table, mostly without incident, while Pabbi ran the wrapper, trying to do justice to Mamma's standard of excellence. It went quickly. I thought so, anyway. I received a few minor recriminations, nothing I didn't deserve, and they were tempered by a few words of praise.

Then everything went shithouse. Like one of Odysseus's shipmates, I fell to the siren song of the long summer light. Pabbi had warned me of its perils and temptations. You go and go, and you want to keep going, finish the job at any cost, because why not? The sun is still shining, the day is still living. It might rain tomorrow, it always might. Maybe you had a little dinner, or maybe you forgot to eat, but in either case you don't feel the exhaustion creeping up on you after twelve hours in the tractor, and you work past your limit, and all it takes is one careless mistake.

Pabbi didn't like to leave the wrapped bales in the field. When he did, the job felt undone, put off. It hung over his head. Most farmers didn't care, they left the bales out there for weeks sometimes while they slowly moved them in. Moving bales became a fill-in job, whenever a sliver of time exposed itself. They might have sheep that wandered into the hayfield, but sheep tended not to disturb the bales. Horses, on the other hand: Pabbi already had a volcanic reaction to neighbors' horses getting on our land. He lived in fear that they'd get into his bales, compromising his wrap. This would be too much, and he'd react badly, and then what? Nothing good.

But tonight, with all the extra time of teaching me, and the fact that I still ran everything several thousand rpms slower than he did, he argued in favor of leaving them out there for a day or two. It was late, he said. Almost 9 p.m. Time to pack it in while all our limbs and digits were still attached. I could see he was tired. Maybe I was too, but I didn't feel it.

"I got it," I said. "You head in and take it easy."

He left me out there reluctantly. Alone and righteous, I loaded bales onto a hay wagon and started ferrying them back to the farm-yard, eight at a time. The route required me to drive Kolkrabbi up and down a few steep, grass-covered slopes. The track, such as it was, had no gravel, just a greasy depression where the tractor tires had chewed it up over two days. What Pabbi forgot to tell me, what I should have known to do in any case, was put the tractor into its low-est gear and engage four-wheel drive. The first trip went well even though I was still in two-wheel, as I just happened to be in a lower gear, low enough to maintain traction, to cling to the ground while 4,500 kilos pushed me from behind. The second trip, heady and complacent, also went well. On the third trip, I realized halfway down the slope that I was in a higher gear—realized because I found myself going a touch too fast. That's when I made my worst mistake. I should've ridden it out, committing to the gear and letting the rpms hold the engine back just enough. I probably would've made it. Instead I tried to change gear. As soon as I depressed the clutch and knocked it into neutral, Kolkrabbi took off running, wholly unhindered by any sort of mechanical control. And now that it was going, nothing in my power could convince it to shift into a lower gear, or any gear at all. Faster and faster. I tried to stop, jamming down on the brakes with everything I had, but they were of no use, the tires just skidded down the slick track as though they were completely bald. The combined force of gravity and a loaded hay wagon were like a rocket booster, only I wasn't pointed at the sky, I was pointed at a ravine, a series of fences, a knot of unforgiving black rock, and certain death. In the moment, was I more terrified or more embarrassed? I was in full view of our house. Maybe Pabbi and Mamma were watching from the window, drinks in hand, mouths open.

It was the wagon that saved me, classic bitter irony, unremarkable to any farmer but a delight to relate while kicking tires in a muddy dooryard. In its unruly descent, the wagon decided that it was impatient for chaos and mayhem, that the deranged tractor was in fact not going fast enough and should pick it up a little. And so it began to swing. If you've ever been on a highway in a little car and been plagued by an eighteen-wheeler that wanted to pass you, it's a bit like that, except if the truck were hitched to your rear bumper. This lurching dance of the wagon made an impression on Kolkrabbi, of course. It began to swing too. That's when I realized that my nightmare vision of crashing into something immoveable and sailing through the windscreen—a ragdoll on the rocks—was wholly inaccurate. No, I was going to roll. They'd find my body inside the cab, all juiced and muddled.

Neither came to pass, in the end. With one final determined swing to the right, the wagon thrust Kolkrabbi to the left, and it just kept turning and turning, 45 degrees, 90 degrees, 180 degrees, and all at once I was jackknifed tight against the wagon, pointed precisely in the direction from which I'd come. The whole apparatus came to a sudden, inexplicable stop. I tried to breathe. I had to get out. I couldn't get out, as the tractor door was pressed against the wagon's side wall. So I opened the rear window of Kolkrabbi and slithered onto the grass like a newborn calf. I lay on the ground, panting. I couldn't see right or think straight. Every muscle in my body was ratcheted to its breaking point. There is an expression, when you're driving and something scary happens: "Your ass chews a hole in the seat." What happens when your entire body is gripping against the empty air? Do you chew a hole in time and space? Do you leave this world for another?

I heard the sound of a four-wheeler approaching, and suddenly my face was being licked hard by an anxious, whining Rykug. And there was Pabbi, just as concerned. Was I all right? I would be all right. No judgment, no recriminations, but a steady assessment of the damage. Nothing too bad, as it turned out. Sometimes, infrequently, nothing too bad. In this case a sheared tie-rod on the wagon, a big chunk of rubber out of Kolkrabbi's rear tire—that was about it. Mamma brought another tractor, one of the Deutz relics. Together we chocked up the wagon so we could unhitch it—a tricky task, pinched as it was—move Kolkrabbi away, unload the bales one by one, and drag the crippled, tire-dragging wagon safely to the bottom of the hill.

Before we left the field, Pabbi looked at me appraisingly. His face was very creased, but his voice was calm. "Next time, before you head down that hill, stop and put it in four-wheel. Check your gear. Put on your seat belt. Ask me how I know."

We left the bales in the field.

18.

The following day it spat rain. Summer session in Bifröst, and Mamma had left the house at her usual hour, coffee in hand, work shoes in a canvas bag. Not that any sort of vanity prevented her from wearing rubber muck boots to a classroom—she just didn't want her feet submerged in a pool of sweat all day. Modern buildings in Iceland, tapped as they are into the shared abundant resource of stinking, bubbling hot water, tend to be sauna-esque.

She seemed cheerful to depart, as usual. Pabbi watched her drive away with a viscous brew of dejection and envy. He knew she liked to get off the farm and use her brain. It was never the plan for her to work the place with him. Still, he often found himself wishing she were around more. Or that he were off the farm, someplace pleasant, anyplace really, with her. That was the thing: Pabbi was very fond of Mamma. He would've claimed all her time if he could justify it.

We sat at the table, drinking extra coffee but with deliberation so we didn't vibrate. The rain was slow, persistent, steamy. The air, stagnant, smelling vaguely industrial. No Baula to the west, no Skarðsheiði to the east, and forget about His High and Mighty Iciness, Eiriksjökull—we could barely make out the next ridge over.

"Did you see any of the weird sheep?"

"I don't think so. They were mangy and looked like they hadn't been sheared in about four years."

"No rainbows or Technicolor?"

Pabbi seemed disappointed. When he heard I'd been to Drunk Stefán's place, dropping Rúna off, it piqued his curiosity. Some years back, for reasons unbeknownst to all but himself, Stefán had bred odd, nontraditional colors into his flock. It was clear that he'd worked hard at it—harder, perhaps, than he'd ever worked at anything, other than finishing a bottle. How had he done it? Where had the peculiar oil-sheen genetics come from? These questions occupied Borgfirðingar at their breakfast tables for quite a while until, inevitably, the sheep got loose and began contaminating the genetics of every neighboring flock. Stefán never could be bothered to maintain his fences. His wandering, horny escapees were called the Bifröst Flock, after the rainbow bridge connecting Asgard to the other realms.

This drama caused such widespread consternation that, at one point, several farmers considered it a capital crime. It was beginning to look like Saga times all over again. But they restrained themselves, for modern Icelanders are very good at repressing all manner of toxic emotions, and in the end they expended their ire by killing every last illegitimate sheep (instead of Stefán). The death count was significant—almost as bad as a disease cull. But there was nothing, really, they could do to Stefán that he hadn't already done to himself, and eventually he lost whatever mystical source of genetic code he'd found. Every now and then someone claimed to have seen a Bifröst sheep, and the rumors swirled, but like a troll or a UFO, they evaded photographic evidence.

"Did you ask her about them?"

"Who, Rúna? No. Of course not. Doesn't she have enough to be embarrassed about?"

Pabbi shrugged. He really wanted to know.

That's when we heard the ravens. A determined, agitated chorus.

It went on and on. We were used to them, of course. A small family roosted in the sharp rocks just to the north of our house, overlooking the river. When we passed beneath, there was almost always a lone raven supervising from a spire overhead, croaking at us in his mild inquisitive way. And when we mowed hay, the raven family usually came down to snatch voles and mice as the vermin scurried for cover. But this was something more substantial. A whole clan gathering. Relatives shouting to be heard, food-related quarrels, politics.

"What in the hell is going on down there?"

We listened for a while, our heads cocked to one side in ridiculous doglike attention.

"Sounds like it's coming from the hayfields," I said.

"Which?"

My ears, relatively youthful in the abuse they'd suffered from piston and exhaust, were better than his.

"The one we just cut, I think."

Pabbi stretched to his feet without much haste, drank the tepid dregs of his coffee, and made for the door.

"Guess I'll check it out."

In farming, there is a fine line between things you should probably check out and things you can ignore. The line exists in the ether and has to be felt with gloveless fingers.

He took off on the four-wheeler with Rykug running behind. Pabbi lived with the bitter shame that Rykug wouldn't ride on the back of the four-wheeler like other farmers' dogs. He'd even fashioned her a special platform over the rear rack with a tacky rubber surface so she could dig her nails in and hold fast, but she refused to use it under any circumstances. Sometimes he could coax her onto the platform with gentle entreaties, but she'd leap off the second he started moving. Maybe the noise, or the motion. Maybe she just preferred to run.

A few minutes later he called from his cell phone. The reception was mediocre. I had follow-up questions but "Need help" and "Bring the tractor and wagon" were the only things he felt it vital to convey.

So I suited up in my rain jacket and rubber boots and waded into the spit. The wagon with the busted tie-rod sat in the grass at a weird angle, regarding me reproachfully. Last night felt like a fever dream. I located the other wagon, which we called Tvær because it had a bent driveshaft and tires cracked with dry rot and it was second most in all qualities to Ein, the wagon that had tried to kill me.

The scene I encountered was difficult to interpret. Pabbi, looking irate, raced the four-wheeler around and around the field in serpentine loops, alternately yelling at the ravens to fuck off, at Rykug to chase the ravens, and at me to hurry up. The dog, looking delighted, ran almost as fast as the four-wheeler but in loops of her own devising, for ravens are unlike livestock and do not adhere to any predictable pattern of movement. They paid her little mind, rising with their heavy flapping only to squawk a few times and circle, unfazed. My first concern was that Pabbi would lose control of the four-wheeler and roll, or run it into a ditch, and so launch himself into eternity. He'd nearly done it a few years back. He'd been chasing a few errant calves who contrived to get on the wrong side of a temporary fence, but in his haste he sped blindly over a rocky drop, plunging the four-wheeler nose-first into the ground from a height of almost two meters. He stayed mounted somehow — if he'd flown forward the four-wheeler might've landed on him — but took the brunt of the impact in both wrists, neither of which had ever been the same.

Now he slowed down and beckoned me over. His voice was already hoarse, and he was out of breath. He looked shocked.

"The ravens," he kept saying. "The goddamn ravens."

I looked around. There were certainly a great many of them. Three families altogether — maybe fifteen individuals at first count? Anyway, more ravens than I'd ever seen in one place. And then, through the Borgarfjörður spit, I saw it. The bales were ruined. Almost every last one of them, shredded, torn, pecked, ripped. Maimed bits of plastic lay everywhere on the ground like fallen leaves. Rain glued it to the mown stubble; there was no wind to blow it away into rivers and glaciers, not yet. And from the bales, great tufts of fresh grass and net had been pulled and yanked so they stuck out unnaturally like ice formations. The damage was beyond comprehension. And to add insult to great injury, the ravens had celebrated their assault by shitting and vomiting on every flat plastic surface, their excretions running in globulous runnels down the wet sides. The bales—the objects of their wrath—stood like desecrated altars. It was mayhem.

"Oh my god," I said.

Pabbi nodded. "All these years, I've never seen anything like it."

We regarded the scene in silence, almost in admiration, for a minute or two. Then the ravens alighted to continue the exorcism of their malice, and that woke us up.

"What do you think? Should I get the wrapper?"

"No," Pabbi shook his head. "It would take us half a day to rewrap all of these, and so much damn wrap. Meanwhile they're spoiling. The hay might be too far gone as it is."

Pabbi's plan was to make his way around systematically, laboriously, and patch every single rent as best he could. The tape might not stick so well on the wet plastic, but it would be better than blowing our wrap budget in an attempt to get three new layers of film over each hole, Kolkrabbi's tires chewing up the wet field in the process.

He rummaged around the milk crate he kept strapped to the front rack of the four-wheeler and produced a roll of ag tape—like duct tape but somehow better for this specific job and priced accordingly.

"While I'm patching, you take the four-wheeler and drive big circles. Try to scare them off. I'll send the dog after them too. When I'm done, we'll switch and I'll scare the bastards off while you load bales and get everything up the hill."

"You don't think the birds will follow us up there?"

"I don't know, but I doubt it. They rarely come so close to the farmhouse."

The process, surely insane to anyone who might witness it, took us all morning. By the time the last patched bale was carted off, the ravens were wandering disconsolately around the stubble, their playthings removed.

We sat at the table, exhausted and wet, with mugs of bitter, over-brewed tea. Both of us watched the window, from which we could see the bales in their neat stack. No sign of black wings against the gray sky. And they'd gone silent.

"What would compel them to do that?" Pabbi said.

"Maybe there were rodents moving under the plastic? Or bugs?"

"But why bother? There are so many rodents and bugs in the field."

"Then boredom, I guess? Just for the sheer hell of it."

"That's what really disturbs me," Pabbi said. "It feels so... *rude*. A personal insult. I've always liked the *krummi*. Always been kind to them, or at least felt kindly toward them. Why do this? Why now? And what the hell do I do next time?"

"Move the bales in right away, I guess."

He shot me an irritated look. Mere hours had passed since I'd absorbed the lesson that sometimes there is no time.

"So will we shoot them?"

Pabbi's face darkened. Death was all around him. Furthering its dominion was like leaving the doors and windows open on a January night and standing on the threshold and saying, *Come*. The prospect of killing a raven was exceedingly bleak to him. To me as well. They were intelligent and charismatic. They were residents of this farm too, and they were Odin's birds. It was bad policy and bad luck put together.

"I heard this story once," Pabbi said, "about the drying racks for cod, and how they're plagued by ravens. Those guys will kill a single raven, pull its corpse in two, and lay one half at each end of the long rack. Apparently it keeps the birds away. Ravens don't appreciate seeing one of their own like that."

"So maybe that would work with our bales?" I said, a bit dubious.

"Maybe. But while I curse their horrible little souls, I don't want to kill even one."

In the coming days, I told this story to a number of people, mostly farmers, and everyone acknowledged how odd it was, and it was well received because farmers love to hear about other farmers' misfortune, and we all laughed.

Pabbi did not laugh. He left me to finish the rest of the first cut on my own, with Mamma wrapping, and he showed not the slightest interest in the conditions or yield.

The ravens had provided an irrefutable sign, and he took it very hard.

19.

Somehow, Mihan and I had managed to cram in quite a lot of talking since we first got on the telephone. She was busy, I was busy, but we found time, pockets where time slows down, like when you're in close proximity to a black hole. But this wasn't dire like a black hole, or at least I didn't think so, and maybe black holes are not so bad anyway, we shouldn't project our petty little human biases onto them.

There were rules, unspoken but at times referenced obliquely, to whatever was going on between us. Or one rule: We were just friends, friends being friendly, friends particularly interested in each other's lives. Friends could wish to spend hours on the phone, poring over every shred of history, every anecdote, every like and dislike. Friends could sacrifice sleep and, if we're being honest, certain responsibilities in order to experience these revelations.

Of course this was a joke, a paper-thin pretense, all part of the flirtation. In another era, they would've called such chaste conversation "courting" and either condoned it or forbidden it, depending on the circumstances. In our era, over such distance and with no background, no history between us, we called it friendship. She'd recently emerged a little shaken from a long, not altogether pleasant relationship and wasn't looking for something new. I knew this; she'd told me early. And I concurred, or at least said I concurred, having just barely, or in the not too distant past, put my own former love life in the rearview mirror.

Who was fooling whom? I believe neither one of us had a lie in our hearts. But we set no concrete boundaries, and the talks grew deeper, became more personal, more invested, and we delved together until we came up hard against a wall—a kind of psycho-emotional Balrog, if you will—that I thought was imaginary and Amihan did not.

There was nothing prurient leading up to this moment, no crossing of that line. Just a certain flash of vulnerability and a magnetic pull that has a way of undoing friendship.

No, it was me, I crossed the line. I believe now that I always expected to cross the line, had in fact seen the line approaching from a long way off and neglected to slow down at all.

We'd been talking about social media, the artifice of it. How little you could really learn about a person's life from how it was presented. When talk drifted to photographs, to the various ways they could be manipulated by doctoring, filtering, or old-school techniques using angle, frame, and light, and the fact that she and I had both steadfastly refused to present the ether with a clear image of our faces, I barreled right through the opening before any better judgment could stop me. As one gets older, I hope, one learns to barrel less.

"I'd like to know what you look like," I said.

She was silent for a few long beats, and then said, "Why." There was no audible question mark.

"I don't know. So I can picture you when we're talking." It was feeble and we both knew it.

"That seems unnecessary," she said.

"You're right. Of course."

That's when I realized that whether or not our pretense was more real to her than to me, I'd never know; regardless, she had no intention of crossing the line. I felt like a worm. I deserved to feel like a worm.

"I liked how this was going," she said. Her voice was bitter, rueful.

I noted the past tense. It's hard to disappoint people, and yet we are always willing to do so again. "Nothing's changed," I said. "I'm sorry I said anything about a photo. Forget I asked."

"I have to go—my sister's calling."

After that, Mihan refused to call me or answer my emails. First I tried various techniques to rectify the situation, being careful not to overwhelm her. Friendly, offhanded texts about innocuous subjects and the like. When that approach yielded only more silence, I gave up. I wasn't about to profess any extravagant feelings—a request to see her face had already taken me over the edge. Mihan owed me nothing. We owed nothing to each other.

And yet the sensation of grief was so strange, so outsized. I tried to logic my way out of it. I told myself, *No big deal, you've never even met this person, what have you really lost? Do you regret the sudden disappearance from your mouth of cotton candy or a yeast donut when you knew it barely existed to begin with?* But I did, I missed the donut. I thought it was a real one, a cake donut, and I'd foolishly allowed myself higher expectations. Its absence burned a hole in my left lung, not my stomach. That's where I felt it.

20.

Amma generally always showed up on July 4 or 5, depending on the day of the week, so she'd be settled and comfortable in time to start drinking the morning of July 6 and be piss drunk by noon in the company of her remaining loved ones.

Dr. Nechama Lacas, who refused most nudges toward assimilation but tolerated the Icelandic grandmotherly endearment "Amma" because it was already her nickname before she ever landed on the shores of our volcanic home, had a conflicted relationship with July 6, aka Lithuania's Statehood Day, aka King Mindaugas's Coronation Day. For who was Mindaugas but the man who had allied with the Germans in the thirteenth century and been baptized as a Christian so the pope would acknowledge him as king? Maybe he never quite fulfilled his promise of converting all the other pagans in the region, or even converting himself entirely, but he did gain the royal title he was seeking—Lithuania's first and last—and therefore a moment of recognition for the little country. It was a day for Lithuanians all over the world to get drunk and sing the national anthem.

Not that Amma sang the national anthem. She would sooner die than sing any national anthem, unless it were a raunchy parody, or wave any flag, or intentionally wear an outfit that displayed the colors of a flag. She had a conflicted relationship with the whole country, not just the day. The whole concept. This sensation of unbelonging, she said, was common among the Jewish diaspora. It ran in our blood.

But she preferred celebrating July 6 to Lithuania's other independence days, February 16 and March 11, even though those two were more politically relevant to her, because they fell on miserable days to visit us in Borgarfjörður. Also, Iceland had a unique bond with Lithuania, having been the very first nation to recognize the latter's true, most recent independence — undoubtedly there would be more — in 1991. This was considered a bold, audacious slap in the USSR's ruddy face, for they were by no means convinced yet of their vassal state's liberation, and Iceland had to scurry to secure natural resources from other parties in case the Soviets embargoed us, because we may be a country of independent people but self-reliance is something we're still working on — just look at what we've got to deal with. But the Lithuanians were grateful for this slap. So grateful that they tried to gather 300,000 signatures to thank every Icelander, but they fell short by around 100,000. This didn't dispel the good feelings all around, however, and Lithuanians had been flooding in ever since we started to allow more people to move here, Icelanders evolving slowly, like always, but at last joining the other civilized countries that are tired of doing their own shit work.

Now, in terms of the immigrant community, Lithuanians were outnumbered only by Poles. And on the two main independence days in February and March, in Reykjavík and in Akureyri, Lithuanians filled the bars, singing, drinking, singing louder. Amma was allergic to this. She wasn't part of the recent influx. She'd come to Iceland in 1972, a special exception, tolerated, recruited for her particular skill in pulmonology. And even if she had come along with this recent surge of Liths, she wouldn't be one of them. She didn't love the flag — she didn't love the people. Sometimes she feared them. But she still loved her home country, in a tormented way, the home she barely knew, the stories and memories that she had heard and now carried. So of course it made sense to drink four beers over the course of a day, maybe four and a half—she wasn't a big woman—and eat a few dishes she remembered how to make, and celebrate the escape from Soviet tyranny, and get wistful about the way the air smelled in Vilna, and damn the eyes of the fucking place. That's the thing. One's relationship with one's origins is rarely a comfortable arrangement.

On these days, Pabbi made himself somewhat scarce. It wasn't out of hostility. He and Amma were close, very close. Sometimes it seemed to me that he was more open with her than with anyone else, and I wondered if Mamma felt that way too. Amma called Pabbi her "crazy son-in-law." She'd never liked Mamma's previous boyfriends, strivers, fawners, self-aggrandizers. Something about Pabbi's directness rang true for her, or reminded her of a relative from the old country—she said he seemed like a Bundist organizer, recognizing defeat from the outset and trying for the thing anyway—but more than that, she saw the way he looked at her daughter. Pure admiration.

"This man is very odd," she liked to tell me, gazing affectionately in Pabbi's direction. "He can never approach a task in the normal way. And I think he likes animals more than people."

When Pabbi and Mamma had their brief honeymoon in a cabin alongside the Norðurá, they got bored and stir-crazy—it was November, of all times to honeymoon—and took several long drives. One drive brought them over the Þverá and past our driveway, where they saw the real estate sign. Pabbi backed up 100 meters in the middle of the main road. They walked around the decrepit old house, uninhabited for a decade or so. There was a hole in the barn wall where rain had splashed up from the concrete and battered it until the wood ceased to exist. They could see right through to the stanchions inside and a chain-and-paddle barn cleaner that had definitely quit before the people did—often there is a correlation between the two. Barbwire fences sagged; posts leaned, clinging to the ground by a rotten thread. Low gray clouds obscured everything to the south. A hellish wind whipped down from the high country, scouring everything in its path. Several disreputable sheep belonging to no one in particular, ancient wool pilled and piled around their scant frames like barnacles, bleated without much hope.

"Look, you can see Baula from here," Pabbi had said, in tones of enthusiasm that surprised Mamma. "And Litla-Baula!"

"The Clit," she replied drily.

"Yes!" He raised his hands to the sky like a seer. "The Clit smiles upon us!"

Amma made the down payment. She called it a loan, but never asked for it back, and I believe never looked for anything of the kind. She cosigned the mortgage too. I suspected that she had made the mortgage payment more than once when we were strapped. This, I think, was why Pabbi made himself scarce. It weighed on him, her generosity. It made him feel a little bit like a scrub. What were his responsibilities to her? What did he owe her, since he could probably never pay back what he literally owed? I knew what Amma thought he owed her, because she told me: devotion to her daughter, devotion to her grandson, and nothing else.

But Pabbi didn't like to sit with that kind of pressure, real or self-imposed. So on these visits of hers, he'd spend much of the time out with the cows, or in his shop, or running errands, occasionally coming back inside for a bite of food or a cup of coffee with Amma. He had no interest in drinking in the middle of the day, it would put him straight to sleep. And he valued his privacy, or he wouldn't have moved to the middle of nowhere. It wasn't a big house. There was only so much talk he could tolerate. Also, like a dog, he resented being watched while he ate.

Amma didn't care. That was just Viðir being Viðir. He'd have to do a lot worse than that for her to take it personally.

21.

So, July 6, 2012, this surreal scene:

Amma, Mamma, and Rúna, crammed together on the couch at 3 p.m., drinking beer, eating smoked salmon and butter on cold toast and talking loudly over the radio, which was hooked to Amma's cell phone and playing Mahatet Masr, a pop station out of Cairo that Amma liked and that made her feel less alone when she was in her apartment in Reykjavík but that was unnecessary, even superfluous, at the moment.

Pabbi, hiding out somewhere, far from the noise and chaos. Rykug, hard at work, fastidiously cleaning the crumbs that fell like volcanic ash between the couch and coffee table. Rúna had been invited because this was a holiday, one of our most important, and when it's a holiday you think about people who have nowhere to go on holidays, or have no holidays, and you invite them over, particularly if you like them. And it was clear that everyone liked Rúna.

Me, sitting in an old chair opposite the couch with a bemused look on my face, I know, because I was bemused, trying to secure a morsel of salmon before it was gone, feeling a little left out but tolerated.

Amma was explaining Jewish things to Rúna. Rúna didn't know

that I was one until that day and, like most Icelanders, especially rural Icelanders, had no experience of Jews, no background whatsoever. And instead of being discouraged by her ignorance, instead of clamming up, she was hungry for more, and so, asking question after question, she received answer after answer. That was a unique thing about Amma. Unlike Mamma, who was easily wounded by anti-Semitism, deliberate or unintentional, who tended to grow silent, glum, and evasive whenever she felt like the subject of Jewish identity or history was on the wind, and she could smell it from miles away, Amma took it upon herself to illuminate. Despite having endured or been in close proximity to more atrocious shit than most people have, she was an outward-facing individual, she always would be. She was a survivor; she was a physician. Maybe there were limits, maybe she didn't always want to get into the particulars, but educating curious people didn't annoy her—even when they said something very stupid, she just baldly told them how stupid they were and corrected the misinformation. She seemed to enjoy it. Maybe Icelanders are uniquely positioned to receive this kind of tutelage, as we don't generally assume we know better than everyone else.

"So a Litvak is not a Lithuanian?" Rúna said. "I don't get it."

Mamma shook her head and said nothing. Amma laughed.

"A Litvak is a Lithuanian, yes. But also not a Lithuanian. A Litvak is a Lithuanian Jew."

"But isn't Judaism just a religion like any other?"

"It is a religion," Amma said. "Maybe not officially recognized by the government of Iceland, but a religion all the same. It's also a *people*. An ethnicity."

I could see Rúna's gears turning.

"But wasn't that one of the fucked up things about the Nazis—they said the Jews were a race? Sorry, I don't know what I'm talking about."

"No, you're fine, you're absolutely on the right track. But it's thorny. What is a race? When does an ethnicity become a race? I don't know. I think the bigger issue is when, race or ethnicity or otherwise, someone tries to kill all of them. All of *us,* as the case may be."

"Right," Rúna said, looking shy and despondent for a moment, and then recovering fast. "So you don't practice Judaism, though?"

"We're atheists," Mamma said, not unkindly.

"We are," Amma confirmed. "But we still carry on with a few silly old traditions, since they tie us to our eroded, in many ways obliterated, past."

"And you're still Jews."

"And we're still Jews."

"And every Jew from Lithuania is a Litvak."

"Well . . ." Amma took a long drink of beer. Mamma shook her head again as though this were impossible to answer.

"There are Litvaks and there are Litvaks. These days, if you talk about Litvaks, most people will think of the extreme Orthodox Russian Jews who immigrated to Lithuania after World War II and then later moved down to Israel, where they multiplied and have been causing all sorts of trouble, working hard to make that place the hawkish, reactionary nightmare it's become. But Vilna, where I was born, and other places in Lithuania too, used to be a place of many Jews, Jews of all kinds. Thinkers, artists, radicals. The Bund. John Mill. They're not in Lithuania anymore, of course, the descendants of those few who made it out. The diaspora of a diaspora. But they made a name for themselves elsewhere. There are lots of great Litvaks. Some greater than others."

I settled back, seeing that Rúna was now in for one of Amma's favorite subjects: Famous Litvaks.

"Take, for example, Bernard Lown. Born Boruchas Lacas. Invented the defibrillator. Started International Physicians for the Prevention of Nuclear War, which won the Nobel Peace Price in '85. Great man. Could be a distant cousin, who knows? Or Nechama Lifshitz, a beautiful soprano. Took melodies from our history, from the Vilna and Kaunas ghettos, and wove them into her music. Not my namesake—she's only a little older than I am—but sometimes I like to pretend she is. And then of course there's Teodoras Bieliackinas."

Seeing Rúna's total incomprehension, she went on: "A scholar of Icelandic literature. Lived here in the '30s and '40s. He translated *Þrymskviða* into Lithuanian."

"And *Iceland's Bell*," Mamma said.

"That's right. He was friends with Laxness. Taught him Russian." She took a drink. "Who else?"

"Philip Glass," Mamma suggested. "Leonard Cohen."

"Oh, I like him," Amma said.

"David Cronenberg."

"I don't know him."

"He's a genius. You might like his movies. Very anatomical."

"Fine."

"Bob Dylan!" I remembered, my one contribution.

"Emma Goldman!" Amma said, ignoring me.

"Saul Bellow . . ."

"Eh," Amma said.

We were winding down. There was about a minute of silent rumination. Munching, gulping, thinking. Rúna looked a little fidgety. I didn't think I'd ever seen her sit still that long. Amma seemed to get this. She sprang up and declared that it was high time for a walk. She was seventy-one—spry, indomitable, restless.

Outside, the air was perfect. Very little wind, a rare thing in Borgarfjörður. Amma led the way through a wire gate and into a hummocky pasture. Three calves reclining in a close huddle waited until we were close and then jumped up in a huff, as though they hadn't heard us coming and were spooked. Tails raised high like little black fence posts, back legs kicking, they ran off dramatically to their mothers, who did little more than look up. Rykug ran ahead, skimming the top from the freshest cowpats.

Rúna had left her beer inside and was now snorting neftóbak. Every now and then she produced a handkerchief, into which she blew discreet wads of brown snot. Amma regarded this with genuine curiosity and said nothing. As far as she was concerned, as a pulmonologist, if someone wasn't smoking, it wasn't her problem.

We walked on. Rúna looked more sanguine again, now that she had a little air in her lungs and nicotine in her blood, and she was more than politely interested in everything Amma had to say. So we covered a fair bit of ground, geographical and historical. When you put it all together, as Amma did sometimes, it seemed impossible that one person could have been at the center of so much. And now she provided the grim outline.

She was born in Vilna in 1940, the same year the Russians occupied, or reoccupied, Lithuania. Of course the Poles had already controlled Vilna for about eighteen years—first, the Poles had to give it back to the Soviets. At that time there were between 160,000 and 200,000 Jews in Lithuania, depending on how many refugees had flooded in from elsewhere in Europe. Then the Soviets proceeded to wreak absolute havoc. A few Jewish communists went to work for them, only a few. Far more Jews were disappeared or deported to eastern gulags along with anyone else of even mild interest. Things were bad for everybody, whether you were Jewish or not. Fortunately— the word "fortunately" didn't quite do it justice, maybe we should say in a stroke of luck so unlikely that it was almost cosmic—Amma and her parents got out, made it to Moscow, were given work there. Amma was never clear on why or how. They weren't Soviet collaborators, they weren't even communists. But they had skills, they spoke Russian, and they lacked the certain red flags that filled the Comintern with fear and rage: too much education, too little, too religious, not religious enough.

Then, in 1941, Hitler invaded Lithuania. The story of those who remained is all too familiar now, but there was something special at work. First the Germans spread a load of spurious bullshit that the Jews had been the source of Soviet brutality, and the Lithuanians, terrified of the Nazis or eager to do their bidding or both, ate it up. So the

Germans didn't have to do all the genocide at first because the Lithuanians jumped to do it for them. The maestros just told them where
to shoot. They didn't even need ghettos or camps to get it done, not
yet—most Jews in Lithuania were still running free like wild deer.
It was a busy year. About 175,000 were dead by the end of it, in the
woods or pulled out of their houses one by one. A few made it out,
thanks to strange extraordinary visa-writing angels like Chiune Sugi-
hara, who got a handful across Siberia to Japan and on to Shanghai,
or Jan Zwartendijk, who sent some to Curaçao and Suriname. And
of course there were hundreds of Lithuanians and indeed Poles who
risked their own lives to shelter Jews, and were mostly discovered and
killed for their efforts. But by the end of the war, Lithuania had lost
between 91 and 95 percent of its Jews, about 195,000 dead in all.

When it was over, for reasons of their own that were murky to
young Amma, still murky today, her family returned to Vilna. There
they watched as the tiny, crushed, bedraggled rabble of surviving
Jews tried and generally failed to resurrect their previous existence
while the Soviets, once again in control, hands over their own eyes,
mouths, and ears, did everything they could to make the whole sor-
did thing go away. A Jewish museum was built in 1944, only to be
moved to the library and jail buildings of the old ghetto and then
closed down in 1949. Everywhere you looked you saw signs of Jewish
culture and life, or of Lithuanian complicity in their anti-life, being
erased or literally paved over. Amma's parents desiccated from the
inside out like grasshoppers that find their way into a house and never
get out, leaving only their chitinous shell, now paper-thin. A weak
breeze would've blown them to pieces.

Fast-forward a few painful years, and eventually Amma left,
unable to take any more of the repressed trauma. Smart as hell,
viciously smart—she would be the first to tell you—she was admitted to medical school in Moscow. She emigrated east; she bought
used textbooks. She choked down her rage and confusion and pain
and directed all that volatile energy, like heat from the roiling magma

beneath us, into her studies, her labs and residencies. She rose from the ranks. She ascended.

Somewhere in there, and yes, it was horrific and she never had one moment's sleep or peace, but yes, it was possible with the help of friends and neighbors and socialized if brutalist day care, Amma conceived and bore and raised her daughter, Emma, otherwise known to us as Mamma. Mamma's father, Vlad, was a nonentity. He was a weak, venal fool, he was another medical student, Amma did not begrudge him anything, she knew what kind of man he was, she'd known what she was doing, she would always know what she was doing, he was not worth speaking of.

And then, the very minute she possibly could, Amma got out. It wasn't easy. She was a refusenik, having applied for and been denied an exit visa, but she was spared the worst indignities of a refusenik's lot—several people she knew had been locked up or fired for "social parasitism"—because at thirty she was already heading up the pulmonology unit of the city's main hospital and therefore wholly indispensable.

But things changed after the Six-Day War in 1967. Russians remembered or admitted just how much they disliked Jews, and they started displaying it more outwardly. And it got worse after the Dymshits-Kuznetsov hijacking affair in 1970, when the refuseniks made the international news and the Soviets were outraged and embarrassed like a child who has complacently pissed in his own pants but dislikes having it brought to the attention of the whole playground. But if this metaphor is to be carried on, the child manifests his vitriol by beating the other children with a stick, by arresting and disappearing the other children, and then when the teacher gives the pisser a very stern reprimand, he responds by finally allowing several of these maimed and terrified schoolmates to leave the yard, which they have been begging to do anyway.

The Soviet Union aliyah—they finally released them. But first Amma had to pay the head tax, about 12,000 rubles, because the state had paid for her education and given her everything, and by the hem of their cheap polyester suits, if she wasn't going to show her gratitude, they would damn well extract it from her.

And though Amma's stamped visa and flight out of Moscow should've been the first full breath of air after years of hyperventilation, things didn't end there. First Amma had to shed her previous unasked-for epithet of "refusenik" and become a "dropout." The aliyah was all well and good, but Amma didn't want to go to Israel. She had no interest in that benighted war zone; she'd seen enough of them. She wasn't particularly keen on the US either, which she had never seen, not then and not now, but which she persisted in calling a shithole. Maybe Soviet propaganda on that score had weaseled its way in. Maybe it was right. In either case, while sitting on a bunk in an Italian processing center with a nine-year-old, weirdly untroubled Mamma, who thought they were on an adventure—at long last, a real vacation!—Amma got the news she had been hoping for. She'd been laying the groundwork for years, and against all possible odds, it came through just in time. An old friend from medical school—not Mamma's father, she was careful to say—was an Icelandic man, by this time an esteemed thoracic surgeon in Reykjavík, and of course you had to discount some of what he said, he was a surgeon, after all, and therefore rash and impatient and maybe a bit heartless, and he certainly drove too fast, but he was also kind and honest to a fault. He said that the hospital where he practiced was in serious need of a competent, no, a brilliant pulmonologist to deal with all the diagnostic work and patient care and *talking* that he didn't have time for. They wanted Amma, and recruitment was the only way in. The Icelandic government was certainly not keen on charity cases or, really, immigrants of any kind.

That brought us up to 1972, Amma arriving at Keflavík, via a long complicated headache in Heathrow, over forty hours with no sleep and minimal belongings, Mamma at her side. They were hungry and bewildered and didn't speak the language—Amma had secretly been studying the basics but still had a long, long way to go—but both of them, they insisted, took one look at the barren moonscape of the Reykjanes peninsula, ocean gray and heaving and remorseless, moss barely gaining a thin foothold against the sideways blasts of wind and rain, volcanoes huddling black in the distance, and thought it was the most beautiful place they'd ever seen.

The story had run its course. Now we only shuffled along. Amma's voice was ragged as an old raven's and her face a little drawn, but her eyes were bright. Mamma held a bouquet of *fífa* that she plucked at idly, watching as the white Seussian puffs drifted away toward Borgarnes.

Rúna looked depressed, which is the appropriate look after hearing such things bluntly related. "I only knew a little of that," she said. "So there aren't many Jews left."

"No," Amma said. "There weren't many of us to begin with, and six million really made a dent."

"And very few here in Iceland?"

"I dare say. Maybe two hundred? That's including the First Lady, of course."

"Who, the fancy one?"

Amma laughed. "Yes. Dorrit Moussaieff. I call her Little Dorrit."

"She's nothing like Little Dorrit," Mamma said.

"I know. That's why it's funny."

"Who's Little Dorrit?" Rúna said.

"I think this girl should go to school," Amma said, and when Rúna clearly took this hard, "She's sharp. She'll go far."

22.

I was out checking stock tanks with Rúna—one of the float valves had quit, probably rusted or plugged up by mud daubers, and Rúna had said she wanted to see Pabbi's strange watering system—when my phone buzzed, alerting me to a voicemail. I'd never heard it ring, but that was no anomaly. Any little hill or boulder on the farm served to blight the signal, which I imagined as a set of toxic little tendrils, like asbestos fibers, reaching feebly out to us from the tower in Borgarnes.

Rúna shot me a judgmental look. She didn't believe a person should be so tethered to their device, but she knew what was on my mind.

"Not her," I said, scrutinizing the number. It had been an eternal three weeks since I'd heard from Mihan. Clearly things were over, and yet I still carried the damn phone.

"Where's it from?"

"The prefix is Akureyri, I think."

"Akureyri!" she exclaimed. "Well, shit!"

"Probably a spam call."

"We're not going anywhere until you listen."

There was a strange voice on the message, not Mihan's. At first the disappointment was like a blow to the sternum. We are forever susceptible to such blows, there is no armor against them. Then I became confused. It was a child talking, not a spammer.

"Who is it?" Rúna demanded, in my ear.

The message was already over almost as soon as it began. I played it again, on speakerphone this time. The caller was a precocious kid introducing himself as Mihan's nephew, Óskar, and saying that he'd like to meet me sometime, he'd always wanted to meet a "cowboy," and that maybe I should come visit.

I stood like a stunned animal, unsure whether I was dead or alive, but Rúna was ecstatic. She'd hated all the moping, didn't approve of self-pity. She insisted that I call Mihan immediately.

"What, right now?"

"Right now."

I pleaded that I had no signal. She pointed to the phone and its two encouraging bars. I tried taking a few deep breaths; they did nothing to steady me.

"Are you going to be quiet?" I said to Rúna.

"So quiet."

"You promise?"

She nodded solemnly. Mihan picked up on the second ring, laughing before she said a word. We didn't waste much time on pleasantries, she had about as much use for them as anyone in my family. I was a little exasperated; she was unapologetic.

"So I got a call from Óskar."

"I know. I was sitting next to him when he left the message."

"He says he wants to meet me."

She laughed again. "So do I."

Was that the roaring of the sea, or blood in my ears? I would've liked the moment to go on longer, to hold it, to make a print of it, but into the void came the sound of Rúna moaning—loud, ridiculous, and yet eerily accurate cow moans.

"Who's out there with you?"

"That's Rúna."

"HI, RÚNA!" she screamed through the phone. I held it away from my bleeding ears. Now Rúna was doing some kind of suggestive dance, I really couldn't identify it. I felt my face contorting into something it hadn't done in a while. And I was perfectly willing to follow Mihan's lead, to be pulled around if necessary, but I thought the physics of the situation should be acknowledged.

I turned away from Rúna and took a few steps up the hill, a pretense at privacy.

"I was starting to think I'd never hear from you again," I said.

"Yeah, I freaked out," Mihan said.

"It's freaky."

"I just—it was so good to be friends. Or whatever we were doing. Felt like it could go on that way forever." She paused. "I really, really don't want to get into another relationship right now. Or, I don't know, *didn't*."

I thought I was genuine in honoring this, though I probably wasn't. Mihan's previous boyfriend had been a shit. He specialized in making her feel low about herself, so she was perpetually uncertain of how she'd offended him or where they stood. He didn't like it if she had too good a time. I hated the man, and wished to take his place. Unless you're replacing a beloved dead person, I guess, you always think you can do better than the last guy. At first, anyway.

"So where does that leave us?"

She didn't know. I didn't know.

"Óskar thinks I should come to Akureyri."

"He does," she said.

"Seems like a smart kid."

"The smartest."

Back to this game. I would cut my own arm off to play it. In a strictly hypothetical sense I told her I could get up there for a visit sometime, maybe in August before the second cut. Just to say hello, eat some lunch together, the way friends do.

We left it in the air, but with a new honesty. Honesty around the edges.

Rúna was still celebrating, and I was doing my limited best to temper her expectations, and mine, when the phone buzzed again.

Mihan had sent two photos of herself. They were still a little obscure, but they were irrefutably her face. I peered at them. I thought, *These tell me nothing,* and at the same time, *These are the most magnificent things I have ever seen.*

I showed them to Rúna. She agreed.

23.

When is a pasture a pasture? In some parts of the world, a pasture looks almost as good as a hayfield, possibly a touch lumpier. In Borgarfjörður, we hay whatever we can hay and we graze the rest. The rest, literally anything above the river bottomland, is so hummocky, so shaped and jumbled by the lacerating stones it has grown over, that it's almost as hard for quadrupeds to manage as for us miserable tilting bipeds. Perilous leg-breaking ground to all but the most sure-footed of livestock, and everyone knows that cattle are not the most sure-footed of livestock. That was one of the many factors to send Pabbi in search of the wooly, almost yak-like Galloways, belted or unbelted, who are nimble, almost like giant sheep in their agility, and since they are more or less happy to eat dubious fare in all hellish weathers, they make a fair living in the British high country. Iceland is not the British high country, but still the principle is the same.

Cows are a bit like second-class citizens here, even as they are revered. The mighty Icelandic cow, ancient in lineage, the precious cargo of our questing longships. And now larger than before, thanks to decent feed! Generating a nearly respectable eight liters of milk per day instead of the shameful old four. Kept inside a great deal of the time, or all the time, they are prized for their milk but not their intelligence — who, I suppose, prizes cattle for their intelligence?

A few determined contrarians who wished to focus on beef production had jumped the necessary hurdles to get seed stock of the bigger, beefier Angus, who can grow to slaughter weight and beyond in a staggeringly short period, provided you give them enough to eat. They don't do well in rough pasture, though; they don't care for it. Their enormous barrel frames are made for gentler use. The forage is too damn difficult; the rocks are too rocky. That left the even fewer, more determined contrarians like Pabbi, contrary to the most contrary notion, who thought a little Galloway's scrappy hardscrabble fortitude was a decent trade-off for the hard truth that it took each animal about three years to come anywhere near slaughter weight.

So, the pasture. Few things grow out of hand here, we have no real weed problem, and that's well and good if you're worried about weeds, but it also means if we want anything to grow at all, a solitary blade of grass, it has to be encouraged, placated, chivvied. Some farmers worked wonders to vegetate the barren ground. Over decades, they spread chaff and manure, often by hand, until slowly, oh so slowly, enough organic material collected that one could almost call it soil, and a thin layer of grass started to grow. Now it was held down at least, now the very earth itself wouldn't take to the air at the first sign of a south wind and strip the paint from every automobile, the siding from every house. But it was brutal work, requiring much more labor and patience than simply planting lupine, as they'd done to hold the rocks down in Reykjanes, and which was now a rapidly spreading blight — the "fucking lupine," as Pabbi called it, choking out every blueberry and crowberry bush, you'd recognize it from miles away.

On our place, Pabbi had begun the vegetation process in earnest, but it quickly made him despondent. Returns were minimal. Fortunately we had some pasture that was already greenish, already decent. That didn't mean we could move the cattle easily, however. Pabbi had read Allan Savory, he'd seen the evidence online of how nominal pasture could benefit from being hit hard by livestock, grazed down, and left to rest and recover. The trick was to move, move, move them. But reading about it was one thing; application, a whole other thing. Each subsection of pasture needed water, temporary fence, shade. And fences were hard enough to build in the stony ground—how in the hell could you set a firm corner post in a rock pile? You couldn't, that's how. Most Borgfirðingar relied, instead, on simple boxes filled with large stones, cheerfully referred to as "dead men."

Still, Pabbi did his best. He moved the cattle as often as he could, until they knew the routine quite well. Except the calves, that is, every year there was a new crop of dimwits.

On this breezy afternoon in July, clouds in a hellfire hurry, *krúnk* echoing down from the outcroppings, I was out there with Pabbi. I'd been doing much of the moving myself lately, but now we were together because back at the house he'd seen a calf that looked like it was on the wrong side of a fence and his binoculars could neither confirm nor deny. He thought I might need help managing the situation and he was the farmer, after all, he couldn't just step away indefinitely.

It turned out to be an optical illusion. The calf was fine. This often happens—a fence line is hard to define at a distance, but there is still nothing like calf stupidity, they are unequaled. I suggested we rotate the herd since we were out there together, and as we called them, the cows bunched around the gate, always eager for the next thing. But the calves straggled, lazy and unsure, some trailing their mothers, others taking their sweet time, strung out along the fence. This was a problem. If a calf followed right on his mother's heels, he could pass through a gate opening without a second thought. Or a first thought. But if he found himself alone at this strange and new hole in space and time, this gap where once there'd been electrified polywire, and was it still there? Was it invisible now? What did it all mean? Then it was anyone's guess whether the instinct to follow his mamma would win out over his nameless, baseless fears, of which he had many.

So we were left with three who abruptly and firmly decided that no, they would not go through the gate, they would fuck off elsewhere. Pabbi groaned. Rykug whined—she'd been sitting impatiently about five meters off so as not to freak anyone out, like she'd been trained, but there was only so much she could stand. Her DNA was vibrating. First Pabbi made her wait while he tried in vain, in predictable vain, to get on the other side of the calves and usher them calmly back toward the gate. I stood at a kind of crux point, aiming to block their escape, but the calves just flowed like a river around a stone and came back together on the other side of me, more spooked than before.

Rykug was up and moving almost before Pabbi finished saying, "Get 'em." She was perfectly silent except for a very thin whine like tinnitus that seemed to come from nowhere in her body. And at first things worked; she'd done this before, she knew the drill. She circled behind the calves like a heeler and darted at them, pausing so as not to overrun their feet, yapping a little for effect. With a few well-timed feints to the left and to the right, she kept the calves aimed at the gate, and when they got there, two fled right through, too terrified of the hellhound to perseverate over metaphysics. But one did not. He, a bull calf of course, stopped at the opening as though it were made of iron rather than air. Now Rykug's overzealousness, her desire to work, to please, to conquer, got the better of her entirely. As the calf pivoted in confusion, the dog gave him a solid nip on his fetlock and sent him bawling away. This was when things went shithouse. The calf's mother, alarmed by the weirdly basso profundo moans from her child, came running back through the gate. She was very pissed off. Quickly the two were reunited, and the situation might've resolved itself peaceably if we'd just let them settle before ushering them through together, but at this point Pabbi was impatient and irritated, I could see it in his bearing, and that kind of attitude is transmissible to livestock like a virus.

"Get 'em," he said to Rykug again, and I winced. Rykug wasn't trained for this—Pabbi relied too much on her breeding to see her through every unique situation, and occasionally this non-strategy paid off. As things stood now, however, a border-collie-type approach, working the head, maybe circling to the rear as necessary, would've been preferable.

Rykug was fairly adept at handling calves. She could dial up or down the antagonism like a sound engineer. But when asked to push grown cows, she easily overran them, and they weren't really afraid of her so much as angry. That's what happened this time. She went after them in a hurry, and before she or they knew what was happening, I think, she was underneath the cow's back legs, and then she fell back with a piercing squeal. But she kept chasing, and they kept on too, until she ran them straight through a two-strand line of temporary electric fence, snapping it, across another pasture, and finally through an old barbwire perimeter fence, and into a non-pasture, the wilds, the void.

Pabbi had been shouting himself hoarse, "No! No! Goddammit, no!" but maybe the pain or the chase had deafened Rykug and she was running them to hell and gone.

"Get the dog," he said. "Make sure she doesn't…" He had no need to finish his sentence. If she got onto the neighbor's land and had lost her mind, she might chase sheep, or she might be perceived to chase sheep, and then she'd be filled with bird shot. But more likely she'd end up on the road, and well, people drive fast in Iceland. In any case, Pabbi was already halfway back to the house, fetching the four-wheeler.

Our misadventure, gathering that lone pair, is scarcely worth relating, it was so ridiculous and unnecessary. Rykug didn't need rescue. She saw me coming to find her, or heard my friendly call of "Rikka, come!" and trotted back to join me, limping almost imperceptibly. The cow's hoof had split one of her front paws wide-open. It would require an expensive trip to the vet, stitches, a cone that we couldn't bear to plague her with—she knocked everything over and looked so abject—and eventually an old sock held on with vet tape that she had to wear at night for a week.

In the meantime, though, Pabbi piloted the four-wheeler out to the wasteland and proceeded to chase the two dejected cattle around and around. The pair jetted shit in a thick stream and their tongues lolled. It was pitiful to see. It was also completely futile. The four-wheeler only increased their fear—they loathed the thing. Pabbi knew this. Everyone knows this. But he was thoughtless in his frustration and concern; he kept on until, watching the cows run in one direction while the machine lurched in another, he forgot where he was and drove straight into the same barbwire fence the cattle had gone through. Alas a four-wheeler can't pass between the strands in the same physics-defying way that a cow can: It came to a dead stop and launched Pabbi into the fence. Fortunately he was wearing decent canvas and not driving too fast or it might've been much worse. He lacerated his leg and hand a little, but it was his pride damaged more than anything else.

So Pabbi calmed down eventually. He had to calm down; it was the only way. Sometimes the pain or shame of a mistake is what it takes to accomplish this. And together, while Rykug lay nursing her paw, happy to concede the battle, Pabbi and I changed tack and lured the tired pair through a gate, and then through another, and then through another, with promises of alfalfa treats and finer pasture and a reunion with the herd. Everything was better with the herd.

24.

ate July interlude, a fine early evening. Rúna and I sat on the porch, sharing the two-person swinging rocker, with a dusty bottle of Danish aquavit between us that she'd found in the back of a cabinet at her place, undoubtedly stashed by Drunk Stefán for later use and forgotten. We took turns slugging and grimacing. Neither of us was a big fan of the caraway.

"I think this dates back to pre-prohibition," I said, peering at the water-damaged old label.

"I think it's from Snorri Sturluson's personal stash," she said.

"I think it was bottled by Ragnar Hairy-Breeches."

"I think it was filtered through his hairy breeches."

"I think it's Slcipnir's piss."

"Okay," she said, "you took it too far."

She'd eaten dinner with us. Nothing fancy, grilled lamb chops — given to us in trade by a neighbor who raised sheep and said the smell of lamb repulsed him — roasted potatoes, sautéed kale. It had become fairly routine, an established thing, that I would never be invited over to dine at her place, that I wouldn't wish to be invited, and that she was welcome at our table anytime she liked, which happened to occur about twice a week.

"So," I said, and waited a beat, because my line of inquiry was obvious. "How goes the quest?"

"The quest for what?"

"A soul connection, of course."

Rúna groaned and aimed a sharp kick at my shin, which I dodged—I'd been anticipating it.

"Not well, if you must know."

"I must know."

She gazed out toward a distant water trough, where one officious cow was lording it over the space, dipping her head to slurp great drafts at her leisure and then butting away anyone else who showed even a mild interest. A thirsty crew gathered at a safe distance, their needs vying with their rock-solid understanding of the hierarchy. Resource and control—you hear so much about herd mentality, but cows are born capitalists, they live to stomp on the little guy.

"Nobody promising online?"

"Not really. How did you strike gold so fast?"

"I think it helps that I wasn't looking."

"Bullshit you weren't looking."

"I wasn't."

"Tell yourself what you like," Rúna said, and she poured a dram of the odious aquavit, drank half the shot, hissed. "There was one woman. Heiðrún. Lives in Reykjavík."

"Oh?"

"Don't get excited, it didn't pan out. We were messaging for a little, then texting, then video…Um. You get the idea. Well, that was pretty good. I thought so, anyway. She's in her thirties, works at a coffee place, but not making coffee. Something behind the scenes—what do they do back there? Roasting? Anyway, she bikes to work all year round. Cool tattoos. Works out a lot. Kind of a badass."

"So? She sounds great."

"Yeah, I thought so too. But then she started acting surly with me sometimes, out of nowhere, right in the middle of a conversation, and she'd get off the phone super fast and then more or less ghost me for a few days. It freaked me out a little. At first I thought maybe she had something stressful happening in her life, I should give her some space, but she never said what, so I started to assume I was saying the wrong thing, and how could I know what it was? It's shitty to keep saying the wrong thing and not know what it is, you know?"

"Very shitty."

"Well, finally I got fed up. I was tired of sitting around, waiting for her to forgive me or settle down or whatever she needed to do and then pick up the phone again and act like nothing happened. So I asked her. And guess what she did."

"I can't guess."

"She broke up with me."

"No! Can you break up with someone you've never met?"

"Yes, of course you can. Or maybe not, I don't know. Anyway, I told her I needed to know why, and that's when she said I was 'experimenting.'"

"Well, that's bullshit."

"Thank you. So I figured it was just an excuse to break it off. And just the other day I came up with a theory about the real reason."

"I can't wait to hear it."

"Well. I worked back through our conversations in my head, reading old texts, you know, and I realized that she always seemed to get the most quiet and surly when I talked about farm stuff. Working on a machine at your place, that kind of thing."

"Jealous?"

"No, not that at all. I think it's that she's pretty butch, and I'm not femme, and there's no room in her worldview for a relationship like that."

"Ahh," I said, but I was still confused. "I'm confused."

"Don't hurt your brain," she said. "It's like this. By doing butchy work, way more butchy than, like, lifting weights or picking up compost in her friend's truck for their community garden plot, I was threatening her concept of herself."

"You were emasculating her!"

"Exactly," Rúna said. "Sort of. Without knowing it."

"Well, she doesn't deserve you."

"I guess. But..." She broke off and stared at the cows again. She cracked her knuckles against the silence. "I'm tired of being lonesome. Feels like I've been lonesome since I was born."

"You sound like a Hank Williams song."

"I am a Hank Williams song."

"Maybe you're Hank Williams reincarnated."

"I would look good in one of those hats."

At this point Mamma stepped outside to take the air. She sniffed appreciatively, then regarded us.

"Shouldn't you lovebirds be sitting closer together?"

Rúna looked pale for a moment, almost horrified, but then Mamma snorted a laugh and sat down in one of the fake-wicker plastic chairs.

"I can't keep anything from her," I told Rúna apologetically. "Sometimes she knows things about my life before I do."

"It's all right," Rúna said. "I guess I figured it might be obvious to your folks."

Mamma nodded vaguely. She was not in the business of telling people what she found obvious about them—she often said the only thing more impertinent than asking personal questions was knowing the answer before you asked.

Books, on the other hand, that was fair game.

"Have you read anything good lately?"

Rúna was a voracious reader. She consumed anything she could get her hands on, making up for lost time, a youth that was in many ways stolen from her, and though she could never seem to remember the titles or the authors' names, she experienced them deeply. Mamma had already lent her a great number.

"Nothing really good," she said. "I read that translation of *Persuasion* you gave me. Or maybe it was *Mansfield Park*? Anyway I didn't like it much. Rich people doing their rich people things. *Pride and Prejudice* was better. At least that one was funny."

"Mmm," Mamma said. "I know what you mean. Well, I have something new to recommend. An Icelandic writer, Jón Kalman Stefánsson. Used to write for *Morgunblaðið*. I just finished a novel of his called *Himnaríki og helvíti,* the first in a trilogy. He's brilliant. I've only started the second, and the third is supposed to come out this year. I'll lend you *Heaven and Hell*. I keep trying to get Orri and Viðir to read it, but they don't take book advice and it's just sitting around. He's completely rewired my brain. I don't know how he does it."

"I do take book advice," I said. "From you."

Mamma ignored this and went inside to find the book. When she reemerged, Pabbi was with her, beer in hand. He liked Rúna—she could be silent for long stretches in a way he approved of.

"Listen to this," Mamma said, flipping through the novel to a marked page. "I haven't dog-eared like this in ages."

She tipped us a particularly good passage and we all murmured in approval. Rúna accepted the book, placing it reverently in her bag.

"Well, I just read one I hated," Pabbi said. For Rúna's benefit, since he'd already complained about it so much that Mamma and I knew every detail, he laid out the promise and disappointment of *The Wall* by Marlen Haushofer. He was invested but had become so fed up that he skimmed the final quarter just to find out what happened.

"Why do I need this kind of bleakness?" he said. "Isn't there enough bleakness in life? And she tells you almost from the very beginning, over and over again, that the dog is going to die, and so are the bull and one of the cats. Jesus Christ."

"I think I'll skip it," Rúna said, a tissue to her nose because she'd just snorted a line of neftóbak and it was trickling back out a little, as it will. Pabbi eyed her with interest. Rúna noticed and raised her eyebrows, dancing the plastic flask toward him.

"Better not," he said. "I never could handle it. Not man enough."

But he reached out regardless and took the offering, tapping a conservative line onto his hand, snorting it, and then erupting in a series of explosive sneezes. His eyes dripped and he chuckled as he handed back the flask with a nod of thanks.

"God, that takes me back."

"Ah," Mamma said, "the halcyon days of youth on Vestmann-aeyjar."

But something had occurred to Pabbi. He raised his index finger, said, "Wait a minute," and disappeared into the house, returning a few minutes later. With a kind of flourish, he handed Rúna a ram's horn flask, obsidian-black with a few jets of yellow and cream, a cork stopper at its end.

"It was my grandfather's," he said. "My own pabbi didn't take snuff, but he kept it."

"It's beautiful," Rúna said, and it was.

"It's yours."

"What?" Rúna looked shocked. She tried to give it back, but Pabbi put his palms flat out before him and refused.

"No, really," he said. "You should have something stylish to keep it in if you're going to snort that awful stuff. The plastic flask is just, I don't know, a little sad. And it's made in Denmark, for Christ's sake. The horn is from Heimaey."

"But don't you want to keep it in the family?" She looked at me for help, and I just shook my head.

"No," Pabbi said, "you take it. I'm trying not to hold on to all these old things."

25.

The drive to Akureyri wasn't far, maybe three and half hours, but I was still wholly unprepared for how short it would feel. I pulled over several times to stretch it out. With every stop Rykug whined and pranced, thinking we'd arrived. She was along for moral support. "I don't need her" is what Pabbi said, I'm glad she didn't know these words, and she passed the hours in the back seat either curled into a tiny ball, her face under her tail, or scrutinizing livestock through the window, her obelisk ears reaching, reaching, and her nose leaving an opaque snotty smear across the glass.

By the time I reached the petrol station near Varmahlíð and realized I had only about an hour left, I was deeply nauseated, running to the clean bathroom—we take clean bathrooms somewhat for granted in Iceland, they are a cultural priority—and hanging my head over the toilet, trying to decide whether it would feel better or worse to throw up. My stomach wouldn't have much to work with— I'd barely eaten all day or the day before. It's moments like these when one questions his life choices. That's a lie, I'd been questioning them beforehand anyway, for weeks.

The night before I left, she and I had picked apart the implications.

If I did come, which was insane, given that we didn't know each other at all, or did we, where would I stay? Her flat, she said. I countered, convincing no one, that maybe I should stay in a hotel, so there would be less pressure. What if we didn't in fact like each other that way? Then we could just have some lunch or something, put a certified stamp on our friendship, and not be stuck in the same charged atmosphere. Sure, something was going on, something potent flying back and forth through the ether, but how could you know what was real until you were face-to-face with someone, smelling their pheromones or whatever?

"It'll be okay," she said. "Just stay at my place."

In the week that followed, I polled the limited demographics available to me. Pabbi and Mamma both thought it was absurd. They deemed it a waste of time, a waste of petrol, a waste of emotional reserves. They were fairly sure I'd be disappointed.

"Will the Twingo make it?" Pabbi said. "Because you can't take the truck."

Rúna, on the other hand, was all for it. She loved the vicarious drama, the sense of possibility. Anything that spoke of newness and escape was electric for her, like the first smell of coffee in the morning when someone else is making it.

"But what about your *beard*?" I said.

"Shut up," she said.

At this point in early August, nothing on the farm was holding me back. We'd taken down a few of the temporary fences and the cows were just ranging around, periodically stopping to holler disconsolately if they saw us moving around the barnyard. I told Pabbi I could feed out a few bales before I left, if I left, to augment their meager later-summer forage. Sometimes that stopped the bawling for a little while. He just shrugged.

And now here I was, having wound my nauseous way around the northwest shoulder of Route 1, stopped dead at the Olís petrol station in Varmahlíð. But nothing came of it. Maybe I was just hungry. On my way out of the convenience store I grabbed a few innocuous snacks and tried to eat them, sitting at the pump with the car door open, but they tasted like moss. Rykug accepted them graciously.

I thought of calling Mihan, but it felt too delicate. I called Rúna instead.

"I'm in Varmahlíð," I told her. "I feel sick. What the hell am I doing?"

"Stop whining and drive," she said.

I drove on.

26.

Mihan's flat was on the ground floor in a squat building with nothing to recommend it other than this one occupant who was, I hoped, I feared, behind the door. I could see Rykug's eyes at the cracked window of the Twingo. She looked attentive, not necessarily supportive, but then you can't ask for unlimited support, even from a dog. I gave her an unconvincing wink. She never responded to these. Dogs wink all the time without knowing it.

The door opened before I could knock and there was Mihan, looking a little nervous, a little amused, hellishly attractive, and I became very aware of my muck boots, my not-quite-beard, and did I have crumbs on my shirt?

"Hey," she said in the voice that had always been disembodied and was now very much bodied, a disarming but wholly logical change.

"Hey," I replied, smiling despite all the myself within myself.

"Is Rikka with you?"

I shifted to the side so she could see Rykug in the car. It pleased me that she used the nickname. Everything that carried our telephonic closeness into the real world would please me.

"Should we take her for a walk? There's a park nearby."

We took her for a walk. There didn't appear to be much to say for a few minutes. Small talk felt pointless. Rykug balked and strained at her leash, choking herself, never quite trained for it, hardly trained for it at all, she wouldn't heel if it were her last day on Earth. But the park was indeed close, and I let her off for a minute. I thought she could be trusted, as there were no other dogs in sight, and no livestock, and she was the kind of dog that thrived on trust. She was a bit feral off the farm, a bit too interested in everything, but she was on good behavior that day. At first she raced around, investigating a number of important spots and jetting a long stream of piss onto the steel pole of a swing set, all the while huffing this weird city. But she seemed to become tired of it in no time at all, or else found it not to her liking. She trotted back and looked emphatically from me to the car.

At this point Mihan and I were standing very close with our shoulders touching, nothing more, and I truly did think I might have a heart attack. Then Mihan squatted down and held out her hands for Rykug, who was generally not too keen on new people, who might allow herself to be petted or scratched by some, so long as she could turn her head in such a way that her eyes were always on the suspicious hand, it was not an affectionate transaction. But in this case she moved forward with her face toward the ground and planted her head in Mihan's belly, pushing with enough force that Mihan staggered back a little and had to throw a hand behind herself for stability, and then pushing more. Now almost all of Rykug's body was between Mihan's folded legs — this was a position she reserved for family members, a gesture that I always took to mean *I am not submissive, but I submit myself to your attentions. Anywhere along the neck, back, or haunches will do.* Mihan was conscious of the honor.

Back at the flat, invited inside at last, I met Mihan's roommate, a fellow student named Birgitta. I also met Birgitta's boyfriend, and I began to comprehend that I was under some kind of scrutiny. This was reinforced by the suggestion, made by Birgitta and seconded a little skeptically by Mihan, that we all go out to dinner together. And so Mihan and I were separated for a period of hours, as though by chaperones, while we walked to the restaurant, waited for the food, waited for the alcohol to take effect. I made small talk with Birgitta and Eiríkur. I tried not to look at Mihan the whole time. I wondered what was really happening and whether it was going well.

I must have passed the test because we found ourselves back at the flat a few hours later, and the chaperones did not.

"They were a bit worried because we met online," Mihan said. "They wanted to make sure you weren't a serial killer."

"Too much Nordic noir," I said.

"Or just enough."

We proceeded to dance around each other for the next several hours, like opposing magnets, inching a little closer only to be repelled farther. Mihan had the day off and her usual late shift at the hotel the following evening, so there was no pressing need for sleep. Rykug settled right down on a pile of dirty towels. The night rolled forward into bleariness. We talked a great deal, watched a cooking show on television, talked over the television. I began to feel concerned that I should've booked a hotel room after all. At one point we almost bickered over something trivial, and then Mihan acknowledged that everything was a bit strange, and I thought, *Is this thing already over?* There were a lot of tricky signals to read, given how much we knew of each other, and how foreign our corporeal aspects. Maybe something hadn't quite transferred from virtual to real. Or maybe we were loath to fuck it all up.

It didn't last long. By about 2 a.m. the magnets gave up their obnoxious little game and flipped around the right way. There ensued some heated wrestling, first on the sofa, then the bed, nothing too serious, but serious enough. During breaks, we smiled at each other like fools. We laughed and raided the fridge, where the only palatable thing we could find, the perfect thing as it happened, was an enormous hunk of Havarti cheese. The worries that had been plaguing me for weeks wandered off elsewhere, they bounced out of the rut and left me

fairly blank, almost carved out. It wasn't a night for pondering implications. This held true even after Mihan fell promptly to sleep and I
was left alone in her twin bed, impossibly uncomfortable, impossibly
untired, even though she lay warm and peaceful next to me, one leg
thrown over mine, for he who wakes while the other sleeps is always
alone. And yet I didn't despair as I so often had in Reykjavík. Sleepless
nights are the ideal venue for unwelcome thoughts, they are like petri
dishes for painful rumination, a growing medium, but on this first
night with Mihan I just watched her and that was all. At about 6 a.m.
I dozed off for an hour, brain conceding defeat to body, and when I
woke again an impatient summer sun was shouting through the
cracks in the blackout curtains, and Mihan was still far under.

I wandered around the flat a little, everything different and harsh
and a bit squalid in the bright living room. The couch looked like
someone had taken out their frustrations on it, and Rykug occupied
one corner, her head and one leg on a pillow. She leapt up when I
emerged from the bedroom. She was hungry, bored, insistent, like a
child who has been awake too long. I took her out to a little patch of
grass where she peed in an unconvincing way, the wind so stiff from
the north that it tried to blow my hat off. She squinted into it, her ears
flapping a little at the tips just like when she rode in the back of the
truck. I retrieved the kibble from the car, which I'd measured out in
fastidious increments for three days, just in case things worked out,
Pabbi having watched with approval while I did this; despite his disapproval of the general endeavor, he liked attention to detail. Back
inside, Rykug pacified for the moment, I found a few coffee beans but
didn't dare grind them. I returned to Mihan's bedroom and was mar-
veling with some horror at her closet—almost nothing hanging, just
a great pile of clothes on the floor, as high as my waist—when she
stirred at last.

"Hi," she said. She rubbed her eyes in the clichéd way I had seen in
a thousand movies but had never seen before.

"Hi."

"How long have you been awake?"

"I didn't sleep much. How in god's name do you find anything in here?"

"Don't you mock me," she said. "There's a system."

"There's a system to this pile?"

"Get out of my closet."

Those first few days together passed in a blur of talk and insomnia, for sleep begets memory, and without it, we're eroded before our time. And there was some drinking, and other things. Mihan was an inexhaustible mine, or rather a volcanic crater that just pulled and pulled from the cracks between Earth's plates, never cooling, or rather, I don't know. I could hardly conceive of a person containing so much fascinating detail. That might be the definition of love, or at least love's initial outlay. And she made me feel as though I too might possess some reservoirs I hadn't been aware of.

A great deal of the time she spent working. If she was at the hotel desk, I couldn't really loiter, even in the lobby. Her manager saw me doing this the first time and noted with displeasure that Mihan seemed distracted, was perpetually looking away from the customers, so I had to stay in her flat, where I was almost content to look through the window she looked through, lie on her bed, snoop around her stuff, in the presence of the things that smelled like her, until she finally came home. Or I walked, and I got to know Akureyri somewhat well, for it's not a big city — sure it's a big city for Iceland but we know it's not a big city — and Rykug got to sniff many things and piss on many things, often those things were the same.

Several nights a week, Mihan also tended bar in the hotel, and I was permitted to hang around for those shifts so long as I bought a drink now and then. It impressed me just how unfriendly she was to the clientele. It was peak tourist season and the place was often packed with chatty folk from elsewhere, but she rarely pretended to give a shit about their lives back home, their children, their animals, their miseries big and small. She certainly didn't smile.

Every so often a patron would get a bit drunk and make some comment, framed as innocent curiosity, about Mihan's background, and where was she from? How long had she been here? Her Icelandic was *so good*. And then her face would close tight and the air in the room would get noticeably chillier, like someone had left the door open in February, and I'd be sorely tempted to stand up and fell the offending person with a barstool, but that wasn't my role in the situation, I wasn't her savior, and anyway she was mostly unmoved. People seemed to get the hint from her emphatic silence, her blinding indifference, and I never saw the situation escalate, though it undoubtedly had in the past.

Eventually I'd get too tired to sit there anymore, my body collapsing under me, and I'd creep back to her flat to relieve Rykug and wait for Mihan—Birgitta, hallowed be her name, never came home the entire time—trying to stay awake but unable since I was finally alone in a bed, the necessary condition, and drifting into unconsciousness while simultaneously worrying about her getting home after closing time.

"I'm fine," she told me.

"Maybe I should come back and walk you home," I told her.

She gave me a very skeptical look, meant to illustrate how ridiculous I sounded, which it did.

"I've been doing this a long time."

"What about muggers? Besotted patrons and other ne'er-do-wells?"

"In Akureyri? No. The worst we tend to see is a group of drunk Americans and they're more obnoxious than dangerous. Their loud laughing is the worst."

In a slow drift, almost a mudslide, the three days I'd budgeted for became five days, and then seven, and then I was well into my second week. The biggest concern was that I was out of money, having been required to buy more kibble for Rykug, only the best, and though I'd saved a little from my ignominious restaurant shifts in Reykjavík, ignominious because I was the worst waiter known to man, and Pabbi had insisted on giving me a cut of the beef sales that summer, these meager financial holdings had been depleted nearly to their copper bottom with beer and take-out food and a couple of movies at the theater. I'd even bought a terrifically overpriced, Icelandically priced, pack of cigarettes with the terrifying photo of a cancerous lung, my first pack in eight months, unfiltered because I thought it was vaguely impressive — we all do things we should know better than to do, whether it's smoking cigarettes or smoking unfiltered cigarettes because we think it looks tough. On this trip I was back up to three or four a day, and Mihan said she had to have a few drags or she wouldn't tolerate the smell, and I watched her smoke, admiring the easy grace with which she did everything, as though life were an art that she might have worked at for many years, or maybe not, but there were no signs of struggle in her present mastery, and I thought, *She looks a hundred times cooler than I do.*

The other concern was that I was a waste, a layabout, literally lying about while Mihan worked. She didn't appear to judge me for this, but I judged myself enough for both of us.

And I missed the farm. Having up to now only texted confirmation of my continued existence, I finally called home. Mamma sounded so genuinely pleased to hear my voice that it almost made me cry, that's how much sleep I needed.

"I figured things were going well when you didn't come back," she said.

"Really well," I said. "Weirdly well."

"When do I get to meet her?"

"We're talking about her coming down sometime next month. The hotel slows down in September, and she'll have three days off in a row."

"Great. When do I get to meet you?"

"You mean when am I coming home?"

I heard Pabbi muttering in the background. His tone could be hard enough to interpret in person. I figured he was saying that everything was fine, the cows were fine, no hurry, which could very easily be lies, or he was complaining about his shoulder, or he was talking to the air.

"Soon, Mamma. A few days."

So I made it clear that this idyll was coming to an end, and suddenly everything shifted into a higher gear, which should have been impossible given that our relationship was already moving very fast, but some engines always have a little more to give.

At this point I was granted access, finally, to Mihan's relations. First, and of the highest importance to all parties, were her sister and nephew.

"If he doesn't like you, it's over," Mihan said beforehand. "No pressure."

Fortunately Óskar was not the judgmental sort. He forgave my obvious shortcomings, first among them that I was not in fact a cowboy, did not have a pistol, did not own a horse, did not even know how to ride a horse. Pitiful.

"We do have cows, though," I told him. "And I am a boy."

He was unimpressed, so I added, "There's a big rifle at the house? And a motorcycle."

This seemed to get me out of the red, if only just.

And his mother, Hiraya, unlike Mihan in almost every way except for generosity of spirit, had, it turned out, been the architect and engineer of Mihan's reversal during the infamous three-week freak-out, had suggested the phone call from Óskar as a reasonable concession, had also approved of me sight unseen and insisted that Mihan write me back after my initial uninspiring note, had been the voice that urged her to continue this dubious courtship.

Hiraya, who went by Hira, told me all these things with pleased complacency, for she seemed to like me a great deal, and liked Rykug even more, she was positively smitten with the dog. Hira was a person who did not have her shit together. She never had. This was her natural state, and she'd learned to thrive within it, or at least find some illogical ember of happiness that could guide her back in the dark, a kind of psychological lighthouse. She was an artist through and through, a painter of grotesque human and animal figures nearly swallowed up by magnificent hallucinatory hellscapes, but she was untortured. Óskar, raised by Hira alone within this swirl of benevolent chaos, had grown a certain self-protective husk of seriousness, but a cheerful seriousness. He'd learned early on to speak like an adult so that adults would tolerate his presence.

I also ate a meal with the rest of the family, who greeted me with varying degrees of warmth and chilliness. It was only at this lunch that I began to grasp a bigger piece of Mihan's cultural dislocation. She'd told me some things about it, of course, but carefully, reluctantly. I knew she'd come to Iceland in 2001 at only eleven years old, and that the shock had been extreme, both in culture and climate. She'd achieved that rare feat, or at least I thought it was a rare feat — she insisted that I was being a fool and there was nothing rare about it, especially among children — of a lightning-fast assimilation at school, maybe at work too, and a firm hold on her Pinay identity everywhere else. Her Icelandic had scarcely any accent, less even than Mamma's, Mamma who had been nine when she arrived, *thirty-nine* years earlier. She also had a leg up on the other Icelandic children with her English, which was already far along before she left Manila. On the other hand, though Mihan had been encouraged to adopt an Icelandic name in school, and her parents had supported this, going so far as to make it official so that it appeared on her documents and driver's license and passport, she never used it anymore, she wasn't born here and didn't have to, they could have their name.

With her family, Mihan spoke a little Icelandic, a little English with Hira when they didn't want their parents to know what they were saying, though their parents knew English quite well, and mostly Filipino. Mihan explained later that they were in fact oscillating between Filipino, a standardized Tagalog from metro Manila that incorporated Spanish, English, Arabic, and about fourteen other colonial influences, and the traditional Tagalog spoken by her grandparents.

I was a long way from hearing the difference. Her mother, Tadhana: garrulous, friendly, if not exactly warm to this white, non-Catholic outsider with nothing particular to recommend him. She was smart, focused, infinitely capable. The kind of person you'd want running a company. She'd begun her Icelandic career in hotel housekeeping, that old cliché of immigrant populations, but she wasn't ashamed of it, and she'd quickly been acknowledged and promoted, so that she now managed the entire cleaning workforce of a national three-hotel chain, traveling periodically to Reykjavík in this role. She'd helped Mihan get the front desk job, and was a far tougher taskmaster than any Icelandic manager, keeping tabs and issuing stern reprimands if she felt like Mihan showed up for work looking even slightly disheveled, or addressed the clientele with anything other than smooth congeniality.

Mihan's father, Ramil, was amiable but almost silent, possibly a bit depressed. His face was closed, an expression I recognized from my own father's face. He had worked for a while at Samherji, the fish processing plant, but he'd loathed it, it had nearly ruined him, and now he picked up about three shifts a week at Vífilfell, the brewery, spending the rest of his time engaged in less productive pursuits that were opaque to Mihan, if not to his wife.

"They loved you," Mihan said on our drive home from the modest little house on the outskirts.

"You think?"

"Eh, I don't know."

"Yeah."

"Hira really does love you, though."

"That I believe."

"One of the first things she said after you wrote me was 'Does he have a brother?'"

It was dry weather but gray, never a glimpse of sun during my entire stay in Akureyri; apparently the place was infamous for its clouds. We decided to stop at the docks and look out across the narrow gap of Eyjafjörður, its water reliably placid and un-Icelandic down here. Every time I'd come to this spot during the last eight days, which was often since I felt stifled and oppressed in town—the noise, the cars and non-animal filth—I'd craned my neck to the left, to the north, as though one final twist of the vertebrae might allow me to see all the way to the open ocean, almost sixty kilometers away. It was impossible. Too many bends and folds in the landscape. Too many mountains. In Reykjavík I'd grown to rely on the balm of big water, its sublimating effects and the way the white-flecked foaming waves shuffled and threw themselves against the sky, becoming indistinguishable. Many days I drove out to the docks, never far in that city, one of its finer qualities, just to breathe a little. When it was inclement—when isn't it?—I'd park facing the water and let the rain or sleet or snow cover up the windscreen and it was still worthwhile. If you can hear the ocean as though it's crashing upon you, you don't necessarily need to see it.

Here in Akureyri, on the opposite side of our icy Atlantic outpost, things were different because I wasn't alone, I was emphatically not alone, but they still felt heavy that afternoon. Almost catastrophic. It was a grim prospect, parting from Mihan, trying to sustain something so new and fragile across untold kilometers—well, not untold: about 300 kilometers of often treacherous roads and tunnels, the high mountain pass of Öxnadalsheiði, and mediocre cell phone signals in between. Mostly I just didn't want to be away from her. I felt that I was awake now and asleep before. Awake in the good way, not the insomniac way. I thought of Sóldís, of course, and how our spark, or my contribution to it anyway, had sizzled so fast as though removed from the stove and carried outside, into a stiff rain. But that was different, wasn't it? This was different. Maybe every new experience feels dramatically different when you're twenty. I couldn't tell if Mihan felt quite the same. We'd issued no proclamations.

"I like your town," I said, lying for the first time since we'd met.

"Do you? I hate it."

"It's a beautiful spot, though, isn't it?"

"Sure," she said, clearly dubious. "I think, though, that it just felt too harsh and different when I first came here, and that stuck with me. And Manila, well, you know how big Manila is?"

I shook my head.

"Fucking big. Something like thirteen million people in the metro area alone? So, to me, that's a city. This is . . . not. I love Iceland, I don't think I'd ever leave, but it's the mountains for me, the rivers and heaths. And I still haven't really seen the interior! Do you believe that? Anyway, there's just too much baggage here in this little town. Feels like I can't breathe sometimes. Like I'm a turtle that got flipped onto my back once, maybe by a hawk? Or a strong wind? But even though I got right-side up again, I was too slow or rattled to leave the place where it happened, and so a part of me always feels like I'm still help-less, wobbling on my shell."

She looked pensive for a moment. Then her face cleared and she laughed. "That sounds ridiculous! But you know what I mean."

"Can I tell you something?" I said. "Something serious. It'll proba-bly make you uncomfortable."

"Maybe you shouldn't," she said. "No, you should. Do you have a bastard? A natural child? I forgive you!" She laughed again. I thought, *I will suffer any indignity the world has to offer in exchange for this sound.*

"No, I don't have a bastard."

"Then what?"

"Okay, it's like this." I suddenly felt a bit queasy and short of breath. I thought Mihan could sense this, was trying to fend off whatever was coming with levity. "It feels like we've known each other a long time, even though technically it's only been a little over a week. This thing of ours is so weirdly lived-in and comfortable—"

"Like an old shoe?" Mihan was trying to compose herself, but she looked very arch, and on the verge of losing it.

"Ugh, fuck it. This is what I wanted to say. I'm already falling in love with you. No. Already *in love* with you."

Now Mihan looked a little shocked, perhaps a touch freaked out. *Of course she does,* I thought, and goddamn that sounded lame, but also, with some satisfaction, *so I did surprise you.* I kept talking.

"Obviously I don't say that with any expectation that you'll feel the same way, but I just thought you should know. This feels really serious to me. If you want to just take it slower, let things play out in a more normal human way, I'm fine with that. If you think there's any hope for us, I'll hold on, I'll wait. I'm a serial monogamist anyway. But there it is."

Mihan searched my face, my eyes. Is true emotion written on a face? Is trust something earned, or something that forms between two people when the conditions are right, when they collide at high speed like atoms in fusion?

"I'm *in love* with you too," she said, "and I appreciate the semantic distinction."

We held hands as we walked back to the car. It seemed very unreal, for happiness is not far from dissociation.

"Jesus, are we in the 1950s?" Mihan said.

On the passenger side of the Twingo I opened the door for her, and she said, "Chivalry is alive!" but then I swept in ahead of her and fell into the seat, raising a cumulus of dog hair.

"You drive, please," I said. "My legs feel like jelly after all that."

Mihan went around to the driver's seat and adjusted all the mirrors down.

"My delicate flower," she said. "You just rest your pretty little head."

27.

ack in the real world. Fewer things are more real than farming, it is far too tangible for unreality. And Akureyri was like a strange, pleasant dream, though perhaps few have described it that way.

The cows now grazed far apart from one another, each one seeking out the perfect mouthful, and often seeking in vain. In some places, we're told, cows can graze well into the autumn, but not in Iceland. When they saw us they gave vent to their dissatisfaction.

Give us hay! they shouted at every opportunity. *It is inferior stuff, it isn't what we want, but we want it anyway!* Or maybe it's more accurate to translate their repetitive moans as *I am nebulously unhappy and I don't know why!* We shouldn't anthropomorphize, but they are a lot like little children in their way.

For us humans, however, the weather was perfect. August had reached its ides and was rolling toward September, gathering speed. The nights were crisp, not yet cold, the skies so placid—for days on end—that you almost forgot where you were. A little rain, an hour or two, a day or two, would come around with its stern reminder and then retreat to the high country, or blow off toward Greenland, they could have it.

I sat with Pabbi on an old bench by the river. The salmon were still running, just barely. Pabbi hadn't fished our little section of the Þverá for several years, as far as I knew. It was easy to miss his opportunity — riverfront landowners are all part of a union that rents fishing rights to a company or fishing society, and the landowners themselves are allowed only a day or two to fish for themselves — but even so. Sometimes it was his shoulder, he said, that kept him from casting, or he was too busy, farmers don't have time for such things, or it was unnecessary: he often traded beef with a neighbor for a box of famous Hvítá salmon. Maybe it was just one more death.

From her vantage on the bank, Rykug watched the big fish with her general unwavering interest in all animated things, occasionally darting into the shallows as though she might make a try, but never past her elbows. A river in Iceland is no stock pond and she knew it.

It was late afternoon, nothing in particular to do, so we did nothing in particular. Pabbi smoked, letting the pipe go out and lie fallow in his hand for long periods. He always said he preferred to smoke indoors, in his workshop, because then he could really bask in the nuances of the tobacco, but it made his lungs hurt and that probably didn't bode well for a person's health, so he forced himself to smoke outdoors, fighting the wind, at least half the time. Moderation can be achieved in various ways.

Competing with Pabbi's weak output, a rare verdant smell drifted from the shrubby birch thicket just upstream. Their waxy leaves danced conservatively, reflecting sunlight and riverlight.

"What does an Icelander do if he gets lost in the woods?" he said. "Stands up."

I chuckled graciously, though I'd heard it about seven hundred times. Pabbi was not a great teller or enjoyer of jokes, but everybody likes that one because it's a truism, and also we are fond of our old Icelandic birches, they are diminutive but hardy like our cattle, sheep, horses, and geographic character.

There was a stiff, perceptible silence between us — different from

Pabbi's usual entrenched reticence. I'd felt it ever since I came home in the spring, and I was only too happy to breach it, or laugh at a tired joke. He was deep within himself.

"I like that pipe," I said.

"This?" As though I could've been talking about another. It was his freehand from P. Holtorp, acquired when he made a pilgrimage to Copenhagen in 1979 and found it used but immaculate, at the legendary Pibe-Dan shop. Holtorp, a regular contributor to Pibe-Dan, was known for his extravagant, often unwieldy shapes. This was a relatively restrained example of his work, light in the hand, minimally bizarre, with a smallish conical chamber. I knew its history and provenance as I knew so many from Pabbi's collection.

Now he handed it over, I thought for closer inspection. The rim was a little rounded and worn, the grain still in perfect contrast, the stem somewhat chomped but well cared for, always stored in the dark. A thin stream of smoke trickled out. As soon as I cradled the pipe, Rykug came trotting over and put her head on my leg, as though someone might finally smoke the damn thing in earnest. She liked tobacco.

"It's yours," he said.

"What? No!"

"Why not? You said you were thinking of taking up the hobby. And you've always admired this one, I remember, ever since you were about four years old and I taught you the difference between the shapes. You had all kinds of opinions. You said you never could love a rusticated pipe."

"But the Holtorp is your favorite, isn't it?"

"Oh, I don't know. Maybe they're all my favorites. Maybe a person shouldn't have so many favorites. Anyway, I'm thinking of quitting."

"Quitting tobacco?"

"It just doesn't give me much joy anymore. I only smoke to... smoke."

Now I was really a bit disturbed. I tried to meet his eyes, but he was looking away at the river.

We sat in silence for a few long minutes while the pipe petered out and cooled off in my hand. Finally he said, "It's that fleeting summer feeling today. Like every good moment will be followed by some harsh reminder of life's cruelty. That's summer in Iceland."

"Grim," I said. "Couldn't you choose instead to enjoy those good moments?"

He barked a humorless laugh.

"You figure out a way to do that, articulate your method, and then maybe I will."

He patted my leg in a feeble gesture of reassurance, as though he regretted opening his mind. "What about you, my boy?"

"What about me what?"

"Your first real season of farming. How did you find it?"

"Actually I've kind of loved it," I said. It was uncomfortable to feel ashamed of the answer, knowing how hard he found it.

Pabbi nodded somberly, but I couldn't tell whether he really heard, or cared.

"I know you don't love it right now," I said. "But is there anything about it you *do* like?"

"Anything I *do* like." Pabbi repeated the prompt in a flat, bored tone, like a child. "Well, I like working for myself. Or I prefer working for myself." His face grew dark, he had his own cloud passing over him, and I guessed he was musing bitterly on whether something could be considered work, proper work, if it caused you to hemorrhage money. It was a subject I'd heard him entertain on several occasions, in tones of the harshest self-reproach.

"I like the cows anyway. Some of the time. Not enough, but too much. It's a paradox."

"When do you like them?"

"Well. I like when they rummage their heads in a new bale. They get feisty and they emerge from the feeder with a wig of hay. They look pleased with themselves, a little confused. I guess they always look a little confused. I like when the calves hit a big pasture for the first time in their lives, two or three months old, and they just run back and forth across it, snorting and kicking, completely batshit."

I smiled in recognition. These were indeed good things.

"How about when you're scratching their backs and they make those weird slurping noises? I like that."

"Me too," Pabbi said. "And I get some satisfaction watching them scratch themselves on bushes and posts—they just put their whole bodies into it—even though it pushes all the posts over and they rake their flesh to ribbons."

At this point a part of my brain, or my stomach, had begun to think about dinner. I knew Rykug was thinking it too because she'd become restless and needy, alternating between a rigid posture and an intense meaningful stare, and tearing a chunk of sod into a thousand pieces. This was how she coped with the interminable period, sometimes as long as two hours, between her realization that it was almost dinnertime and actual dinnertime. It bothered Pabbi that this marvel of biological manipulation and overreach could be such an insatiable chowhound. He was forever snapping her away from the kitchen or the table, only to have her circle back with very little circumspection or stealth and resume licking the floorboards.

But Pabbi didn't seem to notice. He kept drifting elsewhere, as susceptible to the wind as anything else, and if he was feeling even remotely voluble I wanted to encourage him. It was a rare state.

"Did you always know you wanted to be a farmer?"

"Hmm? What?"

I repeated the question. I thought I sounded far younger than myself.

"I already was a farmer. So, no. Unlike kids today, unlike you, I wasn't really encouraged to think about future job prospects outside of the family business, and our family business was farming. Tenant farming, but still."

"You never talk about those days in Vestmannaeyjar."

"Sure I do."

"No, you don't."

"Well, I guess not. Some other time anyway."

I let it go.

"But those years in Reykjavík. Did you spend all that time wanting to get back into farming?"

"No."

I could feel the window of conversation closing, almost with an audible snap. Clearly I'd chased the wrong quarry. So I switched to the mundane — the mundane was safe. I asked Pabbi about the second cut. He said the grass was ready, it was just a matter of waiting for weather. I asked whether he'd ordered his vaccines and dewormers from the vet. He said he hadn't yet, and anyway we were still about a month out from needing those, and I'd be back in Reykjavík by then.

Somehow I'd led us right up to the doorstep of what I'd been avoiding for an hour, for days, weeks.

"Actually, Pabbi . . ."

He turned to me with a look of shrewd expectation.

"I thought I might take a semester off."

"Drop out?"

"No, just a semester. People do it all the time. No one cares."

"For what?"

"To help out on the place. Vaccines, boosters, getting everything battened down for winter. You always said it was the busiest time of year."

"Along with spring," he said.

"Right. Well, don't you think you could use the help?"

"Not at the expense of your schooling. Anyway, I can manage."

He didn't sound particularly convinced that he could manage, and it didn't appear that he would make an issue of my staying, but this wasn't the pleased reaction I'd fantasized about either. Maybe I'd been foolish. I felt a bit crushed. Then irritated. Silently I yelled at him, *Why did you raise me on this farm if you hate it so goddamn much? Do you want my help or not?*

Aloud I only said, "I told the registrar already."

He nodded. *All he does is confirm or deny,* I thought, we should consider ourselves lucky to get one or the other. Then I remembered the Holtorp in my hand, and my annoyance melted into guilt and concern.

"I haven't told Mamma yet," I said.

"She probably knows already."

28.

I figured as much," Mamma said.

She was engaged in some last-minute course prep for the coming semester, and she seemed perfectly willing to be interrupted. She had a weary expression. Her reading glasses a bit grubby and sliding down her nose, one arm at full length to grasp at a faraway paper, esoteric academic materials scattered across the dining room table — she didn't have an office at home; the main room for living and dining was her office.

Only now did it occur to me that my confession was ill-timed, or maybe timed perfectly, hard to tell.

"I'm definitely planning to return for the spring semester, though," I said. "It's just a break. To help Pabbi with the fall work."

"And gather yourself," she said drily.

"And gather myself."

"Well. You've told your advisor?"

"I was going to. I will."

She'd never so much as looked up from her papers. Some people have the capacity to engage with two different things at once, or to appear convincingly that they are doing so. Mamma was one or the other.

I leaned against the doorjamb and watched the fall blowing in, bringing winter with it, and rain in the meantime. A songbird, in a great hurry to migrate or to escape from the resident merlin, or drunk on fallen fermented crowberries, smashed into the glass and fell dead. Still Mamma didn't look up.

"So are you okay with this?"

"Okay with what?"

"Come on, Mamma. You know. Taking a semester off, taking up space in the house."

"You're always welcome to stay. I love having you home. Especially when you clean the kitchen."

"What about university?"

Finally she looked at me. She pulled the descending readers from her face and deposited them upside down on a pile of old syllabi.

"What do you want me to say? I'm concerned. What about all the work you've put in so far? All the work getting there in the first place? What if this is just a preamble to never going back at all?"

"It's not."

"But what if it is?"

"It's not."

We stared at each other. Mothers and sons, there is no rival to the particular way in which a look between them can simultaneously contain so much affection and irritation. But she softened first; she was my mamma.

"Look, boychik, you know how I was raised. You know your Amma. Education is everything. You can never have enough of it. It's the way up, the way out. And here I am, I've dedicated my life to it. Of course I'm going to be concerned. Going to the store, driving around, I see your old friends, your classmates, and they're doing nothing with their lives. Nothing worthwhile, anyway. They work the farm, or some dead-end service job in Borgarnes or Bifröst or Reykholt, or a petrol station somewhere in between, and then they come home, they drink themselves to sleep, they become their parents."

She meditated darkly on these grim outcomes for a minute or two, and I did the same, unsure whether to feel convinced or defensive.

"But listen. Come here," and she held out her hand to me. I approached and, still standing, wrapped my arms around her and squeezed, while she leaned her head on my chest. Her voluminous gray hair smelled like some fruity product, her fruity product. Mine was the physical position of comforting, but I was still somehow the one being comforted.

"I resented Amma's pressure," she said. "It could feel merciless at times, blind to my own agency as a person. And I'm not sure I knew the extent of it back when it was being imposed on me. A few years after university I saw an old friend from upper secondary school who told me how stressed I'd always been in those days, that I would come over to her house and just breathe out this great sigh, and then want to get very drunk as quickly as possible, because the weight of Amma's expectations was so heavy. It was always about getting the highest marks so I could carry that success into university, and then into graduate, postgraduate, et cetera. I was shocked when my friend said this — I'd mostly forgotten, or blocked it out."

"But you and Amma are good now, right?"

"Oh yes. We've always been like *this*." She crossed her fingers. "Together through all weathers. Sometimes more like sisters than mother and daughter. But she can be very judgmental, as you probably know. And there's no doubt that she hoped I'd reach and surpass the level of her career, if not in the field of medicine then in something of comparable merit."

"And didn't you?"

Mamma laughed shortly. "No. Not in her eyes. Teaching, in her opinion, is somehow less than doing."

"But you don't think that."

"Of course I don't. As far as I'm concerned it's a higher calling, not to be left to those who should've been called to, say, knitting. Fishing."

"Farming?"

"No one is called to farming. Shall we have a little coffee? It's still before noon."

We moved to the kitchen and she brought out some ginger biscuits while I put the kettle on. The rain had grown energetic, and was now hitting the concrete pavers with enough force to spatter the kitchen window a meter from the ground. Second cut would have to wait a while longer.

"Do you think she was especially hard on you because you were an only child?"

"Is that a leading question?" Mamma said, glancing at me with shrewd amusement. "You think I'm hard on you?"

"No," I said. "No, I really don't."

"Well, I can't say. We are a family of only children. At least three generations' worth: Amma was an only child herself. Of course your father had five siblings, but I don't know anything about that, or how it was, because he's not in touch with a single one of them. And his father, for your information, was an autocrat. Apparently—I never met him."

My mind, as it always did when he was mentioned, summoned only a black-and-white photograph of a large family, very staged, very serious, and the grim-faced patriarch standing at the rear, looking less into the camera than the void. His name, Steingrímur, *stone mask*, resounding like an incantation.

We carried our biscuits and coffee back to the dining table, slurping the top layer as we went, far too much coffee, we'd both regret it later.

"So you don't think only children turn out a certain way?" I said.

"Not really. Maybe they like to read more? Or maybe they don't. It always seemed to me that siblings read to get away from each other, but peace and quiet is at a steep premium, so they can't do it as often. Maybe they're able to read with more ambient noise. And sleep."

"Do you ever regret only having me? Or, did you plan it that way?"

Icelandic people are not particularly forthcoming with one another, so if you want to pull something out of us it's best to try when the caffeine is peaking. At those times we might forget ourselves and become voluble, but without the danger of overexposure that comes with alcohol.

"I certainly don't regret it, I got to have you all to myself, you weren't part of a feral pack, scrabbling for scraps under the table, but no, I didn't plan it. I had two miscarriages, three actually: one before you were born. Each worse than the other. They destroyed me. I mean, *destroyed me.* And what a stupid word, 'miscarriage,' very bovine-sounding. I carried them fine."

"Mamma," I said. "I didn't know that."

"No, well, the world doesn't like to hear about miscarriages. It wants you to keep silent about them, or else pick up and move on very quickly. I didn't. I ended up needing to take a month off from work, the last time. Your pabbi was good. He has empathy, unlike a lot of men. He was relieved, though, and he tried hard not to show it—he always said that dealing with one helpless parasite was one too many."

"That doesn't surprise me."

"No. But he beat himself up about it, after you were born. Without the benefit of maternal hormones, it took him three months to like you. Really. Three months. And in the meantime he was worried he never would."

Our cups were empty. The top syllabus in the pile, dating back to 2006, had a dark brown ring over the section titled "Expectations." It was past noon and I'd be vibrating until about 4 p.m. We both would.

As for our conversation about my sputtering academic career, there was no need to conclude it. Thorny subjects don't get concluded in life. They rarely even dwindle.

"I'm glad we got a chance to talk," Mamma said, "thanks for the break," and she'd turned away already, disengaged, now deep in contemplation of something wholly speculative.

29.

aying is often interrupted, you must accept it. You hope it's nothing catastrophic. You watch the sky with the anxious expression of a vole in the shadow of a fox and pray it won't be rain. Or a machine breakdown, those are regular occurrences and often terrible. You can get ready to skin your hands and pull your hair and stub your toes as you kick the goddamned piece of shit in unparalleled frustration. But overall you hope it's not death that interrupts you. Death hangs around the act of haying. He can smell it like a carrion bird and he drifts over from wherever he's been and he watches, circling, waiting for the moment when you get a little too tired or careless and make your final mistake. Or he shows up in an unrelated capacity, like when a guest brings a friend without informing you first, and that's still a nuisance and a shame but also it's a relief because he hasn't come for you.

We were back at the house, the three of us, eating a late lunch and preparing to wrap bales. It was the weekend, a joyful two-day window of dry September weather landing on a weekend, which meant that Mamma was home to run the wrapper, and I'd move bales, and Pabbi would bow out to do whatever he did lately. It was a silent, terse, economical lunch, designed to fuel the body and nothing else. I had the distinct impression, a growing conviction, that I was the only contented person in the house, unless you included the dog.

Then Pabbi saw dust rising in a plume from the gray crushed stone that marked the transition from main road to our road, and a minute later Drunk Stefán's disreputable old truck crested a hill, visible.

"Rúna coming to help?" Pabbi said.

"I didn't ask her to, but she's welcome."

She hadn't called, though we'd long since established that such courtesies were unnecessary. And she sometimes used her father's truck. She preferred not to, as everyone recognized it, everyone pulled way over onto the shoulder when they saw it coming, and no one would ever return a friendly wave because they were averting their eyes. But I think we all sensed that something was off. It was moving a little too fast, swerving slightly. And I think we all had the same sudden fear: Stefán himself coming to pay a visit for some unimaginable reason. Whatever it was, it couldn't be good.

It was Rúna. She parked and emerged from the car but failed to close the door properly, one had to slam the hell out of it and she didn't seem to possess the strength. She was always so tall and rigid in her carriage; this slumped, defeated-looking person reminded me with a sharp twist of the Rúna I'd known in school. Taunted, belittled, made small. And she was crying, of all things.

I greeted her at the door. She didn't want to come in—I could see that she was embarrassed. I put my arms around her, though we'd never done this before, and she kind of sagged against me, boneless but unyielding.

Mamma came out next, shifted me gently to one side and proceeded to hug Rúna much harder. She appeared to have divined the essential facts already. How, I don't know.

"The tears are not for him," Rúna said.

Drunk Stefán was dead, at last, the horrible old fool was dead. I didn't ask how it happened. Maybe his life finally gave out, or his rage boiled up inside him and excoriated all his organs at once. Maybe he fell drunk into a watering trough and drowned. Maybe Rúna saw his thrashing death throes and didn't help. Maybe she pushed him in.

We moved indoors. Pabbi laid a kindly hand on her shoulder and then sat back down, gazing out the window. He could've been thinking about the relentless tide of mortality, how sometimes it looked like malice and other times like justice but that was all an illusion, it just was, or he was thinking about the unwrapped bales out there, heating up under their own fermentation; if the cores got too hot they'd spoil from the inside out. After five minutes or so of this dreaded inactivity, he mumbled a few considerate words and stepped out.

Mamma took the opportunity to make a rare afternoon pot, and the coffee seemed to revive Rúna.

She was free now, that was the point. We didn't say it, but we were all thinking it. The mortgage on her place, unbelievably, was paid off. It wasn't worth much. Still, Stefán—could we call him Drunk anymore now that he drank only the cold draught of unknowing?—he'd managed to pull in a few of the government subsidies Pabbi abjured, probably by lying, who cares, but enough to keep tenuously, nominally afloat.

"What will you do now?" Mamma said.

"You mean with his body?"

"It's still there, at your place?"

"No, I called the *lögreglan* and they came eventually, took them fucking forever. They hauled him away somewhere. Now it's just a bunch of questions about burial or cremation, funeral or no funeral..."

"I'll help you with all that," Mamma said, returning her hands to Rúna's, which were shaking a bit, probably not from coffee, as most people can tolerate it better than the Lacas family and their descendants. "I mean, what will you do with the place, with yourself?"

"Oh, that. I was thinking I might give it a go. I know it's just a dry-side farm, but I've had all the time in the world to watch it be mishandled, and I have a list in my head, probably ten years in the making, of about fifty ways it could be improved. A wireless router, for a fucking start. But with some careful breeding and culling, I think I could work the sheep herd into something decent. Maybe even profitable. Could even get a horse or two. Don't laugh."

She looked pointedly at me. I didn't laugh.

"Horses are great," I said.

"Do you think Viðir would let me do a work trade for some hay, maybe?"

"Seems like we could always use a hand. Most farmers with an operation like this have at least a part-time hand. He just can't work with people. Doesn't trust them to do it right; hates teaching."

"This is true," Mamma said.

"I bet we could figure something out for the hay. Anyway, I'll come in the meantime and help with the fence and whatever else."

Rúna looked pleased, in her understated manner. This was a relief—her pride was so intense that it could've gone the other way. I pushed a little further.

"You probably want to clean out the house? I could help with that too."

She turned to the floor, to her dirty socks.

"No. Thanks. I'll take care of it."

The subtext—that the inside of her house, the place she'd grown up in and where she nominally lived, though she mostly resided in an ancient teardrop trailer sitting on blocks, was a shameful place, and no one should ever see it but her—this was plain to me and she knew it, and that's a fine thing about friends, they can tell each other a great deal without speech.

"We're yours now," Mamma said. "And don't forget that other thing we discussed. Could help pay the bills while you get the place operational."

I looked from one to the other and got nothing. It is okay to be excluded sometimes. And what must it be like to never have a mother, just a miserable excuse for a father, and then he dies, and maybe you mourn him in your own way through the cloak of hatred and resentment, and at the same time here is this strange woman intent on mothering you? Disorienting, exhilarating, maddening, all those things.

Rúna stayed that day. She didn't seem to want to go home — who could blame her? So Mamma trained her on the wrapper, and before long Rúna was running it nearly as well. Only once did she spin the hydraulic table too fast and send a bale flying off, where-upon it promptly rolled backward and pressed its bulbous white side against the hot engine, melting the plastic, leaving a sticky burnt-marshmallow residue all over it.

The long day over at last, we sat together on the porch swing, our usual spot, savoring the bubbles and the sour tang of the beer, you can try to replace it with other things but there is nothing better than beer after a day of haying.

"So," I said. "Committing to the farm sounds good."

"Yeah."

"Not so good for your dating prospects?"

She reddened a little. Grinned a little.

"Well, that's the other thing I wanted to tell you about. I went out with someone the other night. An ag student at the university in Hvanneyri."

"Did you meet online?"

"No, your mamma knew her somehow. She set it up."

"Of course she did." I waited for what I thought was a respectful minute or two. "Well?"

"Well what?"

"How did it go, dammit?"

Rúna's grin got wider. She couldn't repress it.

"I stayed over. In her dorm. Her roommate wasn't there."

"No!"

"Yes."

"I call that promising."

We toasted each other, clinking the sweaty bottles, making sure to meet eyes and drink before we set them down.

30.

September crept by without being noticed, and so did the first part of October. That's the best a farmer can hope for: no grievous injuries, no mechanical catastrophes, no surprise animal deaths. But it means you don't appreciate the last vestiges of the decent weather; you come to your senses and it's gone.

Pabbi would've preferred to round up and vaccinate the cattle some other time of year, as he would've liked to reschedule calving, but found to his resignation and dismay that there's a reason so many farmers do the former in fall. It's a miserable job. There are plenty of other tasks to complete as the world begins to squeeze its eyes shut in anticipation of the inevitable, far too many tasks, so we might as well wait until the last possible minute. By then the animals are already lumbering back to their sacrifice yard for the winter. They're a bit more pliable, possibly because they're as depressed as everyone else.

Around the middle of October the precipitation came reliably, and it came cold, you could count on it. Sometimes just rain, pelting curtains of rain, or mixed with wet snow, or frozen hard as it fell and landed, sheathing even the wooliest beast with a lethal lacquer. Then it was time: the forage was long played out, and feeding bales in the summer pastures would only result in the ground, that precious finite resource, turning to mud pit and morass. We called them in and they were ready. They knew the good times were over. They'd soon forget the feeling of warmth on their backs; they'd willingly sacrifice freedom and roaming for a small punched-up paddock with ample shelter and ample hay, all within a short stroll. Not that the Galloways sought shelter very often. Sometimes Pabbi stared at them through the window and wished emphatically that they would.

About a week before the great veterinary intervention, I was on the phone with Mihan. She had a few days off and was planning to come down to visit, to help. That was the plan. But she was nervous.

"What are you worried about? Mamma will love you, I know it, and Pabbi probably will too but it may be impossible to tell."

"Not that," she said. "It's just a lot of white people in one house."

"Right. But my mom and grandmother are Jewish—are we still white?"

"Yes."

Mihan had endured a few less-than-ideal experiences with previous boyfriends' parents. Uncomfortable questions about her background, her command of the Icelandic language. Deep-rooted ignorance about the Philippines in general. They'd been every bit as bad as schoolchildren or bar patrons, except worse because she was stuck trying to make a decent impression, and she resented it, and those comprised only a few meals here and there. She'd never stayed over with someone's family. Not like this.

"Couldn't we just stay in a motel?"

I laughed in apology. "Nothing nearby, I'm afraid. I guess there's the Hotel Bifröst, but I certainly couldn't afford it. Just trust me, it'll be okay."

As things happened, Mihan possessed a stronger constitution than I did. She arrived in Hira's car, a terrifying death trap loaned with the greatest goodwill, seemingly in fine spirits, no stops to throw up in

Varmahlíð, a cheerful greeting for all. And she'd brought presents too, they were odd but welcome.

Rykug, who had been keening and yapping since she detected Mihan through the window, was the first to be greeted, dogs demand this privilege. Mihan presented herself in a squat as she had in that park in Akureyri, but there was no placid demonstration of respect now, no head-in-crotch—everything was far too exciting for all that. She got battered and lathered, the whines changing in pitch and variance to a chatty yowl, as though Rykug were a farmer who had not been around a friend or any other person in a long while, and she had far too much to say. The only way Mihan could extricate herself from this affectionate assault was by delivering her gift, the other half of a pâté-and-pickle sandwich, which she'd saved for this purpose. Rykug took the thing willingly and retreated to a private corner of the yard where she set it down to examine, glancing up at Pabbi a few times to make sure this was real, not a cruel joke; if someone were to retrieve the priceless specimen she wouldn't be in the least surprised. Then she made it disappear, tossing her head back in jerks like a monitor lizard.

Pabbi was handed a six-pack of some higher-end imported bitter, which he received with quiet reverence, studying the label. For Mamma she had a bouquet, partly bought at some exorbitant price and partly scavenged by the side of the road, so yellow greenhouse tulips and bearded iris comingled with dandelion and chamomile, the last faded relics of summer, last survivors of the apocalypse. I didn't know how Mamma would react to this—she was not, as far as I could tell, a flower person.

"No one's given me flowers in years and years," she said, and there was maybe the hint of a crack in her voice, as though she were moved, and after that she grew unusually speechless.

And I, well, I received a flying embrace, legs wrapped tightly around my waist. My nose was in her hair. That faintly herbal shampoo, she was here, she was real again. Pabbi and Mamma were still standing there in the rain, and I thought I saw them exchange a glance, a smirk. Embarrassing but ideal, one of those moments you know you'll recall in perfect clarity forever, seared across the neurons like a psychic tattoo.

Some people can make themselves at home in another house, or maybe it has to be the right house, I wouldn't know because I've never possessed the talent. These people are so quickly woven into the fabric that you can't tell the new threads apart; they may have always been there. Mihan did this. She threw her stuff down in my room, where it escaped her small suitcase and quickly spread across the floor like yarrow. And in the kitchen or living room she began with a polite spatial deference, but was soon jostling and jockeying at the counter for plates, coffee, toast, or allowing herself to be jostled and jockeyed. I'd never seen Mamma and Pabbi so comfortable with a houseguest before.

In my room we pushed the old twin bed frame to one side, threw the mattress onto the floor, and augmented it with another from Amma's room, which we didn't call a guest room because Amma was generally the only guest. We lay there, legs tangled, at the end of Mihan's second day in Borgarfjörður. A long day indeed and tomorrow would be longer. We'd spent several hours rounding up the herd in the bitter rain. Mamma was at work, so it took the rest of us, and Mihan jumped right into it, unsqueamish, unfazed. Pabbi had given her an approving remark when he saw she'd brought her own pair of muck boots and they were already old and mucky. Even Rykug was called into action a couple of times: groups of calves who were huddling dejected under an aspen windbreak got left behind and then couldn't figure out which way to go, ran batshit the wrong way, of course. We did it all on foot. We'd waited too long for this, we always wait too long, and the ground was sodden. This meant we had to stay off the four-wheeler, which loves nothing more than to leave ruts. Bad enough that the cows punched it up with their sharp little trowel feet. And it rained and rained. In other parts of the world people might get away with quaint nostalgic rain gear made of waxed canvas and the like; where the rain is less insistent, it leaves time for the wax to work, it beads up and rolls off. Most Icelanders never looked back when better gear was invented, unless it was to look back at old photos in which people were cold and miserable, but we know that our fancy waterproof membranes wear out eventually, so if we can afford it we replace them every few years. My jacket, as it happened, was overdue, and after an hour of relentless saturation it gave up entirely, it transformed into cheesecloth. By the time the job was done, three humans and a dog were so chilled, nearly cryogenic, bones rattling in their loose sheaths of muscle and tendon, that the shower ran pretty well nonstop from 5 p.m. to 8 p.m., with a short break for dinner, and Pabbi said for the several hundredth time that he wished he'd built a sauna, why didn't he build a sauna. Fortunately most of our houses are hooked to a communal hot-water line; it costs money, of course, but it's abundant, a thick red artery from the heart of the earth. We can cook ourselves for a long time if we need to. We can stay in the water until its life-giving heat penetrates our meager crust and we emerge red and wrinkled in a steam cloud like a troll from a crack in the mountain.

Now Mihan's body next to mine was so warm, more effective than any hot-water bottle; in a stroke of brilliance she'd waited to shower last even though she'd been offered it first, and we barely needed the duvet. I was tempted to place my already ice-cold feet on her legs but knew she would shriek; one should never do such things, though sometimes we do anyway.

"You told me your pabbi has been more withdrawn lately. More reclusive? I guess I don't see it, but then I just met him, and mine talks so little that yours seems almost chatty."

"He's a bit livelier with you around, but yeah. He hasn't really been himself. He just acts, I don't know, worn out by the world."

"Do you think it's rough on him that your mother is the main breadwinner? My father is sensitive about that. He comes from a more traditional family, and if the man isn't supporting everyone, he feels like a lemon. Not a good lemon."

The room was dark, conducive to thinking, even though Mihan's intensely corporeal presence under the covers was less so, and I thought this one over for a minute. In truth, it had never occurred to me.

"Maybe. Not really. Mamma's always supported us, more or less. This place was never the profitable enterprise Pabbi thought it would be, or at least I don't think it ever was. It could be, though. I'm not saying he half-assed it, no, he worked himself into the ground, but I don't know, inflexibility . . . It's the Icelandic curse. Or the farmer's curse."

"Or the man's curse."

We breakfasted efficiently the following morning, food and coffee, topping off the tank, more fuel than we thought we wanted. This wasn't the old days, fishing from a tiny open boat in the huge pitiless sea, but vetting is still hard work.

The rain had reduced its ferocity just a trifle, so a person could think and breathe, so the rain jackets could have time to work, and we were grateful for that.

First we moved the cattle from their winter yard to the much smaller paddock that contained our corral, the decrepit wood-and-metal contraption Pabbi had built for containment, sorting, and veterinary work. Then we had to convince them to enter the thing. This they did not like to do. In the early days, Pabbi made a point of running his herd through the corral at least five times a year, if not more, so they'd know it wasn't so bad, they could survive it, they even got treats at the other end. But this resolution hadn't lasted long. It was simply too much effort; a person had other things to do than spend all day working cattle through a corral for no urgent reason. So our herd had been left to amplify and enlarge upon their natural distrust of all things different. This meant hassling, haggling, coercion, persuasion, every trick in the farmer's saggy old bag of tricks.

But damn the cows could be difficult, and the calves were even worse. It didn't matter how many times we pushed them around and around the paddock, they didn't want to go through the first gate, and cows aren't like sheep, they often act independently and they're stubborn. Eventually we resorted to tempting them inside little by little, small groups of three or four. We stopped pushing, started pulling, it always ends up like that. We shook the bucket of alfalfa pellets, we spoke gently, we slowed our breathing, softened our attitudes. Mihan proved to be particularly helpful with this. Cows don't often like new people, they don't even like when you wear a hat or jacket they haven't seen before, though they will recognize you with sunglasses on. Mihan, on the other hand, they seemed to like. Several curious calves had congregated around her, licking the Akureyri salt from her boots. These five allowed themselves to be led in by her; their mothers observed this and followed shortly thereafter. Sometimes it only takes a tipping point, a wave cresting. The rest of the herd, minus a few determined stragglers and jailbirds, sensed a change in the scales, a collective if wary consent, and they gave up their theatrical resistance.

The vaccination itself was yet another thing that set Pabbi apart from many of his regional peers. It could be argued, and it was often argued, that such preventative measures — onerous, expensive, occasionally traumatic to the cattle, and even occasionally, though very seldom, lethal to a fetus — were unnecessary. Many farmers, as they would tell you at every opportunity, literally every opportunity, had gone generations without such nonsense, and seen maybe a handful of serious diseases. On the other hand, cattle died sometimes, they just keeled over; every few years you might even lose ten or so. Who knew why? That's just how things went. Few wanted to bother with the hassle of ordering all these expensive medicines and poking every animal multiple times; even fewer wanted to mortgage their homes in order to pay for the veterinarian to do it.

But Pabbi had invested a great deal of money and time in procuring the foundation of our herd and then building it, step by careful genetically minded step. He had no wish to leave their health to chance just because blackleg was relatively uncommon in Borgarfjörður. To this point, he'd memorized the things we took caution against and he showed a certain perverse fondness in reciting the litany to Mamma and me, and Amma too if she were visiting, which delighted her medical mind: infectious bovine rhinotracheitis, bovine viral diarrhea (types 1 and 2), parainfluenza 3, bovine respiratory syncytial virus, *Mannheimia haemolytica* (prime suspect in calf pneumonia), and the big Cs, of course: *Clostridium chauvoei* (the aforementioned and evocatively named "blackleg"), *C. septicum*, *C. novyi* type D (bacillary hemoglobinuria, aka "red water"), *C. tetani*, and *C. perfringens*. No one wants to die of "blackleg" or "red water." And let us never forget injectable ivermectin, which purges the bovine body of roundworms and lungworms, not to mention such tenacious external predators as lice, grubs, and mites, aka mange, aka "barn itch." Once you've seen an animal abrade itself until vast swaths of its thick hairy coat are gone, Pabbi liked to say, and then most of the epidermis beneath it, so that the blood and white pus run in runnels down its flanks, every waking second an obvious torment, you might not be so complacent or so quick to use the innocuous-sounding nickname of "barn itch."

But it isn't easy. Each animal has to be in line, and some are more cooperative than others. The shots that can be administered intramuscularly aren't so bad, though they appear to be far worse for the cow, for they're jabbed deep. The tricky ones are subcutaneous. The amateur vet in question, whoever they may be, is leaning, hovering over the animal's back, muck boots wedged between two rails, trying to reach through the fur and pinch up enough of the tight hide to insert the syringe laterally, and do this without sending the enormous goddamned evil needle through one's own hand, which happens about as often as you might expect, too often that is, and meanwhile the cow is bucking, writhing, frothing, snorting, terrified and very pissed off. Adverse conditions for a needle handler.

Mihan was a bit shocked. She felt for them — as Pabbi did, as I did — but the brutality of it was new to her. The fevered, determined resistance.

"These aren't dairy animals," I'd warned her beforehand. All her fond photos online were of Icelandic cattle, fairly placid animals, handled often and accustomed to close contact. Galloways aren't wild, necessarily, they aren't bison, but if there's a spectrum between feral and domesticated, they are somewhere in between.

She rose to the challenge. Even though all our hands were now covered in shit, and there were syringes and vials everywhere, and as the daylight began to wane it all became somewhat rushed and chaotic, she always filled from the right vials to the right mark, and she spoke calmly to the aggrieved patients, she told them it would be all right, they'd soon be free from the chute and back with their families, breathing easy. It seemed to have an effect. We can all benefit from a soothing voice in our ear.

By late afternoon we'd vetted all but a last group of intractable anti-vaxxers. Five steers and two calves were bunched tight between a gate and the chute, refusing to enter under any circumstances. I'd seen Pabbi grapple with this conundrum before. Only rarely could he remain at a safe vantage and persuade an animal to enter the chute who'd developed the conviction that the chute was the gateway to hell, and having seen all of his herdmates enter, spewing every conceivable manifestation of fear, visible and invisible, like an active volcano, and then disappear, well, a steer wasn't about to change his mind easily. Pabbi could shake the rattle-stick all he wanted. Their eyes were now rolling insensibly, their bowels turned to water. At this point, Pabbi had to get in with them and push their discomfort a little further until the chute was preferable. I knew he didn't like it. Who would? In quarters as tight as all that, with no room to flee, cattle are more dangerous than snakes. One careless turn of their enormous bodies and they would crush him. One malevolent kick and his life would be over.

Pabbi'd had some near misses over the years. Every cattle farmer did. It was a chance you took, a trade-off for working with the big animals. Galloways were polled, or naturally hornless, and that was a saving grace, but they still had plenty of strength and bulk and ire. He'd been thrown against the rails a few times. Hooves had whizzed past his fragile body like bullets. One time he took a glancing blow to his left hand and he couldn't use his thumb properly for six weeks.

He internalized these altercations. Violence was inherent to farming, no one could argue with that. But he'd tried so hard over the years to cultivate an operation, an environment, in which its presence was minimal. He'd seen countless farmers do things the old way, and the old way resulted in injured people, frightened animals, or dead versions of both. If he treated the animals with respect and kindness, even though they might be destined for the abattoir, wasn't that enough? What constituted a "good life"? How did an animal make it clear that it wasn't having a good life? By kicking the hell out of you? By breaking your spine?

Violence was everywhere, it grew in the soil like *Clostridium* spores. Some things turned up the same no matter how you went about them. Pabbi had been forced to intubate a surprising number of calves over the years when they couldn't or wouldn't nurse, an experience that he always described with rueful horror, for it was excruciating, an absolute nightmare to the calf whose life he was desperate to save. Or why did it often happen that the friendliest cattle were also the most perilous? They feared him less, so they'd dance and leap and kick and even headbutt at his approach, 600 kilograms of joy. And then, of course, he resented them for jeopardizing his life. This contradiction—the feeling of antagonism, hatred even, for creatures in whose health and happiness he was so invested—plagued him. If there'd been a vaccine against it, he would've pinched up his own skin and plunged the big needle sideways.

It was about 5 p.m. and darkening when six of the last holdouts made their way through the gauntlet of shots and exited the corral. There was one left, a robust and leery steer. Always one left. He'd seen his cohort compromise their ideals, but it had failed to make an impression on him. He was entrenched. Now that there was more room to maneuver in the steer's little area, Pabbi climbed in without too much trepidation. He was tired, moving stiffly, but we were almost done and that was something. I was set to throw boards behind the steer and trap him in the chute the minute he entered, and then to administer the vaccines, a task Pabbi had long since passed on to me since his shoulder was screaming bloody murder. Mihan was on hand to fill the syringes. We were all pretty raw and hungry. The worst time to do anything of consequence.

It happened with unnatural speed. I saw Pabbi climb in, heard him mutter a few words, conciliatory but firm, and then step behind the steer with his arms outstretched. Then he was on the ground, the huge animal dancing over him like a triumphant satyr.

"Pabbi!" I yelled.

"Ah, Jesus fucking Christ," he said. He was clutching his chest. Alive.

"Get Mamma," I told Mihan. I'd seen my mother roll up to the house about twenty minutes before, home from work. She was probably sitting in the dark, cold living room wishing someone had thought to thaw out some fish or something.

I raced around to the other side of the corral and opened that final gate, freeing the steer. He was only too happy to oblige. He'd successfully avoided chutes and needles for another year. I tried to help Pabbi up, but he moaned and grimaced.

"How bad are you hurt?"

"Don't know. Bastard got me—Right in the chest. Hard—to breathe."

The implications were dire. If his ribs were crushed—"stove in," as farmers like to say—his lung could be punctured or collapsed.

And then Mamma was there with Mihan, and we were moving him as gingerly as we could manage into the car, and on the road to Borgarnes, every bump a bitter cruelty.

In the end there were only two ribs cracked, and we all came home that same night, very late, hungrier than before. Pabbi was wrapped up tight, his pain dulled with some defanged opiate but his mind very present. He looked spiritually destroyed.

"Can you get me a beer, please?"

I was in the kitchen with Mihan, the two of us working up a makeshift dinner. Mamma, watching him with a look of profound weariness and concern, sat across from Pabbi, who occupied the sofa—she didn't want to jostle him in his precarious repose.

"Didn't the nurse tell you no alcohol?" I said.

"It's fine," Mamma said. "They just don't trust people to take care of themselves. Alcohol and opiates are a tried-and-true pairing, like wine and cheese."

"If you're the child of a doctor, you're basically a doctor too," Mihan said, and the three of us chuckled briefly at that. Pabbi did not. He was looking out the window, as though he could see past the yellow reflection of us, his little family, as though he could see through the darkness of the cold wet October night into the barnyard, the corral, the setting of his near ruin.

"I'm done," he said. He'd said it before.

31.

"Is he going to be all right?" We stood outside on a Friday morning, glued together for warmth and because even a centimeter of separation felt like an injustice. The rain had stopped, blown off somewhere, and the colder air had a certain styptic quality, as though it could be used to staunch a laceration. That's the sign of coming winter in Iceland—some call it the smell of snow. The mountains had a thin layer of powder and Baula rose above, yellow like an upturned sugar cone. Mihan bore a grave expression.

"Sure, I think so. The nurse said he'd be in pain for a while, would need to take it easy, but he's survived worse."

"No, I meant—Will he be *okay?*"

"Oh." I gave a noncommittal sigh.

"Good thing you're here," she said. "I'd stay longer, but Hira needs her car back."

"And you have a shift tonight."

"And I have a shift tonight."

Rykug had positioned herself beneath the vehicle, a trick she generally reserved for Pabbi. This may have been because the freakishly intelligent creature could sense my desire to go with Mihan, or she knew that Mihan and I were becoming one entity, or just that she adored Mihan. To say that the two were bonded would be a disingenuous understatement.

"*Atay, Atay,* come here. I'll be back soon. Or if you miss me too much you take the Twingo and come to Akureyri again, I know you can drive, yes, you are a very good driver."

I don't know why it moved me so much that Mihan had her own nickname for Rykug—*liver* in Filipino. As I watched the two of them cuddle in the foul October mud, with its telltale oily sheen from spilt diesel, Rikka rolling to present her filthy undercarriage but always training her affectionate side-eye on Mihan, I felt the pulse in my head and a rushing in my ears as though I were on the phone with a conch shell.

Then Mihan blew in Rykug's face, and the wild kelpie, whom I'd never thought of as liver-colored before, made a playful snap at her nose, just shy of contact. This was their unique code for *Things aren't sad; things are fun.* A dog will remind you of this if you forget, but sometimes you have to remind the dog to remind you.

How did I get so lucky? Certainly, as far as Rykug was concerned, it wasn't thanks to Pabbi's planning. He'd been forced to admit during the dog's first winter in Borgarfjörður that kelpies were not ideally suited to Iceland, and perhaps he should've stuck with a border collie. At least collies have coats. And Rykug's paws jammed up terribly in the ice, they were a miserable burden to her, and sometimes she'd spend an hour digging the jagged chunks from between her pads, using her front teeth like pliers.

Of course there was the problem of keeping Rykug's mind occupied when it emerged that she'd actually have very little to do, but as it turned out, she was a bit lazy for a kelpie. This would've earned her poor marks on an Australian cattle station. What did the herding people say? She lacked "drive"? Whatever it was that made the famous kelpies run and run all day across the merciless bush, or that made border collies run from one end of the truck bed to the other ad infinitum. Or maybe that was unfair. She just adapted to our lifestyle, to what was asked of her, as dogs have done for millennia.

Once Ketill asked Pabbi, "What do you need a dog that smart for anyway? Don't cows basically go where you want them to?"

And Pabbi answered, "Sometimes," and it was clear that the accuracy of the comment irked him.

Now Rykug was sulking under the eave because Mihan had the car door open and our extended parting had reached its final act.

"Was that awkward when your mamma asked me about my degree and I said I had no idea why I'd chosen Media Studies to begin with, and I wasn't even sure I wanted to keep going with it?"

"No, it's hard to make her uncomfortable," I said. "And besides, she's far more worried about my degree."

"You're going back to Reykjavík in January?"

"That's the plan."

"We'll be farther away. A longer drive."

"What if you transferred to U of I?"

"What if you transferred to Akureyri?"

We smiled grimly at each other. Invisible heels digging in. It wasn't a real conversation about our future, more like a rehearsal, but still it had teeth. Rocky, fruitless. We'd spent a grand total of maybe three weeks together. I thought it unfathomable that we'd come this far already.

"We got serious," she said.

I nodded, unsure whether she meant the topic or our relationship.

"I feel jealous of everyone who gets to be around you all the time," I said, "but I don't feel *jealous*. Is that weird?"

"Not really," she said. "I guess jealousy between two people could be a sign of instability, volatility. And they mistake that for spark. I think about you all the time, but it feels like we've been together for about forty years."

"Comfortable," I said.

"Strangely easy," she said. "Not like what you see on TV."

And when she drove away, bumping down the rutted road in that wretched old car, I had the oddest, fleeting sensation that the place was mine, and I wasn't a kid anymore, and I was alone.

32.

"Viðir. *Viðir.*"

A dejected mumble from the bedroom was all that Mamma received in response. Saturday in late October, surprisingly temperate, and though it was already close to noon, Pabbi had yet to emerge. Mamma sounded irritated. It had been over a week since the rib cracking. She had no shortage of compassion, but she didn't like to play the part of nurse either, she had no patience for it, especially when the infirmed was a stubborn old fool who resisted all attempts to help or rehabilitate. And she was working on something, furrowed at her computer screen.

"Tell your father Ingi Róbertsson is here. He's wandering around the barnyard like he owns the place. If he comes in here and expects coffee I'll lose my mind."

Pabbi must have heard this because he required no rousing. He was up and nominally dressed before I could do anything, moving with great delicacy, wincing with every step. He rasped his hand over his unshaved face, grunted, and went out to meet Ingi. I followed.

Ingi stood by the barnyard gate, gazing complacently at the cattle, who gazed uninterestedly back at him. His expensive-looking jacket was already covered with Rykug's muddy prints — every farm must have a greeter.

"Fine looking herd you have here, Viðir. Deeply stupid animals, though. Look how that one seems to stare right through me. You'd never see a horse doing that."

He turned to examine us more carefully and I had the unique impression that we were being assessed in much the same way as the cattle.

"Viðir. My god, man, you look like hell. And Orri, how are you? Still home from school, I see. You missed the country so much?"

I shook his hand. Ingi Róbertsson was a neighbor and what passed for an important man in the valley. He was impossibly wealthy by Borgarfjörður standards, one of the few who'd ridden out the crash in style, even capitalized on it. So many farmers had sold out or gone under, and somehow Ingi was always on the spot with cash in hand, either at the farmer's lowest point of desperation or afterward, when the place went back to the bank and Ingi snapped it up at auction. He was savvy that way. Pabbi had told me of one series of events back in 2008 when a dairy farmer made the painful but fortuitous decision to sell his entire herd rather than complete the necessary infrastructure renovation that had been hanging over him, and then the economy promptly collapsed and the unlucky farmer who'd bought the man's herd lost his entire farm, and who was there to buy it, a sympathetic smile on his face? Ingi Róbertsson. Almost as though he knew the crash was coming.

"I think he might be Satan," Pabbi had said.

Which would be rich given that Ingi was a devout man, a pastor in the local church. He never swore, he didn't drink, he was courteous to everyone, in his own bluff manner. He just had a preternatural facility with money.

His business was in real estate. He seemed to buy far more than he sold, but he always had more to spend so he must have been selling at a high price, as when he unloaded prime riverfront property along the Norðurá to a group of investment bankers from Stockholm, who built an ultramodern vacation home and came once or twice a year to drink Scottish whisky and catch salmon.

Ingi was also a farmer of sorts, which commanded a certain grudging respect among the locals. One had to squint to see him as such, Pabbi said, but he did have a sizable sheep herd, and very fine high-tensile electric fences, and he made and sold hay on a few of his properties, or paid someone else to make and sell it. And he loved horses.

Pabbi did not love horses — he didn't understand or believe in them. It was a sore spot with the neighbors, with Mamma. He remained mystified as to how farmers could make any money with the animal. Sheep were bad enough — wool retail being a monumental pain in the ass, and how much lamb could a person eat, really? But horses. What good were they? People like Ingi occasionally made decent money selling registered Icelandic breeding stock to niche enthusiasts in places like the United States, but that was limited, most Americans wanted a big horse, not a funny little thing that looked like an overgrown pony. So what else was there? There were still some horsemeat eaters out there, not many. And there were the ill-regarded blood farms, of course, if you wanted to be cast as a pariah by your neighbors. As Pabbi saw it, most horse people were keeping these expensive animals, who nibbled every pasture down to the dirt and ate their weight in hay all winter, just because they liked to ride them every once in a while, and they looked handsome cavorting around a field. Picturesque, certainly. Profitable, hardly. Driving around, Pabbi liked to count the herds and try to calculate how much the farmer must borrow in order to stay afloat. Unless they had other means, that is, like Ingi.

But Pabbi always rose to the bait when Ingi was around. The truth was that he liked the man against his will. Ingi was intelligent. The two of them had a relaxed banter they fell into.

"A horse will never look placid like a cow because it's always sizing you up," Pabbi said now. "The ideal place to bite you and so forth."

"This from the man who was just kicked in the chest by a steer."

Pabbi snorted. "It was an accident. You'd be upset too if you were about to be jabbed with a needle the length of a fence post."

"And I'm sure the animal had a clear concept of what was coming."

"Well, probably not," Pabbi conceded. One didn't get far defending a cow's perspicacity.

"A horse, on the other hand," Ingi said. "A horse sometimes knows what you're about to say before you do. I think they experience time like a Norn—past, present, and future all at once."

"So does my dog."

Ingi looked at Rykug, who glanced up guiltily, as though she knew she'd been mentioned, lips dripping from the mound of fresh shit that had fallen off the tractor tire.

"A horse is more like a cat anyway," Pabbi said. "There are good ones, but few can be trusted, and too many is definitely bad."

"And you should never let them in the house," Ingi said.

"Very true."

The conversation lapsed into silence for a minute. I pressed boot prints into the half-frozen mud and worked my hands around in my pockets for lint, trying not to think about how much it must hurt Pabbi to stand upright this long.

"Well," Ingi said at last. "Shall we talk business?"

And only then, with these words, and Pabbi gesturing for Ingi to follow him into the shop, but making it clear that I wasn't welcome, did my gut lurch. It hadn't occurred to me that Ingi had been invited, though Ingi never showed up unannounced. He was civil to a fault; he placed a high value on his own time and therefore other people's time as well. He was the opposite of Ketill.

"Mamma," I said, stepping back into the house alone. "I think Pabbi called Ingi."

"Oh?"

She kept her eyes on the computer screen while this hung in the air. It likely meant she knew already. She'd either been told or deduced it. I felt dizzy, frightened, outraged, betrayed. I felt like a child.

After an economical twenty minutes or so, Pabbi hobbled back inside and sat down gingerly on the sofa.

"Well," he said, as though I'd been part of the conversation from the start. "He's interested. He threw out a ballpark that was more than fair. Generous even."

"Mm. What about the cows?" Mamma said.

"Says he knows someone who might be interested. A conscientious farmer over by Akranes."

I couldn't stand the brazenness anymore, the surrealism.

"Jesus Christ!" I shouted. "Are you really talking about this?" I looked to Mamma for assistance, but she seemed so detached, I couldn't reach her.

"It's just a conversation," Pabbi said. "Just exploring options."

"But what about all the blood and sweat you've poured into this place? You built it from the ground up!"

Pabbi's eyes met mine. They were bloodshot, exhausted, sober.

"What have I built exactly?"

I put my face into my hands and stared at the floor. The pulse pushed my skin around in ripples.

"You can't be serious," I said, almost moaning. "This is my home."

"Son," he said, and his tone was a little bit more conciliatory, more fatherly. "It's just a conversation."

33.

November is a time for secrets. Sunlight is minimal, after all, a slim ration. It comes late in the day if it can be seen at all through the miserable squalling first act of the long winter, and it's gone again before you can summon up the will to step outside and sear a few meager rays of it into your protesting eyeballs. You rise in darkness, you retire in darkness, and unfairly, the night is further protracted by demented circadian rhythms. You wander in darkness.

When I was younger, confidence in my world was paramount. I had two parents who loved each other and loved me, no siblings to contend with, and a comfortable place for these phenomena, which I took entirely for granted, to occur. But such things erode, for all things erode. And the speed of erosion is not static but rather a constant acceleration, like the melting of a glacial shelf as it's battered by atmospheric heat and undermined by changing ocean currents and warmer water. The more it loses, the faster it loses.

I think confidence, or rather a youthful sense of security, adheres to the same principle. So my leaving for university the previous year, and finding it not at all what I had expected, was the first block of ice to fall. The foundation was compromised. And when I learned that

Pabbi was thinking of selling the farm, that was a record-breaking temperature, it was a gaping moulin, funneling meltwater to the bottom of the ice sheet. Everyone has secrets, that's nothing new, secrets can be wholesome. They contribute to the illusion of autonomy. But now I felt sure that things were in motion, potentially very painful things, and their nature and trajectory were being obscured from my sight. And yet the household was so divided, so compartmentalized, that the prospect of dragging these secrets to light felt prohibitively difficult, even insurmountable, and would I find any satisfaction in knowing them? Or would their airing bring about the ruin of all?

November. It's a miracle anyone adjusts to anything.

34.

I called Amma from the barn. I was freezing my ass off, and half-frozen rain pelted the metal roof with such force that I could scarcely hear her at all.

"Are you calling me from the barn?" she said. "Why are you in the barn?"

"Pabbi has a secret," I said.

"What do you mean?"

"He's shifty. He's hiding something."

"I doubt it," she said. "Are you upset about this talk of selling the farm?"

"Of course! Aren't you?"

She paused, but only briefly. "Yes. I don't know what he's thinking. I love that place."

I didn't know how to respond. The prospect of no longer having a home, my own sacred home, was still too appalling to contemplate. And yet I contemplated worse things.

"That's not it," I said. "Or, I don't know, maybe it's related. But I think—Amma, I think he might be planning to kill himself."

For a whole minute I heard nothing but the wind, the rain, the roof. The sounds of Iceland.

"Are you still there?"

"Yes. Why do you say that?"

"Well, he's been depressed, for a start. Mamma certainly thinks he's been depressed, and he's almost admitted as much. He seems to hate the farm, the work..."

"I've noticed. Aren't we all depressed this time of year?"

"More than usual," I said. "And that's not all. He disappears into his shop for hours and hours at a time, but he doesn't do anything in there as far as I can tell, he doesn't make anything, he doesn't even smoke. He'll barely talk."

"Sounds like you're describing Viðir."

"No, really, Amma, this is different. He seems...detached? From life?"

"Hmm," she said, the "hmm" of a physician who will never really retire. "I'm not minimizing it. What else? Has he said anything about suicide? Any real indication?"

"No, but he has been giving things away. He gave me his favorite pipe. And a week ago, he gave me his gun."

"Oh. That does sound bad."

Pabbi's gun was our only gun. Icelanders are not a gun-toting people—maybe we would be, given our violent past, but we're not allowed. Civilization can be imposed from the top down. Many farmers have one or two for various farm-related things, but this tends to be an ancient shotgun, almost innocuous as far as guns are concerned. Pabbi, of course, needing to be perverse, needing to be peculiar, had his Sako rifle. He'd procured it about fifteen years ago from another farmer who used it to shoot minks predating on his chickens, or at least that was the intended purpose, it's doubtful he ever got any. This farmer got it from a man who used to guide tourists hunting reindeer in the Eastfjords but who became nauseated by macho Americans and all their posturing and ridiculous gear and offensive talk about "knocking her over" and "dropping her." So the Sako had come to Pabbi eventually. He kept it in fine shape, always well-oiled, and he'd practiced with it for a while until he became a decent marksman, but these days it was seldom used for any-thing more than euthanasia. He'd thought he might want it for foxes, but in the end, we had no poultry, so there was no reason for antagonism toward the species. We rarely saw a fox anyway, and on the odd occasion when he saw one, he said he found himself liking it very much.

I ventured to Amma that maybe Pabbi gave me the rifle because it was too closely associated with dead cattle. Maybe it was a rite of passage that I wasn't aware of.

"Or maybe he's divesting himself of his possessions," Amma said.

"Right."

"Well, I'm not sure what I can do from here, especially if he hasn't said anything about ideation. He has no therapist, no mandatory reporter. And I'm not his doctor anyway, I'm his mother-in-law. You wouldn't want him hauled off for in-patient treatment if he's just got a bad case of seasonal affective disorder."

"It's worse than that."

"No, I understand. But you know what I mean."

"I guess."

"Does your mamma know? Have the two of you talked about it?"

That was the problem. I didn't know what Mamma knew. Mamma was in her own world, with her own secret. And I couldn't burden Amma with it, because I had even less of an idea what it was than I had with Pabbi, and it would eat her up. She'd drop everything and get in the car if she thought something was seriously wrong with her daughter, and Amma only had another month and a half until retirement. This was her victory lap. She was training others at the hospital, she was conferencing, being celebrated and appreciated and tying up about three thousand loose ends.

So we left it in the air, with the extracted promise that I would keep a close eye on Pabbi, and talk to Mamma, and let Amma know if anything took a noticeable turn, and take care of myself while I was at it.

35.

The nighttime is when I first became aware of Mamma's furtive movements. At first I thought it was just our shared affliction.

I was lying in bed, awake but not yet resenting my consciousness after a long call with Mihan in which I'd tried at great length and failed at great length to articulate my concerns about Pabbi before finally realizing with chagrin that I'd been dominating the conversation, and then being reassured that Mihan didn't mind, she genuinely gave a damn.

I heard the soft abrading of a foot on the stairs, the sound a person makes when they're quietly trying to feel their way in the dark. Then the floor creaking in one of its reliable creak spots, and the plasticky suck of the fridge door opening. It is common, I know, for a sleepless person to seek the fridge, even if it contains nothing promising, even if they're not hungry. The fridge is a comforting place, a refuge. Maybe a bite of leftovers, a smear of peanut butter. Maybe a way to turn the light on without the commitment and resignation of an actual light.

Mamma looked a little surprised to hear me behind her. She closed the fridge without procuring anything.

"You too?" she said.

"Ah, not really."

"Things have been better since you came home?"

We didn't have to explain these matters, much can be said with a tired look, and we certainly never spoke the *I* word, "insomnia." The *I* word is a curse. It can manifest the nightmare. There are few nightmares worse.

"Much better, but I heard you."

"Sorry."

"It's fine."

"Well. I'm headed for the guest room. Might have more luck in there."

Mamma's method was to wander in search of sleep. Sleep is elusive — it can slip away from you and hide in corners if you're not attentive, but the paradox is that you must cultivate inattention if you want to find it again.

A few nights later I heard Mamma roaming the house again, like an exhausted ghost, but after several minutes, instead of the door to the guest room closing I heard the front door let a rush of November air into the heated vacuum of the house, the mixing of the sacred and the profane, and footsteps crunching ice in the driveway, and Mamma's car starting up and driving away. I was concerned, even a bit shocked. I listened for a while in case Pabbi was alarmed, but he didn't stir, and sleep returned to me. It clung to my bedsheets though it had forsaken hers.

The next morning she was back. She'd come home before I woke, showered, eaten an early breakfast. The coffee was tepid. Pabbi was still in bed. He was often in bed these days.

"What happened last night?" I said.

"I wondered if you heard me. I remembered some things I needed to take care of at the office, and I wasn't sleeping anyway, so I just drove over there. "

"At three a.m.?"

"You'd be surprised how many academics do it. That's why we

demand a comfortable sofa in our office, not one of those horrible Danish torture devices made of leather or wool that's meant to keep students from lingering too long. Mine is pretty good. So I caught a couple of hours after I finished. Sometimes I have better luck in a new place, away from . . . away from everything."

The explanation was, I thought, credible, if a little too elaborate.

But she repeated this odd behavior, this inefficient crusade. Later that week she went to Bifröst two nights in a row, and the following week three times.

A worm of suspicion, once it enters your flesh and begins to grow or multiply in your organs, is hard to remove. You can't just shoot up with ivermectin or swallow a wad of tobacco. And what a particularly unwelcome sensation it was to feel suspicious of my own mamma, for whom I'd never felt anything but unmitigated trust.

I tried to keep the word out of my head. "Affair," the A word, perhaps even more damned than the I word. I'd been lucky enough to live through twenty years without once applying it to my own parents. And I didn't dare speak it aloud now, even to Mihan. But words and notions cannot be kept from one's head, they are worms.

I willed myself to think charitably about Mamma's secret. It could be a good secret. She was planning a birthday present for Pabbi. A really extravagant birthday present. A vacation! Or it wasn't a secret at all.

Fool. Even a fool can't fool himself into foolishness.

I knew the foundations were crumbling.

36.

Then it all blew up.

I was unfortunate enough to be there when it happened. That's the price you pay when you're the only child in a tight-knit nuclear family and your parents like each other, which also means they have no real friends other than you — you're always there, you're present. If you're not the subject, the protagonist, then you're the third wheel.

It was afternoon on a glassy weekend in late November, already dark, already in its shroud. Mamma and Pabbi were engaged in that oldest of domestic negotiations: What should we have for dinner? Pabbi hadn't cooked much lately. He wasn't holding up his end. Mamma said she'd be perfectly willing to cook if someone would go out to the garage, where we kept the coffin chest freezers, and fetch some meat that would thaw quickly. Ground beef, for example — we could have pasta and meatballs. That's when Pabbi allowed, with some constraint, that he didn't think he was willing to eat meat anymore.

"Oh?" Mamma said.

"I just don't think I can. Every time I look at it, I feel a bit sick. I see a crosscut shank and all I think of is Brauð-Mylsna. Remember we always used to talk about how big his legs were? And his shank steaks are just as big. They're *him*. They're his body."

"Okay," she said. "I understand. And that's fine. But will you be preparing a vegetarian dinner this evening? Roasting some potatoes and cauliflower, perhaps? Tofu with rice?"

These were not dishes she liked to cook.

Pabbi shrugged. He was still in his bathrobe at 4:30 p.m. His face, unshaven. His hair like an unkempt topiary.

Mamma regarded him with a mixture of sympathy and resentment that chilled me. I thought I would never understand the complexity of a long, loving relationship.

"And the business? Beef sales?"

"I don't think I can bear the thought of hocking their flesh anymore. People don't appreciate what goes into it. They think it's just some bucolic lark. They don't understand. I'm selling pain."

He looked on the verge of weeping, but nothing came out of his eyes.

"I thought you did everything in your power to make their lives as painless as possible."

"*My* pain."

"Your pain." Mamma's jaw was clenched. "So. Sell the cattle then? Sell the farm?"

She sounded efficient, a little cold. Like an accountant.

Pabbi shrugged again and looked at the floor. He seemed to have trouble meeting her eyes when things were roughest.

"I don't know. I don't know what else to do."

"You don't know what else to do."

At this point, without any preamble and without uttering a sound, Mamma snatched up the jar of store-bought organic tomatoes that she'd placed on the counter during the initial stages of the dinner discussion, and hurled it with great force at the oven door. The reinforced glass held firm but the tomato jar shattered, and red magma with vitreous shards flowed away in a slow hurry, following the shallow depressions between the floor tiles and the general cant of the sinking, badly leveled house.

Rykug cowered under a chair, too horrified to partake of this sudden bounty. Pabbi and I exchanged a quick glance. Mamma's face was flushed, and a vein pulsed in her temple, but she was composed. Eerily composed.

"Sorry about the jar," she said, her voice flat.

"I'll clean it up," I said, my first contribution to this chaotic parlay, and started in with the paper towels.

While I was doing that, Mamma sat down at the kitchen table, heavily. I saw now just how exhausted she was. She reached across and took Pabbi's hands. He seemed relieved to provide them.

"Viðir," she said. "I'm tired."

"I know."

"I'm going."

"Good idea. Get some air, clear your head."

"I'm going to Reykjavík."

"What's in Reykjavík?"

"Well, my mother's apartment, for one thing. I'll be staying with her, at least for a while. And also, my new position."

"Your new what?"

Mamma looked at me as though I were the only sane person in the room.

"You probably figured?" she said.

I shook my head, baffled.

"Well, I'm sorry. I meant to tell you before, but I wasn't sure at first, and then I still wasn't sure, and it went on like that, and it was hard to say out loud."

She explained. She'd been offered a job at the University of Iceland back in September. Had, in fact, been offered the job a few times over the years. She had colleagues there and they'd been trying to poach her from Bifröst for years. And it had been tempting, for a whole host of reasons. She'd be appreciated, given significantly more room—she could mold her own curricula, teach what she wanted, even cross-discipline. Also, Reykjavík was the heart of Iceland's political landscape. She'd be right at the center of things, watching with great interest, and probably deep frustration, as her own students campaigned for local races and built political careers. Politics in Reykjavík weren't just theoretical, they were punchy and visceral and real—just look at the people in the streets following the crash. Things could change on a dime and she'd have front-row seats.

That wasn't all. The early stages of her academic career had been stunted and marred, she was quite sure, by anti-Semitism. And not just the usual microaggressions either: She'd found herself sidelined more than once by antagonistic relationships with department chairs and administration bureaucrats. Her politics were certainly part of it—for a little while, fed up with the confused, impertinent questions about her decidedly un-Icelandic surname, Lacas, she'd adopted a fake patronymic that she found amusing, thereby rendering herself Emma Goldmansdottir—but anti-Semitism and fear of left-wing ideology often go hand in hand. Now, at last, at the age of forty-eight, she'd reached the stage where her peers didn't give a damn about her background, or were more enlightened, or knew better than to say anything. Her publications were well received. A significant number of international students enrolled in or audited her Bifröst classes online. The city wanted her now—they were ready for her. She could choose how many classes she taught. She could name the length and date of her next sabbatical. She could pick her own teaching assistants.

So she'd been busy, even if unsure. She hadn't told Bifröst yet, but she'd already cast a private net so that she might recommend a suitable replacement for herself—she liked her colleagues, her students too, and was worried about them tipping backward onto their heels with such short notice. It was rare, but not unheard of, for a professor to leave between semesters. She had no contract. And she'd been working out potential new syllabi, new research projects.

A heady prospect, the freedom she could experience with this sudden grant of time and funding. An academic seldom had enough of either one.

And that wasn't all. That wasn't, in fact, the broken heart of it. There remained the tricky thing to say, and she looked as though she didn't want to say it in front of me. She did anyway.

"I never wanted to live here, in the middle of nowhere," she said to Pabbi. "You knew that. You knew because I told you. But you *did* want to. You couldn't bear the prospect of working for anyone else anymore, and you wanted to raise animals, you said. It was all you wanted to do. So I agreed, because who wouldn't? I love you and I want you to be happy. And I sacrificed a number of things to do it. My career, for one. Friends, for another. But look, it's a beautiful farm, and we got to raise Orri here, healthy and strong with his mouth full of disgusting bacteria. So I didn't resent it. I swallowed it because this is where we built our life. But lately it hasn't felt like my life anymore; it's felt like your life. A life you don't particularly want. Now that you seem to hate the place, and hate farming, and you've quit making plans, I don't just feel like you've abandoned everything you've worked for, I feel like you've abandoned me. And I do resent it. And our son is grown now, he's a university student. He doesn't need me to hold down the fort. So what exactly am I doing here, driving day after day to that dismal outpost while my car gets shaken to pieces and stuck in the mud and snow, talking to students on a computer screen, picking up all the work that should be handed off to assistants and adjuncts, then coming back here to a dark house, never seeing anyone else outside of work, and all so you can keep doing this thing you hate? Why do I need to stay here anymore?"

She let the words trail in the air. The hardest question has no answer.

Three days later she was gone. A virulent morning, the first of December, snow falling heavily on a layer of ice that had settled overnight. The valley lay under a filthy-gray cloud. The world was dim, obscured. Maybe things were better toward the south, around the horn of Hafnarfjall, but who could possibly know.

I helped Mamma load the last suitcase into her car, its rusty old leaf springs protesting. I could hardly speak. I believe we all looked equally shocked and miserable. She embraced Pabbi and me and then Rykug, who had the energy of a sodden rag.

"I'll call when I get there," she said to us, and then pointedly, just to me, "See you in a few weeks."

"What's going to happen?" I said helplessly.

But she just shook her head, trying to smile like mothers do, but the tears were all collecting in the corners of her mouth. She climbed in, started the car, and rolled the window down. She gave Pabbi a significant look, as though imploring him to say something, just goddamn say something.

"Be careful," he said. "People will be all over the road."

37.

So that was Mamma's secret, revealed. Pabbi still held his, ready to drop it any moment like a hydrogen bomb. But I was too busy to look up.

Fall was long gone, a distant memory of balmier weather. And we'd wasted it. Fall is the busiest of times for an Icelandic farmer, unless you count spring and summer. Because if you fail to do all the buckling up and battening down that you should before winter grips your world like a vise, then suddenly everything is orders of magnitude more difficult, or it's impossible. I would've done these things months earlier—unbuilding temporary fence to preserve string line and fiberglass posts; wrestling the greasy ice-pick chains onto Kolkrabbi's rear tires; coiling up approximately four hundred hoses and moving them to the heated shop; draining and blowing out water lines, hauling in the stock tanks and mineral feeders; treating the last of the summer diesel with kerosene; cleaning and bedding down every last hay implement and internal combustion engine except for the four-wheeler, etc., etc. There wasn't enough time in the world, but I would've done it, or given it my all, if I'd known what these tasks were. I'd asked Pabbi for instructions repeatedly from September to

November and been told not to worry about it, there was time. This was false, and he was either too checked out or too ambivalent to care. But he must've cared a little. Showing me how to do things right would've entailed some version of doing them himself—the curse of the teacher—which he simply could not be bothered to do right now. On the other hand, if doing things right truly meant nothing to him, he might have just told me what to do from the comfort of his convalescence or disengagement or whatever the hell was going on, and I would proceed to fuck them up. So by that logic, he still cared a little. It's just that his perfectionism and need for control were mired, inert. Maybe I should've taken some heart in this.

Pabbi told me once that efficiency is not like talent. You don't have to be born with it, you can cultivate it, and this is useful for a farmer. Here is how you do it: You walk right up to the unpleasant task that you'd just as soon put off for another few days or months, and even though you're completely depleted and it feels as though your leg bones have been replaced with rebar, you say to your future self, *Future Self, I am doing you a favor,* and then you complete the task. In a few days or months, Future Self sees that the task is done and looks back with fond gratitude on Past Self, rather than detesting him. That is efficiency.

I said I wasn't sure that's what efficiency meant. Seemed like it had more to do with managing the time that's allotted in an organized way. He said that's wholly out of the question for a farmer, I might as well piss in the wind.

As it was, I didn't fuck things up too badly, but I was busy from late dawn to early dusk, and beyond those meager confines. I had no time to be frustrated: Winter was here, and her grip was only tightening. Fortunately Rúna was around to help. She had been left holding the proverbial bag when Stefán took his leave of this world, her farm was a mess, it made ours seem like a well-oiled machine, and so we took comfort in knowing we were in the same boat, though Icelandic boats have a fondness for sinking in unkind weather. Two farms in shambles—it should've been too much for two young people such as us, but she was hardy and uncomplaining like one of the early settlers, I could see her surviving anything this island might throw at her, which was a lot. Sometimes we alternated: a few days working our hands to battered senseless frozen roasts at my place, a few days at hers. Sometimes switching farms halfway through the day. Together we got enough of it done; farmers never get all of it done.

All of this left me little time to reflect. There wasn't much I could do about Pabbi—at least he was close by and I could keep one eye on him. He hadn't said anything further about selling the farm or the cattle, or about the fact that his wife and best friend in the world had taken her leave of him. Mamma hadn't much to report either. Amma's apartment was a comfortable, if mildly oppressive, refuge from the things that had been plaguing her, things that were still somewhat nebulous to me despite her exacting testimonial, because I was twenty and there was only so much I could understand, only so far I could see beyond my own eyelids. Mamma said she spent most days in the library, rereading materials, preparing her courses. The same library where she and Pabbi had met. This allowed her to snatch a little distance from Amma, who was now officially retired but still going to the hospital two days a week in some sort of consulting capacity, maybe they weren't quite ready to let her go, or Amma wasn't. And the library was warmer than Amma's apartment. Icelandic people like their places warm; we value heat so much that we pipe our hot water sometimes hundreds and hundreds of kilometers from a particularly benevolent crack in the earth—that's what the city of Reykjavík does with a giant pipeline alongside the road, which if it were ever breached would produce not an ecological disaster like most pipelines but just a hot, foul-smelling sulfuric pond and a bunch of chilly, irritated city dwellers. Reykjavík even bought up the bankrupt Borgarnes and Akranes water companies and their strangely beautiful monitoring facilities like tiny modernist arks. But these extreme measures don't preclude us from taking heat for granted. We don't pay for heating oil or propane; we don't chop wood all winter. The stuff of life flows into our homes, and we turn up the thermostat. This would never do for Amma, raised on Soviet austerity measures in austere Soviet cities. If her apartment were much above 13°C she would balk. Such extravagances were imprudent, reckless, positively Western.

So I spoke to Mamma of the things that mattered less but were easier to speak of, and for only a few minutes at a time.

And Mihan, with her it was odd—I could think about her every available second of the day, sometimes thinking thoughts that were positively dangerous in their ability to distract, and yet we spent less and less time on the phone. We'd found to our mutual surprise that we weren't keen long-distance conversationalists. All that fevered and feverish talking at the start, those countless hours in a kind of fugue, had run it out of our system. Maybe we liked being together so much that the phone was too pale a simulacrum. At first this was frustrating; we ended up in silence more often than not, and I worried we were cooling off already. But we weren't. It's just that calls became less important, almost a cursory check-in, the sound of each other's voices for five minutes like the long-awaited drink at the end of the day. Pour the drink, ingest, appreciate, wash the glass. There was seldom a need for reaffirmation. Everything about us was undramatic; we just put our joint self on hold until we could see each other again.

That was true, at least, until she and I had our first major disagreement. The first of many, of course. It was a frigid exchange, leaving brittle shards in its wake, like a ship carving a path through pancake ice. The conversation had begun innocently enough. I'd come back inside from a long cold afternoon in the elements, and I was hungry, tired, probably in need of a stiff warming drink. Icelanders know that in certain conditions even children require a stiff warming drink. But I'd had none when I called Mihan. I was only thinking that I wanted to hear her voice, not that a person shouldn't place a telephone call when he's in that condition. He's apt to say the wrong thing.

I'm not sure what got us off on the wrong foot, except I knew it was me, and that's what put the burr in my tone. In the very early days when Mihan and I first connected, before we met in person, we took a certain joy in divulging our flaws. The conceit was that if we knew each other's most difficult or irritating tendencies, we could move forward with our eyes open. We wouldn't be blindsided or mislead the other, as had perhaps happened more than once in past relationships. So we traded flaws, and the exercise was funny, until I realized that my flaws were vastly outnumbering hers, and hers were absurd.

"I'm moody," I'd say. "Unpredictable. Sometimes the chemicals slosh for no clear reason and you won't want to be around me."

"I can be stingy," she'd say. "And I hold grudges against people for a long time."

"Those aren't real flaws. That's like a politician saying his weakness is that he stops too often to help old ladies across the street."

So we'd play-argue about our flaws, and secretly I'd worry that Mihan didn't believe me. Did she not think the exchange was in earnest? And eventually I understood that I was being shown a window into her only major flaw: She had none. None that were serious, anyway, and that's a problem, because a person with no real flaws is used to that arrangement, a lifetime of being relatively flawless has inured them to the conviction that they can in fact never be wrong. About anything. It's the Achilles' heel of the wonderful person. They might make a small interpersonal misstep, the slightest lack of consideration, but almost never, and when they do it will still be your fault. Or their flawlessness will just sit there, silent and almost smug in its perfection, serving to remind you of your own perpetual transgressions, large and small. The latter happened more often than the former.

This rankled sometimes. It rankled on that cold, hungry, thirsty afternoon. And I shouldn't have called, I should've known better, I certainly shouldn't have chosen that moment to assess the stability of our young liaison. I was needy in that moment. I wanted reassurances about our future, and she was characteristically unwilling to provide them, knowing perhaps that I was projecting, that I was the uncertain quantity.

"I think you should move down here," I said, after the brief initial pleasantries.

"I told you, I'm not moving in with your pabbi. I like him a lot, but no. And you aren't settled anyway. Seems like every time I talk to you, you've waffled one way or another. I'd need some kind of long-term plan before I even considered uprooting myself. Aren't you going back to school?"

"I don't know. Yes. I really don't know."

"Well. You tell me when you figure it out."

"What about transferring to Reykjavík?"

"We've talked about this. I'm not just following you around. I've got my life up here. My family. I have no reason to start over in another city."

"What about me? I'm not a reason?" It was too late to retract. I tried to alter course. "You said you hated Akureyri."

"One puny Icelandic city is enough for me. I know Akureyri inside and out. It's familiar, like an old delaminated boot that's still more comfortable than a stiff new one. Why do I always compare things to old shoes?"

"Sometimes I'm not sure how we're going to make it," I said. "Or if it's worth the trouble."

"Why are you doing this right now?"

"I have doubts, that's all."

A charged pause. Ice-cold brine surging over the gunwales.

"You have doubts," she said. "Doubts about us?"

"Well, of course. Doubts about everything."

A long, bitter silence. The sound of a deep-sea drowning.

I thought I'd better pull myself out, fast. "It's cultural. In Iceland we doubt whether the sun will ever come up again, or if we'll make it through the next month alive. We plan for nothing. It's a nation founded on uncertainty."

Another long silence. I was sinking deeper. A solitary bubble or two escaping my compressed lungs as the cod surged around my pallid form.

"You're being a jerk," Mihan said.

"You never have doubts?"

"No. Not about us. Not until you pull shit like this."

"Isn't it normal to have doubts?"

"Maybe you should keep them to yourself."

"I'm really sorry," I said. "I think I'm just hungry."

"I have to go, my shift is starting in ten minutes."

38.

I was too busy for prolonged rumination. Winter, well aware that Pabbi and I had lowered our guard, took every advantage. It came down hard with its attendant trials and indignities. I'd always thought that a farm in winter was a sedate thing, a hibernating animal, socked in and silent. The Tomten treading from building to building on his nightly rounds, etc. Maybe it was that way, in some places, in some times. And things weren't so hard, this wasn't the Book of Sheep, it wasn't fishing for cod in an exposed sixareen or crossing the open heath in a blizzard to ask another farmer for the loan of one of his children to help dig your family out of its collapsed subterranean sod house. But some things change little in the modern world. The animals still had to eat and drink, and simple as that sounded to me in my ignorance, it took all I had. Bitter cold breaks everything. All your tasks are harder, and things — machines, plumbing, simple tools, human bodies — fall apart at the very worst time, it's a rule.

That December I dealt with a host of small obstacles and they felt large enough. Gates freezing to the ground, the heating element dying in the water tank, the frost-free hydrant losing its seal, and perhaps most maddening of all, the cows shitting in their water — what could possibly compel them to do that? And then they'd turn up their chapped noses, they wouldn't touch the stuff. They were never so fastidious when slurping from shitty little cesspools in the barnyard. So the tank had to be drained, cleaned, and refilled — the process took at least an hour and I did it three times that winter.

Of course the old tractor was temperamental. It balked, it coughed, its fuel gelled, it sputtered and stalled, its wheels squealed, its hydraulic hard lines rattled. I could figure out well enough how to maneuver it through the snow, but I hadn't been trained on basic winter maintenance, and I was hell on the grassy areas when plowing snow with the bucket. Sod is a priceless commodity in Iceland, almost mythical, so it hurts when you accidentally dig up enormous chunks of it.

And yet, the labor felt right. I worked hard, I came home tired, I slept. Frustrations had to be dealt with and left behind. How could I stay angry at a cow for shitting in her water, when she just wanted to scratch her fuzzy ass on the rim of the trough? How could I hold it against Kolkrabbi for its fractious ways? It was old, it had been asked to do more than we have the right to ask of most machines, and it always pulled through. This had a beneficial effect on my psyche, I could feel it. My mind was usually like a tin can with a handful of loose change in it, shaken endlessly by a child who likes the sound. Now it was quieter.

On one unkind morning, wind whipping the snow sideways with gale force, I accepted the inevitable at last. Rúna and I stood in the garage, suited up in our worst coveralls, and engaged in mortal combat with the ice-pick chains. It had become ridiculous, Rúna said, the way Kolkrabbi slid sideways every time I drove across the winter yard. It was time.

So we put our strength together, or rather I did what she told me. I couldn't fathom where she'd learned to do things like this. She didn't even own a tractor. But she was clearly the knowledgeable side of our equation, that's how it went, all her agricultural recommendations bore fruit.

"Let's let a little air out of the tires," she said. One set of chains was already half on.

"What?"

The blower from the garage furnace kept up a steady roar. She showed me what she meant: Kolkrabbi's hind end was off the ground, giving us access to both tires, and the enormous things spun freely now, if sluggishly. The only time I'd ever personally witnessed this debacle, it had occurred outside, in the snow, both tires firmly on terra firma, chains laid out on either side like caltrop runways. Rúna declared this ridiculous. She found a heavy-duty bottle jack, a jack stand, several small wooden planks. Now we were relatively warm and dry, and the tires were in the air. Clearly the way.

I watched her let some air out of one tire with an old gauge. I went to do the same with the other side, but she stopped me.

"Rotate the tire," she said. "Make sure the valve stem is at twelve o'clock."

"What difference does it make?"

"They're filled, right? For weight?"

"I have no idea."

"They are, trust me. And if you release air from the bottom of the tire, you'll let out a bunch of molasses. Up top it's fine. They're not filled all the way."

"How do you know it's molasses?"

"Can't you smell it? And haven't you ever seen a tire gash in summertime? Bees come out of the woodwork."

Together we labored like this until I had a decent idea of her method. Minimal talking, maximum exertion.

"Hand me the tongue-and-groove pliers," she'd say, and she'd squeeze like hell while I yanked on one or another of the chains' inscrutable danglers and tried to lock them in place with a slippery little pin.

"I like your pabbi's insistence on greasing the hell out of them in the spring," she said between bouts. "Rusty chains are a bitch. But damn, it makes them hard to work with. And they stink like old sheep. Lanolin, I guess."

When both tires were armored up as tight as two average-strength humans could conceivably get them, Rúna showed me the trick she had in mind. I don't know whether she thought of it herself or had seen it done. Donning a pair of safety glasses, she rolled the air compressor over and started filling each tire back up, little by little. The chains groaned under the stretch and strain. She turned her head to one side, slightly averting her eyes.

"Cover your balls," she said. "In case the chain pops."

When each side was tighter than I'd thought possible, she snugged up all the loose chain danglers with zip ties, tightened all the pins, and lowered the tractor. We gazed at the machine complacently. It was ready to battle winter.

Rúna sat down in a ratty camp chair and I nudged Rykug from the other, which was covered in short red hairs from where she'd curled herself into a bored little ball. Rykug stretched her legs and paced the garage, returning to lay her chin on my left knee and whine briefly. Her face seemed to say, *Are we working or are we resting? I'm with you so long as I know which is which.* Rúna produced her powder horn of neftóbak, Pabbi's gift, and the sight of it caused a wave of concern that rolled, broke, crashed, and was gone. I didn't feel like smoking in the garage so I took a companionable pinch and snorted it, feeling the cured bits of tobacco excoriate my sinuses.

"I think that went all the way up into my frontal lobe."

"Don't snort so hard."

My brain wandered from workaday reflections, like how tired a person's arms could get when he used them to their fullest power, to more pensive subjects. Maybe it was the tobacco.

"I know what you're going to say, but I never realized how much I love this place. And farming in general."

Rúna's look was sardonic. "What am I going to say?"

"Why did it take me so long?"

She laughed. "Why *did* it take you so long?"

I guessed the real question was why did she love farming at all, but I didn't ask. Rúna had been given every reason to loathe it, and yet somehow she didn't. She saw only possibilities.

"Tomorrow we bury the hydrant?"

Drunk Stefán never set a frost-free hydrant on their place—he just did things the old way, stumbling out on abrasive winter mornings, or whenever he remembered, to break ice in the sheep's water tanks. Fortunately this was something Rúna had thought to correct early on, and we'd dug the two-meter-deep trench and laid the water line way back in October, before the ground froze. But her hydrant had been on back order ever since at the store in Borgarnes, and had only just come in a few days ago. All that remained was to set it in the ground, make the connection, and bury it as best we could with dry crushed stone. Then her sheep would join the modern world.

"Not tomorrow, I'm teaching."

"You're what?"

"I'm teaching. Well, substitute teaching. Your mamma put me on the list at the school in Varmaland, and I mostly forgot, and then they called yesterday. The regular teacher caught the flu, and they need someone to step in and finish out the week before Christmas break. Seventh grade."

Her face was a little embarrassed, a little defiant. As though daring me to mock her.

"Well, I guess they'd better pull up their socks," I said.

"Because I'll be such a bad teacher?"

"No, are you kidding? Because you won't take one milliliter of shit."

She seemed to absorb the compliment better than she would have two months earlier, I thought. Her confidence was rising.

"How are things with Gróa?" I asked. Gróa was the ag student in Hvanneyri.

Rúna smirked, reddened. That was answer enough. "How are things with Mihan?"

"*Jæja,*" I said, and shrugged. That was too.

39.

There are so many tricks to learn. If you begin to feel guilty over the course of a conversation, trust that feeling and back off. Never end a phone call on a bad note, and never, ever go to sleep that way. All dissonant chords should resolve before the curtain falls. The difficult truth is that two people must learn to argue, they have to practice, it's not a skill the relationship is born with. But the practice itself can prove the undoing.

Lately, conversations with Mihan had been more guarded, more halting, as though we'd removed to new islands on opposite ends of the earth and there was a delay in the connection.

Akureyri might as well have been so far. I began to feel that the strange, rapid unraveling I'd experienced with Sóldís was not an outlier but rather a harsh truth about long-distance relationships. The connection simply sublimated like so much vapor. And with Sóldís, there'd been a more solid foundation in the realm of the real.

The ties between Mihan and me hadn't evaporated yet, or at least I knew my end hadn't, but they were certainly fraying. Thorny subjects had already become old, well-worn. There were buttons we could push, and we pushed them sometimes, whether we meant to or not.

I was sitting in my bedroom, avoiding Pabbi, while I waited for a blizzard to blow itself out. It had been blowing itself out for two days. The cows were fed, though, the water was still water, all the rudimentary things that needed to function were functioning. You could hardly ask for more on an Icelandic farm in a storm. And yet, winter and darkness were grinding me down to the blunt, essential things within me — my unsubtle parts — leaving little room for grander concerns, or warmth. This provided a window of empathy into Pabbi's descent. The kind of window you want to close just as soon as you open it.

I thought now would be an ideal time to call Mihan, and then I hesitated. The hesitation chilled me more than the wind that slipped in through the loose old window sashes. But the truth in that moment was that I didn't want to hear her voice more than I wanted to keep to myself. What could I say that was worth saying? Even worse, what could she say that I hadn't heard? I wondered if this was the Pabbi in me. Or maybe it was just the telephone, it does evil things to people.

I called. Mihan was getting ready for a shift, intermittently talking to Birgitta at the same time.

"Tell her I said hi," I muttered for no reason, since I did not particularly like Birgitta. She was a good roommate, that was about all that mattered to me.

I heard the door close on the line, and Mihan said, "Ah, she's gone. Now I can really talk."

Soon I found myself listing farm anxieties — complaints, really — an impulse I'd been falling prey to lately, and which I loathed. Wasn't complaint part of the farmer's mandate, I thought? Written into his constitution? But that didn't make it any better for the person listening, even if the only person listening was the complainer.

Mihan countered with sympathy, and then with suggestions for remedy. This was a button she could push. If I was so worried about the fact that none of the cows were pregnant, she said, why didn't I go out tomorrow and buy an Icelandic bull? They were everywhere, and very mellow. Through gritted teeth I explained about purebred stock, and the long-term effects of giving up on breed standards after so many years of building a herd, and I hated the eugenics-reeking taint of all those words, and wondered if I sounded like a racist to Mihan, who had a very understandable allergy to them, and I felt bad for hating them in front of Rykug, who owed her existence to the same demented human impulses.

So I'd become defensive against my will. That was definitely Pabbi in my veins. Mihan had had a viable idea — a smart idea, because who was buying pure Galloway stock in Iceland anyway, so what did it matter? — and I wasn't opposed to it. The problem was that I'd started taking it personally that she wasn't here. I'd convinced myself that she only had a right to make farm suggestions if she was here, seeing every angle and consequence. Here, on the ground. I knew it wasn't right to ask such a thing, and I almost never did, but I wanted it nonetheless, and the more I wanted it, the more I expected it, and the more I expected it, the worse I felt.

Mihan was right: There were a hundred reasons why it wasn't practical or reasonable for her to drop everything and move to Borgarfjörður. The pieces were not in place. I'd given nothing of more consequence than my affection. And for her to make such a commitment, such a sacrifice, I'd need to be willing to do the same. Icelanders are very big on sacrifice.

I tried to change the subject and failed.

"What are we doing," I said, not a question.

"This again," Mihan said.

"I haven't seen you in almost two months."

"Look," and I felt the whip of irritation in her voice. "I don't want to do this long-distance bullshit any more than you do. My dad was over here alone for two years before we moved from Manila, and something dried out inside him. They used to talk on the phone, he and Mamma, and then they just stopped. By the time we arrived, they were like two strangers living in the same house. They still are."

"Jesus, I didn't know that."

"No, you didn't."

"I'm sorry, Mihan. I want us to make it. We *should* make it! How often does something like this—like us—come around?"

"Rarely," she said. "But this isn't working for me."

We sat in silence for a full three minutes while the windowpanes shook and the line clicked in sync with some unknowable radio wave.

Eventually she sighed. "You need to figure out what you want. Let me know when you do. I love you."

"I love you," I said, the words echoing like a hollow refrain in my mouth, but she was already gone.

40.

I was clearing up the dishes after a mediocre dinner of fried cabbage and sheet-pan potatoes. I'd done my best lately to prepare food that Pabbi would eat. If I didn't he might just slink into the kitchen for a few crackers and a smear of old hummus, encrusted like winter soil, that should've been thrown out long ago. But the end result was not inspiring—the only thing that would've made it more like the miserable fare of Icelandic settlers was some salted, fermented cod or bird or whale meat, pulled stinking from a dank hole in the ground. My skills just weren't developed in that way.

Pabbi choked it down nonetheless. He sat there in his chair, holding his ribs and wincing periodically, gazing blearily at nothing, and topping off his nondescript little glass from a bottle of brennivín. I didn't know where he'd got it; I didn't think he'd driven himself anywhere in days, weeks. But he'd been drinking more lately, before dinner and after, and he didn't fall asleep at the table like he used to. A person doesn't drift serenely down like that unless they've been hard at work.

"Join me for a glass," he said, less a command than a timid request.

I finished wiping off the counter, toweled my hands, and sat down across from him. The brennivín was fairly awful. The mosses and whatever else were fine, but I never could love that caraway. I drank it anyway.

"The cows all right?" he said.

I felt a tinge of irritation, suppressed it.

"They're fine. I fed out three bales today."

"Well. They're in good hands."

We stared past each other for a minute or two. Wind rattled the metal roofs on the nearest outbuildings—most of the snow had blown off, leaving the corrugated sheets free to pry themselves loose from rotting joists—and the house windows shivered in their panes, wafting the curtains inside. The room felt quieter and darker than I'd ever known it.

"I'm wondering," he said, and he looked intently at his glass, "I'm wondering if you'd read some of my poetry."

"Your what?"

"My poetry." He set his jaw against ridicule, but with his bathrobe, his state of dissolution, he clearly knew the odds were against him.

I held back, gauged my response. "I...I didn't know you were writing. Since when?"

"Oh, a month or two."

"And how's it going?"

"Pretty rocky at first, but finding my voice now, maybe. I could really use another set of eyes on it, if you wouldn't mind."

"I'd be glad to."

So that was his secret. That's what he'd been doing those long hours in the shop, in the bedroom. Not planning his own death. I felt profound relief, and also bafflement. He couldn't have surprised me more if he'd confessed that he was moving to Bolivia. How could a man this allergic to vulnerability engage with such a flaying art form? Not only this, but Pabbi had always held a cynical opinion of the hallowed place that poetry holds in Iceland's image of itself, as though poetry were a beacon in the storm, the one pure thing that could ever be pulled from the darkness, a millennium of darkness. Capable of redeeming a soul, or a nation. He found it comical.

"So are you joining Ingi's Poetry Club? Is that the kind of stuff you're writing? *Ferskeytlur?*"

Ferskeytlur are an ancient Icelandic form, quatrains with alternating rhymes. And very often, as it happens, a *ferskeytla* is funny. There are many about the miseries of farm life. Jónas Hallgrímsson had one I particularly liked, but could never remember. That wasn't my skill. A certain sort of Icelandic man, on the other hand, could recite ferskeytlur beyond count. Ingi himself knew hundreds.

"No, not like that," Pabbi said. "No traditional forms. I guess you'd call it free verse? Prose poems? I'm not sure. Mostly meditations on farming."

"Sure. I'd be glad to look at them. Maybe tomorrow?"

He nodded absently. I examined his face. A touch of disappointment, or hope — too hard to tell.

I knew from my brief tenure at university that you should beware when someone wants to show you their poetry, especially if it's unconstrained by form. And I wasn't at all sure I wanted to hear my father's impressions of farm life. It might be like reading news of your own death. I also thought, *I do not know him at all.* He seemed to sense the prickly spines of the issue.

"I never thought I'd farm again," he said. "I certainly didn't plan to. But it's so different here from how it is, or how it was, on Vestmannaeyjar. Different enough, I thought."

I held my breath and waited for him to continue. He didn't.

"Different how?" I said. "Harsher?"

"Oh, in some ways. In some ways not. Hard to describe the place. You've never been?"

I tilted my head and squinted my eyes, a quiet sign of impatient incomprehension I'd learned from the dog.

"Ah. I suppose not. Well, I'm sure I've told you all the old stories."

My head was still tilted.

"Well," he said again.

And then he told me.

41.

"Vestmannaeyjar is a strange place. Unlike any other place. It looks as though god snorted a clump of heavenly neftóbak and then sneezed the particles out into the ocean.

"You know the legend? No? Ingólfur Arnarson's brother, Hjörleifur, was killed by his own Celtic slaves, the 'Westmen' as they called them, who then fled to the islands. This was around about the year 900. Not that it did the Celts much good. They were all hunted down and killed. So, Vestmannaeyjar. An inauspicious way to name a place, if you ask me.

"We lived on Heimaey, the only island where anyone lives. There are about ten or twelve others, more if you count the really puny ones and skerries and Smáeyjar. Heimaey is by far the biggest, about thirteen square kilometers. But still very much an island, you know? That island feeling you can't find just anywhere. Icelanders like to talk about Iceland being an island. To us, on Vestmannaeyjar, it's the mainland. What is an island, after all? Is Australia an island? Granted it is somewhat bigger than Iceland. Yes, I know that's obvious.

"Anyway. The islands rise sheer from the sea, great gray-black cliffs striated and pockmarked, full of little caves, teeming with birds, stained with shit; sometimes the sky is so thick with puffins and fulmars and guillemots and gannets and kittiwakes that from a distance they look like a cloud of hatching flies. The sea assaults each rock face relentlessly. And the waves never break until they crash, the water's too deep there, so the water jets up vertically when it hits, you can scarcely imagine how high. One hundred seventy meters wouldn't be at all unusual. On the smaller islands especially it's like being in the middle of a ring of geysers, or the bleary eye of a hurricane. Birds must know which cliffs are the least battered, I can't imagine how. Birds know all kinds of things, or they don't care and they just hang on tight. They're made of tougher stuff than we are.

"If the cliffs are the forbidding face of each island, then the livable parts are the hair—that's how I always thought of it. Short-cropped green hair. Thicker in some places than in others, but always hummocky, often punched up with puffin nests, or crisscrossed with sheep trails. And mixed in with bald spots—bare or nominally mossy rock, jet-black or sometimes almost a vibrant red. Places where nothing can take hold, or where it's too much bother to try. Not unlike here, come to think of it. But out in Vestmannaeyjar, the Gulf Stream keeps things a touch warmer than the mainland. There's very little snow; it's positively civilized in winter. Rain, of course, more rain than a person should be asked to endure, and wind like you have never seen—no, literally, you have never seen it, the southern headland of Heimaey is the windiest spot in the world, I can see you don't believe me, I'll show you the records later. Anyway, what I mean to say is that each island is like a compressed Borgarfjörður. Each has its own unique valleys and mountain ranges, but in miniature. In certain places the ground is pinched and tented in the center, climbing to the rim of its crater, its progenitor; elsewhere it slopes up and up and then disappears. Just a perilous drop-off into the void.

"There aren't many beaches to speak of, nor simple ways to land on most of the islands. Often a person has to stay in the boat, pitting life and livelihood against the perpetually disordered sea, sailing within range of the rocks only long enough for his mates to jump out, grab hold of the ropes, and begin their horrific ascent. But then there's Heimaey, good old Heimaey, almost a paragon of comfort, because it has a protected harbor. You've probably heard that Vestmannaeyjar has the best harbor in all of southern Iceland—some say the only harbor, really—and that's why its fishery is so important. That and the huge numbers of cod, haddock, capelin. I'm not boasting about it. I have no reason to boast.

"But it's a hard life, son. It was hard for me, certainly. A kind of communal solidarity grows up in a place like that; it has to if the people are going to endure continuous hardship, which they do. I mean, the abject poverty that existed on Vestmannaeyjar, pretty much until the invention of the motorboat—it was unrivaled. Well, maybe other parts of Iceland were just as bad. But we didn't even have reliable drinking water until they laid the pipeline to the mainland in '68. It comes all the way from Eyjafjallajökull himself. So the folks have always banded together to make their lives more bearable. There's the big festival in August, the long Christmas celebration, the abseiling contests, catching the puffins that are deranged and disoriented by artificial lights and releasing them into the ocean, plenty of things like that. But not my family. We engaged with almost none of it.

"You never met my father. To call him stern would be an understatement. He was devout, self-sacrificing, mostly humorless. He held himself to a higher standard. I honestly think it drove my mother to an early death. She had no other particular reason to die when she did. I was then ten or eleven years old. I don't think she hated him; I think she was exhausted by him. And she had six children, god help her.

"We farmed there, you know that. Icelanders will farm anything. So unlike most of the people on Vestmannaeyjar, who either worked in the fishery or in some other capacity to support the fishermen and their families, we didn't live in town. The only town on Heimaey, of course: Vestmannaeyjabær. This meant we kept ourselves apart, or we were kept apart. Not just geographically but socially. We went to church once a week, that was about it. I suspect my father had a certain chip on his shoulder about not being a fisherman, because every man on the island is a fisherman dating back a thousand years. It's the heart of the male identity. He knew how to fish, of course, but he was busy with other things and I think it's possible that he disliked the ocean. Maybe I pity him now. Maybe I understand him a bit better. Who wouldn't fear the sea, out there?

"We lived and farmed on Kirkjubær. Along with Vilborgarstaðir, it was one of the largest farms on the island. They date back to the sixteenth century. We didn't own it, naturally. My father was a hired hand, given a ramshackle old house to live in and paid to keep the operation running. His children, his wife, we were his unpaid serfs. There's an old line farmers always say about having as many kids as you can and then making them your farmhands as soon as they're old enough to hold a shovel. Maybe I should've done that. But then, I don't really like children.

"The real owner of the place didn't live there. He was a rich guy from the mainland with a fancy summerhouse on Heimaey, right in town. He came out to gaze at his holdings and shake my father's hand two or three times a year. I believe those moments of being patronized wounded his heart. I think they withered his soul more than farming an implacable land ever could. I have a theory that farming any land but your own will kill you. Absolutely, farming your own place can kill you just as easily, it often does, but bleeding yourself dry on someone else's ground will do it without fail. Every time.

"I don't know if he liked his work. I don't know if he liked anything. But there were things about it I enjoyed. It was a sheep operation, of course. We had a few horses, a handful of cows, but it's taxing to support the frame and needs of cattle on a tiny island. So we pastured the sheep, we made a little hay, we produced milk and cheese, we grew potatoes, cabbages, beets. Most of our hay we had ferried in from the mainland. Eyjafjöll and thereabouts. The owner paid, of course. That's how most of the farmers in Vestmannaeyjar do it; there's simply not enough room or flat ground for hay.

"When I was about thirteen years old, my father sent me out to Elliðaey for the whole summer. Elliðaey is the third biggest island, I think, almost half a square kilometer. There are sheep pastured on all the islands, or almost all of them. Anywhere an Icelander can put sheep, he will put them. There are probably sheep stumbling around on top of Eiríksjökull right now. Most of the time in Vestmannaey-jar, on the small islands, they're unattended. They get dropped off to crop the grass, live their unknowably dim sheep lives, and then one day they're hauled away, often in nets, for shearing or slaughter. But Elliðaey, along with our closest neighbor Bjarnarey, has the best grazing of the little islands, so naturally it has the most sheep, or at least it did. My father, or maybe his boss, decided it was worth the seasonal loss of one of his underage hands in order to keep an eye on the livestock, or maybe the house felt too crowded, or maybe I asked too many impudent questions. I was the oldest and rankled under his authority from the day I was born. I was a bit terrified, but I still rel-ished the prospect. I'd never had a moment to myself. So I was hauled out there in a tiny pitching boat, and my father and I were dumped ashore with a meager pile of supplies. He helped me up the rope walk—nobody said don't look down but I believe I knew not to—and once at the top, we hoisted the cooking stores into the air with a kind of primitive gallows or yardarm that hung out beyond the realm of humanity. He stayed long enough to show me the location of the dis-reputable little shack that was to be my summer home—they've since built a beautiful new lodge up there, I hear—told me to count the sheep every day and study my Bible, and then disappeared over the side like a sinking cloud.

"I had a moment of panic when he left, maybe a few days of panic, but it quickly subsided. With no one to care for but myself and, to an absurdly small degree, the sheep, I unfolded. My mind spread out and exhaled like an old mattress that's been rolled tight for a decade or so.

I promise you I didn't spend any time with that Bible, unless it were to wipe my ass with. The days were filled with nothing, and yet they sped by. I scarcely wanted to sleep unless I should miss one moment. I knew how unlikely it was that a chance like that would come again. It didn't.

"My duties were few. After a couple of discarded mishaps, I learned to cook well enough to live. A little flour, a little salt, a can of grease, some smoked puffin. They weren't feasts, scarcely fit for polite company, but a person can get by like a settler if he has to. At dawn I began my wandering. Count the sheep. Walk the periphery. Avoid the puffin holes. Climb as far as I dared up the steep slope that rose above my little hut—it rose and rose into the atmosphere and then just ended without resolution, an unfulfilled melody, a truncated mountain, sheared off by some impatient god. I'd stare north, an unimpeded view of the mainland, no other islands of Vestmannaeyjar in the way, and try to make things out. On clear days, rare to be sure, I could easily see Eyjafjöll and Katla, her capricious majesties. I liked to imagine beholding that coast for the first time from the deck of a longship. Would I feel hope or despair? Would I prefer to jump into the sea? Then I'd turn around and stare south, across the length of the little island, toward what? Western Sahara, maybe. Mauritania and Senegal. Places I could only dream of. Places where a person could wear short sleeves.

"Over time my fear of the cliffs diminished. My fear for the sheep's safety did not. I was amazed that the dim little things, waddling under their burden of wool, didn't slip and plunge to their wet deaths on a regular basis. They weren't mountain goats, after all, even if they were Icelandic. But they didn't. All that summer I failed to lose a single one, even during a particularly fuggy spell when the clouds descended as though depressed and would not lift. I was too frightened to wander more than twenty meters from the shack—the visibility was so poor I even considered tying a rope to the hut so I could find my way back—and I didn't dare venture closer than absolutely necessary to the invisible gulf. I was sure I'd be missing at least a handful of ovine souls when the soup cleared, and yet, they knew better. They must've huddled like I did, except they had each other and I only huddled with my knees. At times like these the noise of the sea became overwhelming, a constant barrage on the senses, terrible even for a boy raised on Heimaey. I think because I could no longer see it, no longer define its boundaries, its tiny limitations, I began to feel oppressed. Like it was all around me, which it was, but also upon me.

"For almost an entire week in August, my idyll was interrupted, invaded, by a group of bird and egg hunters. They came every year, I'd been warned, but I hadn't been told when. They had some sort of communal ownership of the island. When they showed up, six loud men clambering up the cliffs and over the edge like pale ungainly spiders, I was appalled, I experienced a compulsion to run for the shack and hide, I even considered the outhouse. But a person can't hide on Elliðaey. Not unless he transforms into a kittiwake and takes to the cliff walls. And I was no kittiwake. So I choked down my shyness, my natural disinclination to be with other men, and I tried to play the host. I welcomed the strangers to their own island, which I already thought of as mine, of course. I helped them haul up their gear, I worked the gallows when they descended the cliffs to hunt, I even cooked them breakfast a few times when they were too hungover. In the evenings I sat with them as they drank and told bawdy stories, always as far from their tents and lamps as I could reasonably get, edging into the darkness, wishing myself away, or rather, wishing them away. I can't tell you how relieved I was when they finally left.

"Anyway, it was a brief respite, just that. I've tried to convince your mamma that it wasn't some sort of punishment, like solitary confinement on an island prison, even if it may have been intended that way, but I don't think she believes me. I only wish that I'd kept a journal, or taken some photographs, something to hold on to that I could show you. I had nothing like that. But I kept it in here. In my head. I think that was the first time I knew I was a real person, alone, with my own thoughts and dreams. Not just some genetic variant hanging around the house, getting in the way, like an ill-regarded parasite.

"It was only a few years later that we left. You know all about it, I suppose? I think they taught you the basic facts when you were in grade school. I remember you asked me about it at the time. You didn't realize that my Vestmannaeyjar was *the* Vestmannaeyjar. You thought these things happened in some far-off place. Kids are like that — they can't fathom that history is being made all around them. Or maybe it's how we teach them.

"I was in my bed, of course. All of Heimaey was in bed, I guess — it was about 1:30 a.m., after all. January 23, 1973. My brothers and me in one bed, my sisters in another. Even the fishing fleet was asleep, about eighty boats held in port the previous day by a nasty storm. What woke us was the house shaking. Pabbi kept a couple of fancy ornamental plates on the wall, the kind with ugly paintings of ships — I think they belonged to my mother's mother — and they crashed to the floor. Then the din started. I can only describe the noise as unearthly, but that's a ridiculous word for it, nothing could be more earthly. Like thunder, I suppose, but with simultaneous lightning, because I could hear the cracking of the electricity, and rocks rolling, falling. I don't know. My memory isn't the clearest. Mostly I was just too shocked to take much of it in. I recall that the house was filled with light, much too bright for a midwinter dawn even if we'd all somehow slept very late indeed, and entirely the wrong kind of light. Orange light. I really did think we'd been bombed at first — you can live your whole life on the Mid-Atlantic Ridge, straddling two tectonic plates, and still not believe it when a volcano blows up in your face.

"My father didn't have to tell us to get up and get out. We gathered together on our front step and looked toward the abomination. There was Helgafell as usual, stately, monolithic, and yet no longer alone. Just to her left the island had cracked open. Bright lava crept insidiously from a hole in the earth, and a vast plume of smoke and ash was lifting toward heaven. Lightning slashed across it. Nothing had fallen from the sky quite yet.

"Pabbi didn't hesitate. He barked instructions. The eldest children were to help him gather the animals, get halters on the big ones, and drive them right through town, down to the harbor. We would save as many as we could.

"'Stay together,' he said.

"It was easier said than done. If the cows were spooked, the horses were fucking terrified. One of them broke free of her stall and nearly trampled me in her panic. She ran from the barn and off into the orange flickering night. To this day I don't know whether she caught up with others of her kind being driven down the mountain and was evacuated, or if she ran straight off the edge of Heimaey in a last desperate flight to escape the cataclysm. I don't blame her. She was a good horse, I'll say that. I don't like many horses.

"So the group of us made our clumsy way into Vestmannaeyjabær and through the streets, driving the sheep ahead of us, leading the few frightened cows and horses, trying to keep our younger siblings from being kicked or trodden over. And we joined with the throng at that point: a great number of animals, and an even greater number of islanders. Heimaey had a population of over five thousand people in those days. Every one of them headed to the harbor.

"The situation took a drastic turn for the worse as we walked, for the laws of gravity are immutable, pitiless. The suppurating crack had begun to cough and belch, and the hellish plume above it was spreading. Lava bombs fell like mortars. Behind us we could hear windows shattering, roofs caving in. And then the tephra started to rain down. You know the word? It means anything airborne from a volcanic eruption. In this case, mostly hot ash, pumice, the like. It wasn't exactly landing on us yet, or I don't think it was, but I remember looking at the wide back of the cow nearest me and observing that big flakes of what I took to be dirty snow were piling up inexorably on her mottled hide.

"We sped up, but we never ran. I don't really understand it. In my memory the whole scene takes on a gauzy, dreamlike quality, and yet, it really was slow. Or deliberate, I should say. People still talk about the calmness of the evacuation, that it's evidence of some kind of magical trait inherent to Icelandic people, or a key element in the Icelandic character. Conventional wisdom is that we are accustomed to ecological disruption, if not always eruption, and so take it with a certain idiosyncratic complacency. But does this make sense? Most Icelanders haven't experienced more than one disaster. Could it be generational trauma? Genetic memory? Or utter bullshit, and ours is just a culture that valorizes repressed emotion? On Heimaey we certainly placed great value on fearlessness, hardiness. We showed this by fishing the merciless sea, abseiling for birds and eggs, or perching on a cliff's edge to hold a rope, attached to which is another human being, dangling above his certain death, or waving a long net far out over the abyss, trying to catch a scared little bird.

"The scene at the docks should've been chaos, but it wasn't. The townsfolk were being shepherded onto fishing boats. A number of people, mostly the men, were forced into the holds in order to make room—I shudder still to think of their voyage across. The farmers, all of whom knew one another, of course, gathered together in a different area with their animals. I recall no fighting amongst the horses. There were only about thirty of them. Somehow they were given berth on the overcrowded ships. People will always prioritize horses. But the sheep, someone decided, could not be accommodated. There were simply too many, about six hundred fifty in all. They were vital, however. They were our livelihood. Around this time someone from Mayor Magnus Magnusson's office came to tell us that the sheep were actually going to be airlifted to the mainland, every single one, and that the farmers would have to drive them back up through town and to the other side of the island, where we had our rudimentary runway. My father volunteered for this task, as did a few other men. He proclaimed our fates as well. He put my sister in charge of our other brothers and sisters, told her to get on a fishing boat and wait for him on the mainland, wherever we were being housed. He didn't appear to possess any trepidation on this score. He certainly showed no affection or fatherly concern. My task was to be more complicated. The cows could not go, he said. It had been decided by the few farmers with a stake in this question. The animals were too heavy; they weren't valuable enough. Pabbi didn't say the words 'They have to die.'

"'It's a pity,' he said.

"But he wasn't through with his edict. No, my lot was about to get worse. I, he said, would be the one to 'put them out of their misery.' I have always disliked that expression. It sounds condescending, because it's seldom used by the dying themselves, though I suppose some things are more miserable than death, yes, surely some things are.

"'Why me?' I said. I think they were my first words spoken since I'd gone to bed the previous day, that stormy January day that spoke of nothing more awful than bad weather.

"'Because I volunteered you,' my father said.

"If there was any sympathy in his eyes, I couldn't see it, just the reflected glow of the volcano. No one wished to see cows running wild-eyed from one end of the island to the other, their backs on fire. If I couldn't absorb that hard truth now, I never would.

"So, in a warehouse on the shores of our protected harbor, at about 3:30 a.m., I was handed a captive bolt gun and told to get the job done. There were about forty Icelandic cattle on the island, a number that had remained basically unchanged since people started keeping records around 1880. There were about forty cattle before me now. Frightened but trusting, it's a look that cows specialize in. Domestication hasn't cured them of their innate fear, the perpetual fear of a herd animal, but it has made them acutely aware that they're in our hands, so they turn to us to cure them of whatever they think is at their heels. It's that look that drives the knacker to drink. Because we are not their friends.

"Fortunately an older farmhand saw my situation and offered his hand with a knife. The bolt gun only stuns a cow, as you know; it still has to be dispatched. He followed behind me as I went from victim to victim, holding my body very still, holding my breath, holding my mind, and I tried not to look into their eyes as I placed the pistol against each fuzzy forehead, but cows are always looking at you, they never stop looking at you unless they're truly at peace, chewing cud, dozing in a shaft of sunlight, and they turned away only as they fell, their eyes clouding instantly. Their bodies slumped to the ground, legs juddering. Cows are born with voices, loud voices, ready to bawl as soon as the fluid is licked from their faces, but not one of these uttered a sound. Behind me I tried not to hear the slashing of their throats, a sound like cutting through leather, because that's what leather is. It was a good thing I was in my rubber muck boots. Blood ran deep in the place. The stench of copper and fear was choking; it mingled with the ash I'd begun to taste, like porridge burnt to the bottom of a pot. I could feel my nose hairs curling against the smoke, the vapor.

"It's dim after that. At around twenty-five cattle, I was stumbling over the bodies. Someone else was trying to haul them off with chains, I don't know where, but they couldn't keep up. By the time I got to the last cow I was barely present. I existed only to stand and kill. I'd forgotten why I was there, or what was happening around us. I remember being ushered to the gangway of a fishing boat that was about to shove off, and a man scrutinizing the gore on my boots. He held a hand to my chest, halting me, then sprayed my lower half not unkindly with a hose, and shoved me aboard. I turned to the ongoing explosion as we made our careful way through the harbor and out to sea. Instinctively I searched for our farm, for Kirkjubær and its vibrant green fields. It was gone. It lay under a roiling, sludgy mass of magma and semi-liquid black rock. I turned away.

"The diesel engine coughed a little louder as we increased speed, passing Bjarnarey on our right and then Elliðaey, the only place in my life I'd ever had any affection for. I never saw it again. I was seventeen.

"*Jæja*. Not much to tell about life on the mainland, after all that.

"Many Vestmannaeyjar men returned in the ensuing days to volunteer, either for salvage or volcano fighting. My father didn't. He said he had to stay for a while and make sure we were safe, see us into temporary homes at the very least. Maybe he was afraid, I don't know. Maybe he felt, with the farm and the animals gone, that he had nothing left to care about on the island. I would never have called him an altruistic man. But other people came and went—we heard the stories. Things were getting worse. Prevailing winds had kept the town from instant destruction long enough for everyone to get out, but now the tephra was falling thickly over everything, crushing roofs under its accumulating weight, lighting others on fire. In February the cone of the new mountain, which they named Kirkjufell or Thorbjörn—now they call it Eldfell, no one is satisfied—it collapsed and sent a thirty-meter-high slag beast creeping into town. They called it 'Tramp.' Noxious vapors spread through the island and collected in shallow areas. That was the cause of the only human casualty we know of, a fisherman who wandered into a basement and choked on the bad air. The evacuation itself had seen no loss of life, no accidental loss I should say, other than a horse who ran demented into a river of fire.

"At a certain point it looked as though the harbor would be sealed off by encroaching magma. The island was reshaping itself. That would've spelled the end of Heimaey—without boats we were nothing. But legions of brave souls had had decent luck holding off the slow flow with jets of seawater, bigger and better pumps were sent from the US, and they used this method to save the port. The entry was left a little narrower then before—in fact the entire island grew by about two and a half square kilometers—and this proved to be an unforeseen stroke of luck, as the harbor is even more protected now.

"They declared the eruption officially over on July 3, a little over five months after it started. In the end, about a third of the town was ruined or buried. Some people went back. They were determined to dig out, to restart their lives. There seemed to be a kind of machismo in it, a native pride. Many did not. We did not.

"A few of the Heimaey farmers earned enough from livestock auctions to at least put one foot in front of the other. Not us. Pabbi had always regarded animals as little more than animate property, I think, but they weren't his property. When you don't own the land, you have nothing.

"So we shuffled from the de facto refugee camp in a school gymnasium to a kind person's house for a while. Pabbi did not approve of that family at all or their potential influence on his children—he seemed to think they were sinners or libertines. Eventually he found a job as a straight-truck driver, a local route delivery driver, and with that, a small flat for us in a nondescript white-painted cinder-block building on the outskirts of Reykjavík.

"My sisters and brothers went to school. They seemed shocked, deeply unhappy. I never finished school. I worked a few menial service jobs until I turned eighteen, and then I got my commercial license and joined Pabbi, who by this time had graduated to ground shipping across Iceland. It wasn't like father and son in business together, nothing like that. We each drove the basic highway system in our rented long-haulers, I did some local routes too, and we seldom saw each other at home. It wasn't a home. He was, if possible, more reserved and harsh than he'd been before. But I think he might've taken some grim satisfaction in having it confirmed that the world was every bit as bad as he'd supposed. He wasn't a parent, he was never made to be a parent. My two youngest brothers, they struggled. They went into state care. Iceland has been doing that for ages: take the kids you can't support and put them with other people, separate them forever, except in the old days it was the parish, not the state. I was sure it was my fault, my responsibility, even though I was working hard to keep us fed. I don't . . . I don't want to talk about that.

"What else is there to say? My pabbi died within two years. They said it was heart failure. He was in a motel room somewhere in the east when it happened, maybe Egilsstaðir. In his bed. At least it didn't happen while he was driving, he might've killed someone. I never saw the body. He was cremated and I misplaced the ashes when moving out of that horrible apartment.

"I think about Vestmannaeyjar sometimes. Certain times of year, I think about it. But you can understand, I hope, why I don't want to go back. Why I can't. I don't even want to drive along the coast in that direction. I might see Elliðaey, and that would be fine, I wouldn't mind that at all, but you can't see one island without seeing the others, and there would be Heimaey, with its new shape, its new mountain. People always talk about the incredible rebuilding efforts, how the town preserved its original character, or how it's even better now. But the town wasn't my home. My home couldn't be rebuilt when it was wholly eclipsed by a barren rocky wasteland, a farm of moss and sandwort, the foothills of a new mountain, where tourists come to gawk and read dramatic signage, already faded now, about the great devastation. If your home is annihilated and replaced with something else, even if it wasn't the happiest place to begin with, there's no reason to ogle its grave."

42.

There is a human tendency, when it's a cold night and the sun is bestowing itself on some other part of the earth, some place we can scarcely imagine, to hole up. *We should be in a burrow,* the body says. *We should be sleeping.*

Those of us who find the latter difficult may benefit from our biological maladaptation. I mean, it destroys us, slowly or quickly, but it also pushes us, drags us, under the stars.

It was 3 a.m. I sat in a ratty old camp chair that I'd found in the barn, its seat and back half covered in bird shit and its plastic legs sloughing off some kind of toxic white powder coating. I wore my insulated overalls and two down jackets, one over the other. To my left, the Twingo, smelling of rust. To my right, Pabbi's truck, reliably smelling like a petrol leak, it would leak forever. Under my boots, an unkind medley of ice and gravel, and upon my boots, a dog who had no trouble sleeping and would rather do it inside but was always eager to see whatever caught my attention, provided it wasn't something on the television, which she wouldn't acknowledge under any circumstances, or in the sky, which was beyond her ken, the birds could have it.

I was looking at the sky. A remarkably clear night. We Icelanders will never cease remarking on clear weather. If you're going to
make it through the winter here, you might as well embrace the dark,
but you can still be pleased, or relieved, when the sky is full of stars
instead of clouds. Tonight, a staggering array — the kind that literally
makes people stagger because they crane their necks back too far, but
I was in a chair so it was safe. A few satellites passed in a red stutter,
forgettable. No moon to speak of, no moon necessary. The stars lit the
world, and the snow flung it back. Crystalline focus and ample illumi-
nation, all shades of gray with no glare or haze — human eyes aren't
well adapted to it, but we get along. I could see everything I wanted
to: the glitter reflected in Rykug's eyes as she watched a cow lumber
up, lick the forelock of another cow for a minute or two, and then
fold back to the earth with a sigh; the humped bulk of the Skarðsheiði
range far off to my right, Baula's stark knifey silhouette to my left,
and above us, with red or yellow orbs in amongst their burning white
hydrogen benefactors, our smear of a galaxy. White at the edges, with
a thick black line running down the center of it, blacker than the sky
itself, like an abyss or a road. We call it Vetrarbrautin, the Winter Way.
I mused those old musings we never tire of, about how destabilizing it
is to see your galactic home up there, as though from a great distance,
and yet reconcile yourself to the fact that you're well inside it. We are
just animals, we can never reconcile it, and this makes us feel small.
It's good to feel small sometimes.

I thought of Pabbi in the dark house. Asleep, probably, I hoped.
Healing through hibernation. He could sleep the entire winter away
and be the better for it. Wake up to the call of the lóa, a line of verse
ready to be written down. In the meantime I would keep things
running.

I thought of Mihan, with whom I hadn't spoken in nearly a
week. I thought of all the clichéd things I'd like to tell her right now,
things that I meant, because twenty-year-olds can mean things very
emphatically. If she were here, I thought, seeing these same stars and

silhouettes, with Rykug making sure to have at least one body part on each of us, then the moment would be whole. Then the night could go on and on while the rest of the world slept. At least until it was grazing season again.

From the pocket of my innermost coat, I extracted the phone. It was still awake, though the cold outside would murder its battery in a matter of minutes.

"I need you," I wrote. "That's all."

Mihan would be asleep, her phone off. I expected no reply, then or maybe ever. I trained my eyes upward, at the things that are too large for us, and was attempting to rebury the phone inside my many layers when it buzzed, startling Rykug. I fumbled at it with numb fingers.

"I'm right here," she said.

43.

Every so often, or very rarely, something occurs in your life that you know you'll hold on to. It'll live like a tiny ember in your chest, you'll return to it when you're in pain, when the wind has blown away everything else good that was inside you, leaving you scoured. Your mind will curl fetally around it in the middle of winter, the middle of the night. And eventually, if you're lucky enough to make it out the other side, you can use it to rekindle yourself.

For me this was dancing with Mihan, a King Floyd album on repeat, in the kitchen, in our underwear. I believed right then that my life would never get any better, and I was probably right. It didn't matter that the speaker was a tinny little thing covered in toast crumbs, or that I am no dancer. King Floyd will make you a dancer. Mihan held it as a point of pride, well deserved, that she had full albums by the best semi-forgotten American soul legends, rather than just the few hits they were known for — King Floyd was her favorite, along with James Carr, O. V. Wright, Clarence Carter, and the great Eddie Floyd, massively overshadowed, she said, by his former bandmate Wilson Pickett, who was also great but, you know, he wasn't Eddie.

Birgitta had absented herself again, of course. So we danced with abandon, and at one point I knocked over the coffeepot, which shattered into about forty pieces, and this would otherwise have been serious, very serious indeed for an Icelander, but we didn't care. Rykug was interested, a little riled by all the wild activity. I tried a couple of times to dance with her, holding her paws, but she just bit my hands, a dog's way of dancing is irreconcilable with that of a person.

I'd been in Akureyri about a week. On the drive up, I'd failed to so much as turn some music on, electing instead to spend several silent, sweaty hours wondering if Mihan and I were still a thing, still two atoms in energetic collision, or if the dog and I would be driving back home in the middle of the night. I needn't have worried. Rykug preceded me into the apartment with a brief, casual greeting and then I was on the step and Mihan was there on the threshold—I could smell her skin from five feet away—and I barely made it through the door before the magnets engaged. Strong magnets. I thought, in rapid succession, *I can't ever be away from her again,* and *How the hell am I going to sort that out?* and *Later, Orri, sort it later.* I needed time to think or, rather, not think. It was a profound relief to be in Mihan's presence, and also overwhelming, vertiginous. Love is a cask-strength drink. Winter, and the telephone, had merely put it on ice.

Mihan was on her break between semesters, and this was my last hurrah before I returned to school in Reykjavík. Pabbi had assured me, he'd sworn up and down that he was fine, that his ribs were feeling much better and he could easily manage feeding out the cows, checking their water, etc., he'd call if he got into a bind. And I could take Rykug if I wanted, he didn't need the company, no, he'd be far better able to concentrate on his poetry without her snoring at his feet. I chose to trust him. He did seem improved. As though the revelations of his long story had purged something ugly and gangrenous that squirmed within him. And it had seemed, in the days immediately afterward, that we were closer. Some veil of formality that had grown up between us during the last few months, or maybe over the course of our life together, had unraveled and drifted away. The wind in Borgarfjörður chases off the good and the bad.

"So do you think it was his foundational trauma, killing all those cows?" Mihan said. I'd told her the whole tale.

"I don't know. I'm not sure he has a foundational trauma. He certainly doesn't think so."

"I thought we all had a foundational trauma."

"Maybe I don't?"

"Maybe you don't."

Worn out from our dancing, we reclined in a sweaty heap on the sofa, watching the last streak of winter sun walk its way across the wall and disappear. This time of year the day lasts scarcely more than seven hours. It was good to be together when darkness made its premature arrival, stage right.

"Weird about his poetry, though."

I nodded. It was a bit weird.

"Are his poems any good?"

"Well, not really. Not great. But he's new to it—maybe they'll improve?"

"Maybe," Mihan said. "It seems like a strange choice for him, based on what little I know of him. He's kind of a contrarian, right? And poetry is such an Icelandic cliché. The Edda, the skaldic era, the rímur, Jolabokaflod, and all that."

"Jolabokaflod isn't just for poetry. It's any kind of book."

"Oh, is that right?" she sneered. "Thank you, I know what Jolabokaflod is. What I mean is there's this truism, and everyone seems to adhere to it, that people who've been forced to endure such misery, for centuries and centuries, have to find cultural satisfaction somewhere, a kind of artistic release, or they'll die. And maybe they're right. And maybe Icelanders don't have much else to celebrate in terms of the things that they—that we—have done well. But there's also something pompous and self-aggrandizing about it. Like the place is still trying to live in its own myth."

"Sounds like a lot of places."

"It does."

Mihan was right about things, she specialized in it. And she was right about Pabbi. Composing poems felt like an odd turn for him. But then, he had been more emotional lately. Maybe it was a function of age.

My mood turned, sank. The afternoon's enchanting melee crept dutifully into its hole where it would have to live in times like these. Tomorrow was my scheduled departure, and I didn't wish to depart. Not just from Mihan, and that felt harder, harsher than previous partings, because I was going farther away, and falling back into a way of life that would keep us on separate sides of the island, a tortuous welter of volcanoes, rivers, glaciers, and *Grimmia* in between. It was also the prospect of university that lay on me like an anchor. An old, rusty, deep-sea anchor. The plan was for me to stay with Amma again, at least for a while, in an apartment that would now contain three generations. Mamma was there, Mamma without Pabbi, a very different sort of entity altogether—a *single* person? My mind recoiled at the thought, I simply couldn't address it.

And then I'd always dreaded returning to school after each summer, each winter break and holiday and weekend. I preferred being home on the farm with my parents—why should I wish to be anywhere else? Now it was somehow worse because there was no absolute imperative. No concerned child welfare official was going to call if I failed to show up. University was supposed to be something you did because you wanted to, for one reason or another—you knew what you'd like to study, or you needed a degree so you could enter the workforce, or you had to get away, get high, cut loose. So what did it mean if I'd only done it because I couldn't think of anything better and it's what was expected of me?

Mihan knew just what I was going through. She had a similarly ambivalent relationship with her schooling. Media Studies was her third major in two years. She'd chosen it almost at random, or in opposition—many of her classmates at the University of Akureyri studied Police Science, a department for which she held only contempt. But things were different for her, she hadn't needed to leave home, *this* home anyway. Her family was all around her. She could go back and sleep in her childhood bedroom at any moment; she could drop by and eat her mother's *sisig* or *adobong isda* or trusty old chicken adobo whenever she wished. She wasn't cast off. Maybe that was oppressive in its own way, an umbilical cord you couldn't get rid of, but it sounded preferable to me.

I felt despair rising in a bitter tide. It's unpleasant to feel so sorry for yourself, to be so wrapped up in your own petty woes. The resultant self-loathing is often more insidious than whatever sparked it. I circled my own drain.

"We'll be all right?" I said.

"We'll be all right."

How was she so certain? Could a person cultivate certainty? Maybe drama would find us after all.

Drama did find us about two hours later, when we were cleaning up from dinner, but not in the way I'd feared. My phone rang. It was Mamma. Her voice sounded hollow, like she was calling from inside a tin can.

"Where are you?" I said. "A tunnel?"

"The hospital," she said. "I'm at the hospital."

In tones as stripped and limp as an old cabbage stalk, in a rush to get the essential information out of her mouth, she told me that Pabbi was there—

"Pabbi's in Reykjavík?"

Pabbi was there, in the intensive care unit of the hospital that had been more or less a playground to Mamma as a kid. Pabbi was there because he'd tried to kill himself.

44.

Amma picked me up at the airport.

I'd caught the last flight from Akureyri to Reykjavík, a short forty-five-minute hop that barely registered. I hadn't read or put my headphones on or even looked out the window, just stared at the tray table the whole time. Mihan would follow the next day with Rykug in the Twingo, a nearly five-hour drive. I'd attempted to argue with her—she should stay, I said, I'd come back and get the dog in a few days, a week—but I didn't have the strength and she was firm.

Now, as I stumbled blearily off the escalator, my grandmother greeted me with a hug, a coffee, and a pâté-and-pickle sandwich, the same sandwich she'd been handing me since before I had teeth.

"Have you eaten dinner?" she said.

"I don't think I can."

"You must."

She was in doctor mode, I could tell immediately. Calm, authoritative, a bit didactic, but not chilly, never chilly. She could switch this on and off, I'd watched her do it my whole life.

Amma knew all the details and she was the ideal person to deliver them. She was in close contact with the physician on call, and her friend the trauma surgeon had dropped everything to check on the situation. The initial report was fairly promising.

"He'll live, probably," she said. "Whether he wants to is another question."

"What the hell happened?"

She told me. Pabbi wasn't talking, he wasn't awake yet, but the sequence wasn't hard to put together, and it looked like this: Bóndadagur. The 25th of January, midwinter's day, Farmer's Day, Husband's Day. He sat down in the shower about noon and opened a vein in each wrist. If there's one thing farmers know how to do it's find a major highway in the cardiovascular system. And he'd done it right, no hesitation or bungling. But beforehand, likely so he wouldn't lose his nerve partway through, he'd ingested every single one of the painkillers he'd been prescribed for his shoulder, his ribs, everything else over the years, and which he never took, never threw away. Amma said it was a good thing no doctor had given him any benzodiazepines, because if he'd taken those too, combined with the opiates, he'd have died before he ever picked up the knife.

Things would've proceeded in their usual course if Ketill hadn't stopped by. He'd been looking for a few square bales but forgot to call first, he generally forgot to call first—this was a perpetual source of irritation, especially for Mamma, who preferred not to wear pants once she got home from work. Ketill saw Pabbi's truck and he figured Pabbi was just avoiding him. He tended not to take these things personally, except that his dog started barking at the door to our house in a very agitated way, dogs almost always know things before we do. So he knocked, and hearing no answer, he let himself in. Gúrka led Ketill right to the bathroom, where he found Pabbi, who still had a faint pulse. Ketill tied off and bound each arm with towels, dragged the limp body to his own truck, a big one-ton, and hoisted him into the cab. He wasn't about to sit there watching Pabbi bleed out while the emergency services took their sweet time, he'd seen enough death in his life. So he drove like hell to the clinic in Borgarnes, all the while calling the paramedics, calling Mamma, even calling Amma, and this mad web of panic and shouting somehow coalesced, largely due to Amma's taking firm control of the situation, into something like a plan. The clinic was ready to airlift Pabbi when he got to Borgarnes—the nurses there were simply not equipped to deal with something quite this bad—and the helicopter arrived before he did.

"Ah god," Amma said. "Your poor pabbi."

"You mean poor Mamma." I was still in shock and honestly a bit angry.

"Yes, her too, but no. You must always reserve your biggest sympathy for the suicide. Remember, we are all in pain, but his pain was so severe that he couldn't bear it a moment longer."

I found Mamma in the waiting room. Her face was ashen; she looked much older. She and I chose two of the horrible plastic chairs that didn't have an armrest between them, a cross between a love seat and a torture device, and we held on to each other as though the wind might blow us apart.

After a little while, she produced a crumpled note.

"Here," she said. "This was in his pocket."

It was classic Pabbi. Terse, no flourishes. It read: "Son. I'm so proud of you. Take care of Rykug for me. I didn't use the gun because it had too many bad memories and besides it's yours now."

Something spasmed in my throat, a spontaneous sob.

Mamma handed me another. This one was for her. The handwriting was a bit neater, as though he'd thought it through more carefully: "Not your fault. There's just nothing left that I want to do and everything hurts. I love you."

"Oh my god," I said, and after a while of making each other's jackets very wet, the tears would dry white on them like seawater, "I really thought he was doing better."

"So did I."

"This *isn't* your fault—you know that? He was right."

"I know, but it still feels like I chose the worst possible moment to leave. Maybe it was the last straw. I wanted him to see reason. I hoped he'd follow me."

They declared Pabbi's condition stable at about 10 p.m. He was awake and communicative, and we could see him so long as we didn't make him agitated. They were still evaluating whether he needed to be put under observation for a few days. Amma held back while Mamma and I went in together.

My stomach lurched when I saw him like that, the tubes, the bandages, his pinched mouth, his sallow skin, all the machines beeping and humming. I thought for a moment I might faint. Mamma held my arm steady. Her face had assumed a rigid, fierce countenance I'd seldom seen, as though she were going into battle.

Pabbi regarded us from his disadvantage. He seemed less than before, sucked dry. In a way he was, his stomach having been pumped, but then he was also full of someone else's blood. Maybe multiple people's.

He licked his cracked lips and cleared his throat. His voice was raspy, brittle, old pumice stones rolling down a dormant cone.

"What a cliché," he said.

We each took a hand. Mamma said, "Because farmers are always killing themselves?"

He nodded, swallowed hard. "Farming. Try to do things differently, you just wind up straight back in the same place as everyone else. And here we are. Couldn't even get this one right."

Something danced in his eyes. It startled me. It almost seemed, without so much as a twitch in his face, like he was laughing.

"Do they have you on meds? Antidepressants?"

"They want to," he croaked.

"Maybe it's not such a bad idea?"

"Oh, he's tried them all," Mamma said, and I was stunned for the second time that day.

Pabbi nodded again. "Always the same," he said. "First like I'm being plugged into an electrical socket, then worse, like I don't care about anything, but not in a nice, breezy way, more like *Maybe I should step in front of a truck.*"

I winced.

"Ketill saved your life," Mamma said.

"I heard." He groaned, and it made him cough. His throat was scoured from the breathing tube they'd pulled out only recently. "Damn him. Another magnanimous act I can never repay."

"So does this mean you weren't writing poetry after all?" I said.

He looked confused for a moment. It was an unusual expression for him.

"I was. What, you didn't like it?"

Mamma kicked my shin below the bed.

"I really did."

We sat there for a while, the three of us together, alive in this world. People should stay together, I thought, as long as they can.

"I'm moving to Reykjavík," he said at last.

"What?" Mamma looked as though she was trying to contain something. Rage, or hope, maybe both.

"I've just been lying here thinking, and it's so clear. I've actually never felt so clear. It scared the piss out of me, dying. Even with all the codeine."

"It scared the piss out of *me,* Pabbi," I said.

"I know it did. And I'm sorry."

"You were in pain." I wondered if the past tense was accurate.

"Well. That's true. But listen. As soon as I understood I wasn't dead, I clung to it, I clung like a goddamn barnacle. Maybe that's what it takes to come back—really wanting to. But the physical pain, Jesus Christ, it's like the worst hangover in the world. I feel like I got run over by Kolkrabbi. Kolkrabbi wearing ice-pick chains... What was I saying? Oh, right, crawling back after officially signing off from the world and then right away seeing in one volcanic blow what a self-absorbed ass I've been... Well, I wouldn't wish it on anybody."

"If that's what it takes," Mamma said, and she gave him the tremor of a smile. He returned it. Each face had the kinetic uncertainty of a reanimated corpse.

"I've been on a doomed crusade. It's high time that I stopped worrying about what I did or didn't want to do with my life; what does or doesn't make me happy. It's your turn. Your move," he said to her, and there was that odd light in his eyes again, as though he'd burned off a few layers of cornea and we were all a few millimeters closer to his undiluted self. The sensation was unnerving.

"I already moved," Mamma said.

"And just look how I followed you in style. Who chases his wife in a helicopter?"

She shook her head, unamused.

"You hate the city. You always have."

"Emma, I'm here now. Your career—Your life takes precedence. I'm just sorry it took me this long, but I'm ready. I'll find work—I don't care what kind. I'll do all the cooking, I'll take your polyester work clothes to the laundromat, I'll even go to those awful faculty dinner parties and I'll wear clean pants. I'm here. If you'll have me."

Mamma made a noise like a seal barking and covered her face. Her shoulders shook.

"You will *not* go to a dinner party," she said in a muffled choking voice.

And she gripped his hand with such violence that her knuckles turned white.

45.

They kept him under observation. Everyone seemed to notice that there was something almost fey about his behavior, and they didn't trust him entirely. They were probably right. When a person tries to disappear himself from the world, he forfeits trust. Everyone in his circle will forever keep one eye on him, in case he should repeat his performance. There's a certain air of criminality about it that still hangs around from the Dark Ages like a tenacious vapor.

But he was too weak to be released from the hospital anyway, he could scarcely rise from his bed, so it made little difference.

Mihan rolled into town around sunrise the next day. She must've left Akureyri before 6 a.m. Her coming marked, I think, the first time I'd breathed properly since the evening before, when I'd gotten Mamma's phone call. It felt like seventy hours had elapsed, not seventeen.

We spent three days alternately walking the city, walking and walking until Rykug had enough, and flitting like moths around the locked recovery room where Pabbi convalesced. Everywhere people hunched against the cold. It always feels colder in cities; maybe it's the added burden of all those charged souls rushing around in commerce and mutual avoidance. Sometimes, when the old smells and sounds started dragging me back to an unhealthy place, a place where I could only cower, like a man adrift in a life raft, the waves looming above me, I had to push against the dark, the cold, the things I associated with loneliness and misery—dryers belching chemical bubblegum breath onto the sidewalk, streetlights with their antiseptic flicker—and I'd say to myself, almost out loud, *You are not alone.* And sure enough, there was Mihan, walking or reading next to me. And I felt so grateful for her steadying, warming presence, so properly magnetized to her vibrant self, that I would've transformed my body into a jacket, a noisome human leather jacket for her to wear. I would be happy that way.

In the evening we retired to Amma's apartment. She had an air mattress—not terrible as far as air mattresses are concerned, though they are all terrible—which we blew up and set in the middle of the living room. Mamma had the guest room, of course—she'd been living there for over a month. We would've taken it in turns to stay overnight in the waiting room, cramped and righteous in a plastic chair, but the psychiatric wing forbade it, and so did Pabbi.

Mihan and I waited until the apartment was quiet before attempting any serious conversation. Our future meant everything to us, but we knew it wasn't everything. Bigger questions were in play, and we weren't sure how we fit into them. Sacrifices had been made. More, undoubtedly, were coming. We talked with animation, though, and with increasing eagerness.

I checked in with Rúna once or twice a day. She was handling things back home, capable of handling anything, that was obvious. She'd even reached an uneasy détente with Ketill, who insisted on "helping." He could be trusted to water the animals, but she was under strict orders, well, strong advisement, or at least she was politely begged, to keep him away from the tractor at all costs. I'd shown Rúna the basics of running Kolkrabbi before I left for Akureyri, how to move snow and feed out round bales, and it wouldn't surprise me at all if she were already a far better operator than I'd ever be.

Toward the end of the third day, I'd braced myself to talk to Pabbi. I wanted to catch him in a good state—he'd been up and down, a bit unpredictable, but more than anything he just seemed restless, edgy. He balked under the nurses' patronizing authority. Confinement was taking its toll. We were told he was ready to be discharged shortly, though of course discharging patients from hospitals is a process that must take approximately eight or nine hours.

At one point I poked my head in the door, only to find Mamma on the bed with Pabbi. She was slightly elevated, his head in her armpit, their hands clasped on his chest. They were talking together in a quiet voice. I withdrew.

When Mamma emerged, she looked exhausted, but almost tranquil. She confirmed that Pabbi was still awake. He'd vowed not to spend another night in there.

"Pabbi," I said, walking in, "is this a good time to talk?"

"I am a captive audience," he said.

I shuffled a little, sat down on the edge of the bed. My heart was hammering absurdly. The air in the room had that particular desiccating quality of hospitals that makes your eyelids stick together and your tongue grow chalky and brittle in your mouth like a dead starfish. I decided to come right out with it.

"We want to take over the farm," I said. "Mihan and I."

"I thought you might say that."

"You did?"

His expression became nearly triumphant.

"See? Every now and then I notice something before your mamma does."

"I'll bet you three thousand krónur she knows already."

"I won't take that bet."

He straightened up a little and folded his arms expectantly. He looked like himself. I wasn't sure how to continue. I had a speech prepared and it evaporated before him. Both my parents had that ability to vaporize arguments.

"So?" he said eventually. "How will you pay the property taxes?"

"Amma says she'll cover them for a while."

"She's in on this scheme of yours?"

"She's in favor of it. She says she wants to semi-retire out there and be treated like royalty as she descends into decrepitude. She says it's too crowded in her apartment now."

Pabbi chuckled briefly. "What about operational costs? Utilities?"

"Amma says she'll give us a small business loan."

He inclined his head with a knowing tilt. "And you think you'll be able to pay it back? I never could."

"We thought we might kind of tighten everything up for a season, reevaluate, focus on meat sales this spring and summer, clean out the inventory, build up some cash reserves."

"Ah. Well. It's a sound plan. Not that you're asking." That wry tone, that subtle flash in his gray eyes, so much more transparent than the deep brown of mine and Mamma's, and yet unreadable. "And what about school?"

I sighed. The sigh was jerky, hampered by my nervous heartbeat. "I think I'm done with all that. For now."

"Mihan too?"

"Her too."

"So you're serious, then."

"About the farm or about Mihan?"

"Both, I guess."

"Yes, Pabbi. Deadly serious."

"Well."

While he was regarding me, a nurse stepped in to say they had his discharge paperwork ready, for real this time, someone would be along in the next twenty minutes to wheel him out, no arguments, he'd be wheeled out whether he liked it or not. The nurse left again in an officious clatter of plastic badges and sticky-soled clogs.

Pabbi rolled his shoulder around in its protesting socket. "Finally!" He stood up, already dressed in a clean set of clothes Amma had bought for him. A fancy new wool hat from 66°North that he'd decried as a pointless extravagance but was clearly enamored with. He put his arm over my shoulder, whether in need of support or in a gesture of affection, it didn't matter, I received it willingly. We shuffled over to the window together and looked out. The tireless lights of Reykjavík screamed against the night. The night is inexorable.

"If you're taking over the farm," he said, "I have a few maxims and injunctions."

"I'm ready."

"Remember that every mistake in farming takes at least two years to undo."

"Yes, I think I've learned that one already."

"You haven't. Take care of your body. Don't plan on farming your whole life. Every year you'll hurt something and it will never fully get better. You don't want to wake up one day like Ketill, bent over, lurching around on two busted hips. Already my shoulder feels like something foreign in the bed with me, like a malevolent entity."

"These are fun," I said.

"Don't go into debt buying machines. And promise me that you'll never get horses."

"I can't promise that. I like horses."

Pabbi shook his head ruefully. "Then just don't let them graze willy-nilly, chewing every last blade of grass down to the nub."

"I promise."

"Don't open a damned bed-and-breakfast. I'm serious! It will kill me. Promise that you'll never fix up an outbuilding and start renting it out to Americans."

"You have my solemn vow."

"And take care of Kolkrabbi. If you keep a close eye on it, change the fluids and filters religiously, and sometimes the coolant and the copper washers, it'll do everything you need. Until one day, of course, when something goes wrong and it'll do nothing at all, and that will be that, and then I don't know what you should do. Give up, I guess."

He seemed lost in a grim reflection for a moment.

"It's strange to consider that my worst year in farming is the year you decide you want to be a farmer. Just...just don't imagine that you'll be able to do it very differently. No one has the solutions. If they did, they'd have thought of them already."

46.

When Mihan and I first turned onto the farm road and pulled up to the house, I was anxious. The place felt empty. Almost deserted. I'd just turned twenty-one years old, young to assume all these responsibilities. Responsibilities that had proved too much, in one way or another, for my brave, strong parents. And where was Rúna? I'd hoped she'd be there to greet us, to say all was well, we'd made the right decision.

But immediately on unfolding myself from the Twingo, I heard a machine sound coming from far away, getting closer. A single-cylinder whine. Then from behind a pile of rocks she emerged, Rúna on Pabbi's old motorbike. She was helmetless, squinting, hair flying everywhere, a huge grin on her face. She pulled up and dismounted, embracing both of us, and submitted to a shrieking toothy embrace from Rykug.

"You got it running?" I said, incredulous. The bike had been declared dead these last six months and more.

"Oh, sure. It just needed a little love. Love in the form of a carburetor tune."

"What kind of tune?" Mihan said.

"Nothing major, not a re-jetting or shimming the needle or

anything," Rúna replied modestly, missing the joke. "I just pulled the welch plug, gave the fuel-air screw a few half turns. She was running too rich, that's all."

"You're amazing, Rúna," I said.

"That's what they used to call me in school, The Amazing Rúna. Well, you guys look hungry. Or thirsty? There's some beer in the fridge."

And now it was February, almost exactly a year after the phone call that had brought me home from university, home to Borgarfjörður.

We were working hard and hatching plans. Rúna and Mihan had schemes to make the farm more profitable, sustainable, ethical, that seemed to build naturally on each other; often I just sat there and listened appreciatively. I was ready to listen. Both were convinced, and nearly had me on board, that we should abandon the cow-calf model entirely. In other words, stop overwintering cows, stop breeding. Avoid all that overhead, all that maintenance and vetting and worrying and attachment and death. We could buy a bunch of steers and heifers every spring, fatten them up over the summer, and send them to market in the fall. Winter could be a time for other things, maybe even travel. Pabbi had considered this idea, of course, he'd considered all ideas as far as I could tell, but he'd rejected it. For him, there was beauty and dignity in raising an animal from birth to death on the same farm, in knowing bloodlines intimately over countless generations, in controlling every aspect of production. Yearlings raised elsewhere could be unruly, untrained to electric fence, dangerous in the corral, fed on grain, or worse yet, neglected and abused. Then you were selling pain. You were propagating it.

But the model had merit if you went about it carefully, and if Pabbi's endeavors had shown me anything, it was that no livestock system was free from pain.

Mihan had strong feelings about the breed too. She'd always been an appreciator and observer of bovine behavior, and she knew more than the average non-farmer. Galloways might be tough, but they still weren't built to withstand the Icelandic winter. They weren't musk oxen. Overwintering them outdoors was a losing game—you exhausted all your resources just keeping them alive. But overwintering indoors wasn't viable for us, so abandoning the cow-calf model would help.

Also, she thought we should gently jettison Pabbi's ideals about rare British breeds. Galloways were hard to find in Iceland. Sometimes exceedingly hard. Angus might be an option, but they'd be sold at a premium. Why not just get Icelandic cattle? So what that they didn't produce quite so meaty a carcass? Dairy farms were always looking to get rid of their bull calves. They were everywhere, they could be had cheap, they knew how to subsist on shitty forage, and their disposition was good.

The retail end could stand to be overhauled too. Mihan wanted to build contacts with the little markets in and around Reykjavík that sold local beef. She'd be perfectly willing to truck our wares down to the city once or twice a month, and Amma claimed she knew of at least a dozen doctors and administrators who liked expensive steaks and could easily be turned into loyal customers with some light arm-twisting.

Meanwhile there was a great deal to do. So many things left undone or underdone during the period of Pabbi's maturing ambivalence. We worked very hard indeed, the three of us. The fences were in a sorry state. Fortunately in Iceland you can repair fence all year, so long as it's not buried by snow, because the posts are never deep enough in the frozen ground to get stuck there.

Rúna showed us how to work on the machines. We tore them all down, rebuilt the carburetors, replaced the air filters, cleaned the gas tanks and bowls that had been corroded by the vile ethanol. We spent countless hours at her place too. It was shaping up nicely. With her sheep, and our cattle, it seemed a natural conclusion that we should join forces and incorporate as a business, an LLC. Gróa—we were now permitted to call her Rúna's "girlfriend"—was invaluable in this. She'd been studying the commercial side of farming; she knew exactly what we needed to do and how to organize our paperwork. They say don't go into business with your friends, but they must not have met Rúna.

Just like my own father, I began to sleep like a child. Long, trusting, uninterrupted sleep. But not only in bed, and never in my parents' bed, that would've been far too strange—I slept all over the place. At the table, standing next to the kitchen counter, on the sofa watching TV with my head in Mihan's lap. The labor, the cold air, the burnishing wind, they did something to me. Something good.

I called Mamma periodically. The new job had her scrambling somewhat, but she sounded pleased. More chambers in her expansive brain were being cracked open, dusted off. She lived for the work. She was surprised, however, at how many Polish students she had now. Poles had been coming in waves, outnumbering the Lithuanians. Mamma said she'd been working to acknowledge and redress her own biases, having grown up with a mother who despised Poles out of hand. It wasn't altogether rational, the Lithuanians having been just as bad, historically, but the Polish annexation of Vilna from 1922 to 1940, their enthusiastic collaboration and murder during the war, after the war, all of it left a mark. Mamma had, therefore, some inherited trauma to untangle.

Pabbi seldom came to the phone, but sometimes I'd hear him offering a comment in the background. He'd found work quickly, as he said he would. Before he became a farmer, and after his initial stint as a truck driver, he tried about fifteen other things: short-order cookery, stevedoring, stocking shelves at various places, and his favorite, of course, the library, the one place where his interest in books had been useful, or damning, it depended on how you looked at it. So he thought he might seek out something similar, something he'd never tried, and work in a bookshop. Amma found him the job. She was a regular there; he almost certainly would never have been hired otherwise.

"Does he seem happy?" I asked Mamma once, about a week after he started.

She paused. The line crackled. Cell phones are not supposed to crackle like the old landlines but they do. Maybe it's just the plastic insulated jackets we require in Iceland, always rustling against the receiver.

"No. He seems like him. But he said the other day that he thinks he's just not a particularly happy person, and he's fine with that if I am."

"Are you?"

"I'll keep him."

We laughed. I missed her.

"I spied on him last week," she said. "You should've heard how he was arguing with the university students who came in to buy some Laxness. He started lecturing them about the Book of Sheep and what an offensive farce it was. 'To hell with Bjartur!' he said. Just like the old days."

47.

The place positively came alive when Amma showed up. The occasion was Lithuania's Independence Day, March 11, the day of restoration. She usually didn't come out this time of year, but she was making an exception. This was a new era, she said, the farm under new management. It was worth celebration. We set out a creditable board of smoked salmon, pâté, little cornichons. I baked a fresh loaf of bread, which turned out to have the consistency of concrete, so we transformed it into toast points. Rúna came too, of course, she was expected.

The room was full of noise. We sat around the table, talking over one another, or mostly they talked over one another and I watched in stunned, semi-drunken benignity. Rykug scavenged, obeying perfunctorily when snapped away and then returning to our feet. The day was crystal clear. Through the kitchen window and two valleys over, Baula stood above everything, stoic and buttery, a rhyolitic monolith raised by the roiling forces beneath us. I thought, *I never want to be out of sight of her. Never.*

Mihan was telling Amma about her plans to learn the art of hoof trimming. There was a dire need in Borgarfjörður—the area's last hoof trimmer had fallen too deep into drink or ill-health or both and stopped returning phone calls. How hard could it be? Mihan had seen a listing online for a used hoist unit somewhere out east; it lived on its own trailer and wasn't very expensive. She could really augment our income with one of those, and she was good with cattle, she knew it perfectly well.

"Not a farrier!" Rúna said. "Then you'd have to deal with horse people."

"Just a trimmer."

"Well, I support this idea," Amma said, and she held up her beer bottle to clink everybody else's. "I'll even put up the money for this horrific-sounding torture device."

"You can't!" Mihan protested.

"I can and I will. I hear you have a birthday coming up, and anyway it's my right as official farm benefactor and soon-to-be rustic gentlewoman farmer. Why did I slave my life away peering at maltreated lungs if not to waste my hard-earned money on a pointless enterprise? Speaking of which, I really think the farm needs a name."

"It has a name," I said. "Þverárhlið. That's what it says on the beef labels."

"No, a real name. Þverárhlið is just this little region by the Þverá. Every farm around here is in Þverárhlið. You need something specific, something evocative."

"Did your pabbi really never name it?" Rúna said, her tone incredulous. Icelanders will name anything. A farm, a rock, a particularly lovely patch of moss. But Pabbi hadn't, for reasons of his own. Maybe it was too ingrained in him to never think of a thing as his.

"How about Urðarstaðir?" I said. "Or Grýttustaðir?"

"Not bad, but a bit ominous," Mihan said. "What about Rauðhundsstaðir instead? It's a little warmer, at least for Iceland."

"*Rauðhundsstaðir*." Amma rolled it around in her mouth and gazed indulgently at Rykug. "Red Dog Farm. It's perfect."

I looked around the table, and I tried not to articulate, even along the outskirts of my mind, the word that you should never say, the feeling you should never feel, because its caprice is infamous. But I said it to myself regardless—*lucky*—because how often do you get the opportunity?

Spring was around the corner. Soon the lóa would be here, calling us from our winter sloth, but she was in for a surprise, she wouldn't catch us resting. We were awake, and everything seemed possible.

I knew this was foolish. I knew it right then, in that moment, despite foreseeing so little of what would come. I know it now, twelve years later.

My daughter will be born within the month. What could be more perilous? And yet, of all the things that could and should consume me, like whether she'll be healthy or whether the Icelandic government will hear my petition to register her name — *Tala,* Tagalog goddess of the morning and evening star—what I dwell on most is this: I hope I like her. Maybe it'll take me half a year, like it did for Pabbi. A crooked smile, a laugh, and suddenly I'll find her the slightest bit charming. Another year—or two, let's not rush things—and a spirited conversation about moss or birds or death, and I'll find her indispensable.

There is a line—a line that Icelanders are particularly good at walking, even when drunk—between acknowledging the precarious nature of existence, letting it sharpen your awareness if not always your appreciation (that last part is next to impossible), and allowing the dread of calamity to hobble you into paralysis. This is what it means to build a life under the shadow of a volcano, even a dormant old cone. It's like pledging your fealty to a destroyer god: In remaking, there is hope.

I still permit myself these rare glimpses of sky in an otherwise cloudy theater. Amma said I got this from her, despite her having seen a good deal worse than bad weather. She said her finer parts skipped a generation, even if I planned to squander my potential on things like roundworm prevention. She said she liked Iceland because you could see troubles coming from very far off, but you couldn't run from them because there was nowhere to go. You just hunkered against the rock, and while you were down there, hunkering, you admired the moss.

So back then, at the end of one thing and the start of something else, in the flush of alcohol and possibility, at the scene of our violent remaking, I knew it could all go wrong. Some of it undoubtedly would. Farms go under all the time. People get hurt, animals languish, relationships wither, machines die. But what is youth if not dreaming that you can do something new in this world?

GUIDE TO PRONUNCIATION

á like the *ow* in *brown*

í like the *ee* in *breech*

ö like the *u* in *sure*

ó like the *oa* in *float*

æ like the *i* in *crime*

ú like the *oo* in *soon*

ei, ey like the *ay* in *day*

é like the *ye* in *yesterday*

y like the *ee* in *screen*

Þ like the *th* in *theremin*

ð like the *th* in *loathe*

ACKNOWLEDGMENTS

With thanks to:

Eilis O'Herlihy, center of all things, more essential than oxygen

Ned Maturin Miller O'Herlihy, trusted reader, BKE

Matt and Tina Miller, a hard goddamned act to follow

Ben George, Esmond Harmsworth, and Maya Guthrie, three extraordinary pillars holding up my corner of the labyrinthine edifice that is publishing

Maÿlis de Lajugie, unflagging champion across the sea, working with you will always be my beach

This novel would never have been possible without the aid, expertise, patience, fixing, and friendship of two incredible gentlemen:

Guðmundur "Gummi" Ingi Þorvaldsson

and

Ólafur Darri Ólafsson

... I love and owe you both eternally.

And with particular gratitude to these crucial, generous, kindly folks:

Delaney Davidson, Renato G. Umali, Kristal Umali, David Arnold, Thao Thai, Lena Khidritskaya Little, Kate MacLean, Bryce Andrews, Þorvaldur Jónsson, Ólöf Guðmundsdóttir, Páll H. Zóphóníasson, Jómundur "Jói" Hjörleifsson, Margrét Friðjónsdóttir, Karen Miller, Halldóra Lóa Þorvaldsdóttir, Haraldur Ari Karlsson

And to Bonaparte, tireless friend, office mate, *Canis familiaris,* I say this: "Drop it."

ABOUT THE AUTHOR

Nathaniel Ian Miller is the author of the critically acclaimed debut novel *The Memoirs of Stockholm Sven,* which was longlisted for The Center for Fiction First Novel Prize and has been translated into four languages. A former journalist for newspapers in New Mexico, Colorado, Wisconsin, and Montana, he now lives with his family on a farm in Vermont.